I0826061

LOCKE AMSDEN,

OR

THE SCHOOLMASTER:

A TALE.

BY THE AUTHOR OF "MAY MARTIN,"
"THE GREEN MOUNTAIN BOYS," &c.

"In every scene some moral let us teach;
And, if we can, at once both please and preach."
POPE'S EPISTLES.

BOSTON:
SANBORN, CARTER & BAZIN.
PORTLAND:
BLAKE & CARTER.
1855.

STEREOTYPED AND PRINTED BY S. N. DICKINSON, BOSTON.

TO THE

FRIENDS OF POPULAR EDUCATION

AND SELF-INTELLECTUAL CULTURE,

IN THE UNITED STATES,

THE FOLLOWING PAGES,

WRITTEN LESS WITH THE HOPE OF GAINING LITERARY FAME, THAN OF AWAKENING AN INTEREST, AND IMPARTING USEFUL HINTS ON AN IMPORTANT, AND, WITH ALL OUR BOASTS, A STILL SADLY NEGLECTED SUBJECT,

ARE RESPECTFULLY DEDICATED

BY

THE AUTHOR.

THE SCHOOLMASTER.

CHAPTER I.

"To me more dear, congenial to my heart,
One native charm than all the gloss of art."
GOLDSMITH.

OUR story, contrary perhaps to fashionable precedent, opens at a common farm-house, situated on one of the principal roads leading through the interior of the northerly portion of the Union. It was near the middle of the day, in that part of the spring season when the rough and chill features of winter are becoming so equally blended with the soft and mild ones of summer upon the face of nature, that we feel at loss in deciding whether the characteristics of the one or the other most prevail. The hills were mostly bare, but their appearance was not that of summer; and the tempted eye turned away unsatisfied from the cheerless prospect which their dreary and frost-blackened sides presented. The levels, on the other hand, were still covered with snow; and yet their aspect was not that of winter. Clumps of willows, scattered along the hedges, or around the waste-places of the meadows, were white with the starting buds or blossoms of spring. The old white mantle of the frost-king was also becoming sadly dingy and tattered. Each stump and stone was enclosed by a widening circle of bare ground; while the tops of the furrows, peering through the dissolving snows, were beginning to streak, with long, faint, dotted lines, the self-disclosing plough-fields. The cattle were lazily ruminating in the barn-yard, occasionally lowing and casting a wistful glance at the bare hills around, but without offering to move towards them, as if they thought that the prospects there were hardly sufficient to induce them yet to leave their winter quarters. The earth-loving sheep, however, had broken from their fold, and, having reached the borders of the hills by some partially trod path, were busily nibbling at the roots of the shriveled herbage, unheedful of the bleating cries of their feebler companions, that they had left stuck in the treacherous snow-drifts, encountered in their migrations from one bare patch to another.

The owner of the farming establishment, in reference to which we have been speaking, was in the door-yard, engaged in splitting and piling up his yearly stock of fire-wood. He was a man of about forty, not of a very intellectual countenance, indeed, but of a stout, hardy, and well-made frame, which showed to advantage in the handsome and appropriate long, striped, woollen frock, in which he was plying himself with the moderate and easy motions which are, perhaps, peculiar to men of great physical power. A rugged and resolute-looking boy, of perhaps a dozen years of age, having thrown himself upon one knee before a small pile of prepared wood, lying near the kitchen door for immediate use, and having heaped the clefts into one arm till they reached to his chin, as if in whim to see how much he could carry in, was now engaged in trying, with a capricious, bravado-like air, to balance an additional stick on his head, by way of increasing his already enormous load.

In another part of the yard, and as near his master as he could remain undisturbed, lay the well-fed house-dog, reclining upon his belly, with his muzzle, which was pointed in a direction most favorable for a look-out, resting on a clean, broad chip, with ears attent, and eyes keenly following the slow, creeping motions of a small carriage, that was now seen in the distance winding along the road from the south, of whose approach he, from time to time, as he considered himself in duty bound, gave notice by a low growl, which, as the vehicle at length emerged from some partially screening bushes into plain and near view, was raised to a lazy *wow!* The carriage in question proved to be a light, open wagon, drawn by one horse, and containing a middle-aged man, of a fine, gentlemanly appearance, and by his side a small female figure, closely muffled in hood and cloak. Carefully guiding his horse, and turning him from one side to the other of the still icy road, to avoid the most sidling and dangerous-looking places, the traveller at length came abreast of the house; when the animal lost his footing, and after two or three violent but fruitless flounders to regain it, by which the carriage was nearly overset, finally landed flat on his side, and lay as if dead.

"My stars!" exclaimed the farmer, pausing with uplifted axe to see the mishap, "if that was 'nt a narrow escape from capsizing, it 's no matter!"

A second thought now seeming to occur to him, he suddenly dropped his axe, darted forward to the spot, and, seizing the prostrate horse by the bits, held him down.

"Clear the wagon," he said, hastily motioning with his head to the traveller, "the horse will be as likely to overturn you in rising as he was in falling. Jump down, and lift out the girl, and I will then let him up."

This advice was instantly complied with; when the horse, being spurred to an effort, soon safely regained his feet.

"Your beast has lost a shoe, sir," said the farmer, approaching the panting animal, and lifting a suspected foot; "yes, here is the foot, as bare as your hand. But you must have another put on before you drive him another rod in that wagon over these sidling ice-patches, unless you want your neck broke."

"I have no very particular wishes for that, certainly," said the gentleman with a smile; "but where can I find a smith within any reasonable distance?"

"There 's one, and a good one too, about a mile from here, on another road; but I think the horse can be taken across my pasture to the shop much nearer."

"Should I be likely to meet with any difficulty about finding the way?"

"Why, yes, you might; and I 'll tell you what, sir — you had better let me clap my boy on to the creature's back, after unharnessing, and he will take him over and get him shod, while you take your little girl into the house, and remain here. Ben!" continued the speaker, shouting for the boy who had gone in with the wood, with which we have noticed him as loading himself, "Ben! Ben Amsden! show your profile out here in the yard, if you will."

The boy promptly made his appearance.

"That boy?" asked the stranger, doubtingly. "My horse has considerable spirit — can he manage him safely?"

"He will think so, I guess," replied the farmer, laughingly. "What say you, Benjamin? We want you to ride this horse over to neighbor Dighton's to get a shoe put on; and the gentleman appears to have some doubts whether you can manage him, seeing he has some spirit — what do you think about it, sir?"

"Why, I guess I 'll agree to find neck as long as the gentleman will find horse," said the boy smartly.

"Well, then, lead him with the wagon into the yard; strip him of the harness; take our bridle, and ride across the pasture to the shop; tell Mr. Dighton to put on a new shoe, and charge it to me, as we have deal; though you may ask the price, that the gentleman may hand it to me if he wants to. Come, Mister, now you and your little girl go with me into the house."

"I will assist the boy to unharness first."

"O, no, it will be nothing but fun for him. Come, come on. It is strange," continued the man, after pausing a moment to see the wagon got safely around into the yard, "it is strange what a natural difference there is in boys. Now this chap, as little knurl of a thing as he appears, will mount and manage any thing in the shape of horse-flesh, even to the breaking of colts; while my other boy, now tending the sugar place over in the woods yonder, though nearly four years older than this, don't appear to have the least notion about a horse, or any thing else, scarcely, in the way of active life, so long as he can get a book to read and think about."

Mr. Amsden — for such, as the reader may have already inferred, was the farmer's name — now ushered the travellers into the house, and introduced them, as such, to his wife, a dark-eyed and finely-featured dame, who received them with simple kindness, and at once proceeded to assist the little girl in unrobing herself of the thick outward garments in which she was encased to guard against the damps and chills of the season.

The girl, who proved to be the gentleman's daughter, was apparently just entering her teens, neatly rounded, and rather slender in form, and in feature and countenance the softened and beautified image of her very fine-looking, though now somewhat pale and emaciated father. The personal appearance of both father and daughter, indeed, was of a character to awaken at once the attention and interest of the beholder; while the countenances of each exhibited so finely blended an expression of benevolence and intelligence, as to carry along with it the assurance of qualities within, which should secure the interest and make good the prepossessions that outward comeliness had created. The gentleman, as just intimated, had slightly the appearance of an invalid. Indeed, he soon stated, in the way of accounting for being on a journey at such an unfavorable time, that, being about to take a sea-voyage for the benefit of his health, he had broken up housekeeping at his late residence, in a village some fifty miles south of the place to which he had now arrived; and it had therefore become necessary to take his daughter, who, with himself, now composed all his family, to reside, in his absence, with a relative, to whose residence another day's ride would easily carry them.

A few moments, with the gentleman's easy and social turn, was sufficient to place him on a footing of familiarity with the family. And having effected this, and seen his daughter beginning to appear cheerful and at ease, through the delicate and motherly attentions shown her by the amiable hostess, he proposed to Mr. Amsden a walk to the barn for an inspection of his stock, and such other things as should afford samples of his management and skill as a farmer.

"Certainly," said Amsden, evidently gratified at the interest which one, who did not appear to be of his calling, seemed to take in his farming affairs, "certainly, sir, we will go. And you, wife," he continued, turning to the dame, who was already giving signs of culinary preparation, "you can look round a little while we are gone, and see what can be done in the way of a dinner. These folks, as well as ourselves, would like one soon, probably."

"By being allowed to pay for it, we should," replied the gentleman.

"Time enough to talk about that when you get it," rejoined Amsden good-humoredly, as the two left the house on their way to the barn.

On arriving at the yard, its various and thrifty-looking tenants were successively pointed out to the observing stranger by the farmer, who proudly descanted on the virtues of his oxen, the qualities of his cows, the breed of his horses and colts, and his mode of tending and rearing each, and the profits he respectively derived from them. After this, Amsden took his guest to a little elevation near the barn, and directed his attention to the different portions of his farm, describing the uses to which the various fields in view were devoted, and dwelling on the advantages which, as a whole, the farm possessed over those that surrounded it.

"It is a good farm, evidently," responded the stranger, "and as evidently well conducted. But yonder is your sugar-orchard, I think you said: I should be pleased to see your manner of managing that also."

"Well, I have as good a sugar-place as any body else in all these parts," replied Amsden; "but I can't say much for its management, as, considering sugar-making no great object further than for the supply of my family, I have, late years, left it almost wholly to the boys, who are allowed to carry it on pretty much as they please. However, we will walk out there, and see what is going on, since you have named it."

A short walk brought them to the border of the forest, where a body of three or four hundred straight, tall, and thrifty rock-maple trees, standing on an area of about five acres, composed the sugar-place. The tops of the trees were gently swaying to a moderate west wind; and the sap, as usual in a wind from that quarter, with the required *freeze* of the preceding night, was dropping freely, and with pulse-like regularity, from the spouts at the incisions, into the cleanly looking tubs placed beneath to receive the pure and flavorous liquid. Taking a path leading to a central part of the sugar-lot, Amsden and his guest soon came in sight of the boiling-place, as indicated by the cloud of mingled smoke and steam which rose from the seething kettles and the hot fires beneath them. The farmer, now espying some tubs at a short distance from the path, that needed adjusting on their sinking foundations of snow, stepped aside, bidding the other go on; and the latter accordingly proceeded, with a leisurely step, alone towards the boiling-place. On arriving within a rod or two of the spot, he paused, and looked around for the one in superintendence; when his eye soon fell on the person of a boy of about sixteen, lying on some straw at the mouth of the shantee, which opened towards the row of boiling kettles in front. The lad had a ciphering slate, and a large, old, cover-worn volume spread before him; and upon this he was so absorbingly engaged, that neither the sight or sound of his approaching visitor appeared to make the least impression on his senses. Hesitating to disturb one evidently so little expecting it, the stranger stood a moment, now looking around for the absent farmer, and now glancing with an air of interest and surprised curiosity at the picturesque attitude, shapely limbs, and finely-turned head of the boy; who, with bosom thrown open, hat cast aside, the fingers of one hand twisted in his curly, raven hair, and those of the other grasping the nimbly-plying pencil, was thus engaged in an employment so little looked for by the other on a common farm, and least of all in the woods. The gentleman was not allowed, however, much time for his musing upon so unusual a spectacle; for, the next moment, our little student of the woods leaped suddenly upon his feet, and, with the exulting shout of Archimedes of old, exclaimed aloud, "I have done it! I have done it!" adding, as he turned back and shook his fist at the book, "now, Old Pike, just show me another sum that I can't do, will you? you are conquered, sir!"

Having thus delivered himself, the boy turned round, when, his eyes for the first time falling upon the stranger, he instantly dropped his head, and stood covered with shame and confusion.

"Locke!" exclaimed the farmer, emerging, at this juncture, from the bushes on the opposite side of the fire, and going up and peering into the steaming kettles, "why, Locke, what have you been about? This smallest kettle has boiled down into sugar, and is burning up, dirt, settlings, and all together! Where on earth," he petulantly continued, hastily swinging off the kettle, "where on earth can have been the boy's eyes and wits, to stand by and let ten or a dozen pounds of sugar spoil for want of putting in a little sap! What is the meaning of it? What is the case? Zounds, sir, why don't you speak?"

But the now doubly confused object of this tirade of the provoked farmer, was unable to utter one word in extenuation of his delinquency; and, after one or two ineffectual attempts to speak, sunk down on a log, and hid his burning face with his hands. At once appreciating the feelings of the boy, and touched at the sensibilities he exhibited under the mingled emotions arising from wounded delicacy and conscious fault, the stranger immediately interposed, by observing, as he pointed to the slate and arithmetic still lying where the owner had used them,

"Your boy is a mathematician, I perceive, sir; and yonder is the innocent cause, and at the same time the excuse for his oversight, as I have reason to suspect."

"Yes, yes, I'll warrant it," replied Amsden pettishly, "it's just like him. His head is always so full of ciphering questions, grammar puzzles, and all sorts of bookish wrinkles, that there is no room for any thing else; and I can scarcely trust him to manage the most simple business, he is often so absent-minded and blundering."

"And yet," rejoined the other, "I should feel proud of his faults, while they sprang only from such causes, if I was his father. Come, come, my lad," he continued, turning and soothingly addressing the boy, "cheer up; you have committed no very serious offence, I suspect. At all events, I will venture to take the sugar which your father thinks is spoil. d off his hands, and pay full price for it, to give to my little girl down at the house. She is very fond of the maple sweet, I believe."

"Pay for it? — buy it? No, you sha'nt, unless you really want to buy some for yourself, and then you should have some better than this," quickly interposed the father, taken wholly aback by this unexpected proposition and course of the stranger; "no, indeed, sir. Why, it is all nothing. I was only a little vexed at the boy's carelessness, that's all. I care nothing about the sugar, even if it had been burnt up, as it is not, I presume. But we will now see. And at any rate, the little girl shall have as much sugar as she wants, without paying for it either. Locke, bring us a clean tub to turn it into, and we will see what can be done with it."

"You are quite mistaken about the quantity of what might be made of all that is in that kettle, father," said the boy, now brightening up, and bringing the receptacle asked for; "I took the syrup from the kettle but a few hours ago, and, gathering a few pails of the clearest sap I could find, and straining it, I filled up anew, thinking I would boil down a few pounds as nice as I could for brag-sugar."

"Well, it does look pretty clear, and it is not done down to sugar yet, I see. I was deceived by there being so little of it," remarked the father, in a moderated tone, as he turned off into the tub the rich, red fluid, which, after all, had only boiled down to the consistency of a very thin molasses. "O, yes, this may be brought to something quite decent. Have you any milk or eggs for cleansing, Locke?"

"Yes, sir, both."

"Well, then, beat up the white of an egg, and add a little milk, if you please; and by the time you have prepared the mixture, I will have the syrup cool enough for clarifying. We may as well finish it now, perhaps."

In a few moments, the liquid was sufficiently cooled, the

mixture stirred in, and the whole placed in the kettle over a small fire, before which the farmer, with skimmer in hand, took his station, to be ready for the process of cleansing. The liquor, beginning almost instantly to feel the heat, at first gave out a sharp, singing sound, which, as the greenish-gray cloud of impurities rapidly rose and gathered in a thick, mantling coat over the surface, gradually changed into a low, stifled roar, growing more bass and indistinct, till it suddenly ceased with the first bubble that rose to the disrupturing surface. The feculent coat, thus collected and broken, was then quickly skimmed off, leaving the pure and brightly contrasting liquid to rise, as the next instant it did, with diffusing ebulitions, to the top of the kettle in a fleckered mass of yellow foam, resembling some fantastic fret-work of gold.

While the father stood over the kettle rapidly plying his skimmer to prevent the contents from boiling over, the stranger turned to the son, and entered into conversation with him, with the apparent object of drawing him out; asking him many questions relative to his studies, and often manifesting both interest and surprise at the answers which were promptly returned.

"Your son bears the name of a great and learned man," observed the gentleman, turning at length to the father. "Do you intend he shall try to rival his namesake in knowledge and fame?"

"Don't know any thing about that. But you are wandering considerable further than you need to for his name. He got that from his mother: her maiden name was Locke."

"O, ho! But don't you think of giving him an education?"

"Education? why I *am* giving him one. He attends our district school regularly every winter."

"I meant a public education."

"Then I say, No; I intend him for a farmer."

"That is right — it is a noble calling, but one, let me tell you, sir, that affords no argument against a public education. I am well aware, that it is deemed unnecessary, by the people of the Middle and Northern States, especially, to give liberal educations to any of their sons, except those destined for the learned professions; but I cannot but consider this a great error, and one whose consequences are seriously felt by the agricultural interest, which, in its various relations, must ever remain the great and leading interest of the country."

"How so?"

"Why, the first and direct consequence of the course I condemn is, that it places nearly all the science, and most of the intellect, of the country in the professions; and from this spring a train of others, all tending to the same point. The business of agriculture is thus left to be conducted by the unscientific and more unthinking portion of community, and its advance in improvement will, of course, be comparatively slow. Grades are thus established in society, in which the farming is made less honorable than professional business, operating as an inducement for all the most enterprising and ambitious to leave the former, already too much neglected, and crowd into the latter, already so much overstocked as to have become the fruitful source of demagogues and sharpers. And besides all this, the farming interest, under the present order of things, will never be efficiently or adequately represented in our legislatures, where those interests will always be best protected and promoted which furnish the most talent to advocate and forward them."

"Well, some part of that may be true, sir, especially your notion about too many quitting work to go into the professions, and become idlers and sharpers; but I really can't see what use high learning is to a man in carrying on the business of farming — can you?"

"Yes, sir. Even in the mere management of your grounds, a thorough knowledge of the sciences will give you many and great advantages."

"What advantages, I should like to know?"

"One, and a great one, too, will be that it will show you the true nature and capabilities of the different soils of your farm, which can be accurately known only by a knowledge of chemistry and geology. It was through these sciences that plaster was discovered, and its use in supplying the place of some ingredient which, by the same means, was found to be wanting to make the soil fruitful. You have used this article, perhaps, on your own farm?"

"Yes, I have; and if the article came by the sciences, I should be willing, for one, that the sciences should take it away again. A year or two ago, I laid out about a dozen dollars in ground plaster to sow over an old, worn-out piece of bottom land of mine; and I might have as well sown so much ground moonshine, as for any good it did. Well, the next year, I put a lot on to a heavy, wet piece of land, to see whether it might not help that; and I come out with just about as much benefit as before. In both cases, my money was thrown away."

"And yet, sir, that is one of those facts which go strongly to prove what I have said. Without chemical analysis, it can with no certainty be determined what ingredients are lacking in any soil to restore its fertility. The knowledge I contend for would have taught you this, and enabled you to lay out your money where, instead of being thrown away, it would have been doubled. It would have taught you, that alluvial soils, or meadows, are rarely, if ever, benefited by plaster; lime, potash, salt, or a mixture of some other soil being required, to produce the necessary change. And so with wet, heavy soils, whose defects are better remedied by an addition of peat, loam, or gravel; while high and dry soils are generally made productive, to an astonishing degree, by plaster alone."

"Is that a fact? Well, I never knew it before."

"Yes, sir; this, and much more of the same character, has already been ascertained, not by practical farmers, but by men of science, who have made these discoveries by only occasionally turning their attention to the subject. And if so much has been done by those who made it not their main object and business, what might not be effected by a whole community of educated farmers, whose whole energies and interests were devoted to the work of improvement? Indeed, sir, I seriously believe, that if our legislatures would establish a fund for the liberal education of young farmers, with the condition that they should remain such, they would do a thousand times more towards promoting and elevating the great interest of agriculture, to say nothing of the general benefits which would follow — would do a thousand times more than by all the premiums they could offer for best products, or all the societies they could establish."

"Well, I confess, sir, that your ideas, which are new to me, look kinder reasonable. But what is the reason all these things cannot be learned in our common schools? We have them in all our districts, both summer and winter, and generally keep our children in them more than half of the year, from the ages of four to twenty."

"Perhaps most of the sciences might be acquired in our common schools, if they were conducted properly, and by teachers of adequate qualifications. But as at present managed, and with the low wages now given, it is next to a miracle to find a teacher thus qualified. Now, for instance, as regards your son here, I very much doubt whether you will ever have a teacher in your district, who will be able to instruct him much more, especially in those higher branches which he is now evidently capable of entering upon with profit to himself. No, sir, you should send him to the public schools. It will give him advantages in life, which he can never otherwise obtain. *Knowledge is power.*"

"Well, sir, if knowledge is power, as in some respects it probably is, it is often used, I fear, by those who have it, to take advantage of the weak and honest laboring people, who don't happen to be so well educated."

"Such advantages may be, and sometimes doubtless are, taken by some, who have knowledge without moral principle. But the proportion of unprincipled men among the well educated, I am satisfied, is much smaller than among an equal number of almost any class of society. Allowing, however, the proportion to be the same, or greater, how would you disarm them of that power? In no other way, certainly, than by placing the same weapons of knowledge in the hands of the many, instead of the few. I am no advocate for power to be used in the manner you mention. I am no advocate for the doctrine,

'That those who think, must govern those who toil.'

I believe, sir, as I have been endeavoring to show, that those who think and those who toil should be one and the same class; and, as I have already intimated, I believe this desirable object can never be effected, without affording the means of a more general and thorough education."

During the foregoing dialogue between Mr. Amsden and his guest, — who stood over the kettle of boiling sugar, occasionally dipping into it with their slender wooden spoons or paddles, to sip the pure liquid, or the less cloying sweet of the snowy scum continually gathering in concentric and surgy lines around the point of ebulition, — Locke stood like one spell-bound to the spot, eagerly drinking in the words and opinions of the courteous stranger, who had so eloquently expressed the feelings of his own breast, and given a definite shape to many a confused idea of a similar bearing, which had often risen in his own mind. His heart, swelling with irrepressible emotions, gratefully responded to every sentiment he had heard; and he felt as if he could have fallen down and worshipped, as a superior being, the man who had uttered them. He had often before, as just intimated, harbored thoughts, feelings, and wishes like those of the stranger; yet they had been vague and uncertain, and he never dared cherish them as practicable for himself, or indulge in any expectation of their fulfilment. But now the train, which had long been preparing in his bosom, was fired never more to be extinguished.

By this time, the now slowly boiling sugar had settled low in the kettle, and assumed that deep, orange hue, which indicates a near approach to that point at which granulation takes place almost as soon as the mass ceases boiling.

"Come, Locke," said Mr. Amsden, raising aloft his skimmer, from which each falling drop was followed by a fine, silken harl, that stiffened and shivered in the breeze; "come, it throws off the hairs pretty smartly, I see; we may as well call it done, I think. You may bring," he continued, lifting off the kettle, "you may bring me a clean pail to take it home in. And hav 'nt you a tin cup or something, Locke, into which you can take some by itself to carry to the gentleman's little girl? — it might please her better."

"We have nothing fit for that, here, father, I believe," replied the boy. "But stay — I made something the other day that will do, I think; and I will give it to her, sugar and all, to carry off with her, if she will accept it."

So saying, he ran into the shantee, and returned with a small, neatly-made, oblong box, holding, perhaps, about a pint, which he had chiseled and cut out from a solid billet of the beautiful bird's-eye maple, having provided it with a curiously carved slide-cover, and tastefully stained the whole with the pale pink of some vegetable coloring-matter that he had found in the woods.

"Upon my word!" said the stranger, glancing at the box, as it was being filled and set aside to cool by its ingenious and free-hearted little owner, "upon my word, Master Locke, you seem to have a genius for every thing. That is one of the neatest specimens of mechanical skill, considering your means of making it here in the woods, which I have seen this long while. My daughter, I think, will feel quite proud of her present."

"O, the boy knows enough," said Amsden with affected indifference, as he, with the pail of new sugar, and his son, with the box, having filled up the kettles with sap, and replenished the fires, now started with their guest for the house, "he knows enough, no doubt; and if he would only turn his mind on business to some account, he might make considerable of a man."

On reaching and entering the house, our young hero sent a sheepish and inquiring glance around the room in search of the object on which he had promised himself the pleasure of bestowing his sweet and pretty gift; but when that fair object met his admiring gaze, with her brightly blue eyes and sweetly expressive countenance, his courage suddenly failed him, and he found himself unable to approach and make the offering, till her father, interposing, directed her attention to the present, which he told her his young friend, Master Locke, had generously proposed to make her; when, feeling that there was now no retreat for him, he timidly advanced, and silently presented the box to the smiling girl, who received it, at first, with a playful "thank 'ee," and then, as she drew out the cover, and ascertained the contents, with lively expressions of grateful delight. This breaking the ice of his bashfulness, Locke soon found himself engaged with his fair friend in a sociable conversation, which was maintained on her part with that sort of unconscious frankness, or forwardness, perhaps we might say, which characterizes the manners of the sex at the age of the one in question.

The company were now summoned to the excellent dinner, which the provident and ambitious mistress of the house had prepared for the occasion. The meal, which she had spread on her best cherry table, covered with a cloth of snowy whiteness, the workmanship of her own hands from distaff to hemming and marking, consisted, in the first place, of ham, eggs, and other varieties of the substantial food usually found upon the farmer's table. Then came the fine meal Indian Johnny-cake, mixed with cream, eggs, and sugar, and forming, when rightly made, perhaps the most delectable esculent of the bread kind, that ever gratified an epicure's palate. This last, and the light, hot biscuit, for those who chose them, together with pies, both apple and minced, stewed fruit, gooseberry preserves, honey, and new sugar, constituted the desert, — the whole making a repast which gave proof that the farmer has ample materials of his own raising, if he has but a wife of competent skill in cookery to manage them, to furnish a table which may be made to rival the boasted banquet-boards of princes.

As soon as the dinner, which had passed off with great sociability and good feeling, was finished, the travellers, pleading the necessity of diligence on their way, immediately commenced preparations for resuming their journey. The horse, which, in the mean time, had been returned and well cared for by the boy who had taken him in charge, was now, by the same active little groom, speedily cleaned, harnessed, and brought up with the carriage to the door. And, the next moment, the gentleman, with the sprightly little Mary (for such, it appeared, was the girl's name,) emerged from the house, followed by the family, who now gathered round the carriage to witness the departure of those who seemed to have succeeded, in two brief hours, in awakening an interest which is usually created only by a long and intimate acquaintance.

"Now, Mr. Amsden," said the stranger, turning to his host, after placing his daughter in her seat, "now, I will settle with you for the shoeing of the horse, our dinners, and all other trouble, to say nothing of the hospitable kindness with which you all have made us feel so much at home. What, sir, will be your bill?"

"Ben, what did Mr. Dighton say he should charge?" asked the other, turning to his boy.

"Forty cents, sir," was the prompt reply.

"Well, forty cents, then, is the bill," resumed the farmer.

"Yes, but the rest of your charges?"

"We will trust you for that."

"I should prefer to pay, sir."

"You may, if you will allow me to direct the manner of payment."

"Very well, sir; speak on."

"Why, when you get settled down in life again, give some other traveller a dinner, if he is as good company as you have been, and that shall square the account between us."

"I will, however, make your boys a present."

"Better see whether they will take any thing first, sir."

"O, no, no, sir," quickly interposed Locke, as the gentlemen was opening his purse.

"Not a cent for me, Mister; that aint the way I get my living," chimed in the spirited and proud little Ben.

"Ah, I see you are all determined to have your way at this time," smilingly remarked the stranger: "however, all may come right hereafter, perhaps. But as the matter now stands, I have only to express my sense of obligation to each and all of you. And one thing more, before we part, Mr.

Amsden — let me repeat to you my advice, to give this elder son of yours the chance for a good education."

"Do you think he has capacities which would warrant such a step, sir?" asked the gratified mother of the boy.

"Indeed, I certainly do, Madam; even to sending him to a college," replied the other.

"That would be impossible in my circumstances, provided I thought as you do on the subject," remarked Mr. Amsden.

"Let him go to a good academy, then," rejoined the stranger.

"Well, now, I don't exactly know about that," replied the other. "He may go winters to our district schools as long as he pleases; and I think, for the present, at least, that he should, and will be, quite satisfied with that. Is it not so, Locke?"

"Why," answered the boy diffidently, "I should be satisfied to go to our district masters, if they could tell me the reasons of things, which I always wish to know."

"That is right, Master Locke, responded the stranger; "you have expressed, in almost a word, the great aim and essence of all true knowledge and philosophy — '*to know the reason of things*.' Yes, my young friend, let that still be your ambition; and, if your father will give you the opportunity, I doubt not you will do honor to the motto you have chosen."

"Well, I would be a scholar, Locke, if I was you," added Mary, with charming *naïveté*; and if you will, and come and keep school where I live, I will go to school to you, and become a great scholar too, if I can."

The travellers now took their leave of the family, and drove from the yard, attended by the repeatedly expressed good wishes of the good-hearted farmer, and his equally kind and more high-minded companion. And, in these wishes, they were joined by another, who, though he had uttered less, yet felt more than they had expressed! That was our young hero; who, as the rest of the family returned into the house, stood mutely gazing after the receding carriage, till its last traces were lost to his sight; when he slowly turned away, the big drops of tears standing in his eyes, and his lip quivering with emotions which had been awakened by this brief, but to him, as will appear in the sequel, important visit of these interesting strangers.

CHAPTER II.

"The dream, the thirst, the wild desire,
Delirious, yet divine — *to know!*"

BULWER.

THE accidental call of the travellers at the house of the farmer, as narrated in our opening chapter, formed an era in the life of Locke Amsden. By that call, new thoughts had been suggested to his mind — new feelings and hopes awakened in his bosom; and, as the slumbering energies of his intellectual and moral nature became thus aroused, young ambition began to point him upward to the temple of science, over whose distanced-hallowed pinnacles floated the mystic banner of fame. At first, every word of the revered stranger was recalled, every position revolved over and over in mind, and every argument carefully weighed; and the result of the process was faith and conviction. Then came the inspiriting words of the beautiful little being, who, in angel shape, had thus appeared in his path to incite him onward; and, "*I would be a scholar, Locke,*" continued to ring in his ears. "Ay, and I will be a scholar!" he at length mentally ejaculated; "and then I will go where she lives, and she shall know that I have worthily done her bidding, and justified the good opinion of her father. But where does she live? — yes, where?" For he now recollected, that he had not learned from her, or her father, the place of their residence; and, under the proud and joyous impulse which his reverie had imparted, he flew to his parents with the inquiry. But neither of them could answer it. They had not ascertained even the family name of their visiters. Mr. Amsden had thought of asking the man these particulars ; but, it occurring to him that his wife would naturally find them out from the little girl, he desisted. And this Mrs. Amsden had intended to do ; but her attention was so much engrossed in the cares of preparing the dinner, that she had neglected it, till the return of the gentleman into the house deprived her of the opportunity of doing so, without appearing obtrusive. The Christian name of the girl, therefore, with the fact, that she and her father came from a place some fifty miles to the south, and were destined to another nearly as far to the north, was all that had been ascertained concerning them, other than what their personal appearance indicated. But, although our young hero was thus left in ignorance of the names, residence, character, and calling of his new friends, and for many years was doomed to remain so, yet the event of their visit was not the less destined to exercise an important influence on his future life and fortunes. It seemed to be, indeed, one of those trifling incidents which so often seem to change the fate of individuals, and impart an enduring impulse towards a destiny to which, in all human probability, they otherwise would never have been called. Such an impulse had been imparted, in the present instance, by the mere call of two entire strangers ; and that simple incident would probably have been sufficient of itself, had no other grown out of it, to give a new and continuing direction to the energies of him on whom it so peculiarly operated. But there yet remained to be added another occurrence arising from the circumstances of the first, which was directly calculated to strengthen every impulse already received, and every resolution formed under it.

About a month from the time the incidents we have been sketching transpired, a strong board box, directed to *Master Locke Amsden,* was left at the door by a teamster; who, saying he had received it from another teamster, with directions to leave it at this place, went on his way, without giving any further information respecting it, or those who sent it.

Wondering what might be the contents of the box, the receipt of which was so unexpected to him, though partly anticipating the source from which it must have come, Locke flew for his hammer, and knocked off the cover; when, to his joyful surprise, he found the box filled with books, upon the top of which lay a neatly folded and superscribed little billet, directed to himself. Eagerly snatching up the paper, he opened it, and read, in the finely-traced characters of an unsettled female hand, the laconic contents: —

"A lot of old, musty volumes, in return for your nice little present. Father has picked them out from his old college books, and given them to me to send to you, saying you would like them. If you think, as he says, about them, I shall be pleased to have you accept them from

"Your friend,

"MARY."

With a low shout of irrepressible joy, he now hastily caught up his treasure, rushed into the house, and, calling on his mother to come and witness his good fortune, fell to unpacking the books, greedily running over the title-pages of each, as, with many a half-suppressed exclamation of pleasure, he successively took out the different volumes, which, to the number of eight or ten, the box contained, and spread them around him on the floor. The collection consisted of a complete set of mathematics, from common arithmetic to fluxions; a standard work on natural philosophy; another on astronomy; together with separate treatises upon geology, mineralogy, and chemistry; while the whole was accompanied by a good set of mathematical instruments.

From what we have already shown the reader of the

character and inclinations of Locke, it may be easily imagined with what rapture he doted on this munificent and appropriate present, not only from its intrinsic value, and the untold advantages which he was to reap from it, but for the fair giver, and her prompting father, by whom it had been so delicately and flatteringly bestowed, — with what pleasure he looked forward to the time when he should be allowed to devote himself wholly to the great, but coveted task, which, in these books, he now saw set before him. By most others, perhaps, the course of mathematics here presented, had been viewed only as a labor of almost endless toil and difficulty. He, however, looked upon it but as a labor of delight, so much the better for its promised length, since that would add so much the more to the fund of his happiness. For the first week, his leisure was given to looking over the subject matter on which the volumes of his prized little library severally treated, and arranging the order, in which his own good sense and discrimination rightly taught him they should be studied. Having settled this, and accordingly determined to make mathematics his first study, while he should proceed with geology and the like as his light reading, he began with algebra, assiduously, and with his usual systematic perseverance, devoting to it every hour he could snatch from his customary employments on the farm. And thus, making what progress he could, in the brief intervals allowed him for the purpose, and leaving all knotty points to be thought over and solved while at work in the field, he alone, unassisted and unprompted, steadily pursued the course he had marked out for himself, neither seeking nor asking any other recreation or pleasure than what his studies afforded. But, although this course was a source of constant pleasure to Locke, not so did it soon become to his honest but simple-minded father, who, rightly enough attributing his son's growing inadvertencies in business to these books, often wished, in his heart, the whole collection at the bottom of the sea. And these inadvertencies, which so naturally grew out of the course he was pursuing, were, it must be confessed, not unfrequently of a character to cause vexation to a business man of a less petulant turn than Mr. Amsden. For, if the latter had reason to complain of his son in this respect before, he had much more cause for doing so now; since, with the greatest willingness and undoubted capacities for work, the boy too often effected but little, and as often did that little wrong. In those kinds of labor, to be sure, where he could induce his father to task him, he would apply every energy of body and mind, till his task was completed, which was generally by noon; when, for the remainder of the day, he might be seen lying on the grass, under some shady tree, with his book and instruments spread before him. But in work which would not admit of this, the problems that he took with him in his head into the field, often led to singular oversights in the business about which his hands were employed. If he was sent on an errand to some other part of the farm, he would sometimes wholly forget what he went for. Sometimes he would leave the bars down, the cows unmilked, or the hogs unfed; and sometimes, when hoeing alone in the cornfield, and when some mathematical question occurred to his mind which he wished to solve, he would stop work, and making a smooth bed of earth to serve for slate or paper, fall to figuring or making diagrams with his finger in the place he had thus prepared, and think no more of his hoeing, perhaps, till roused from his study by the loud note of the tin house-trumpet summoning him home to his mid-day or evening meal. All these, as innocently done as they were, cost him, as may well be supposed, many a scolding and fretful expostulation from his impatient and driving father, who, as the season of outdoor labor drew to a close, expressed himself heartily thankful that the time for beginning the winter school had at length come, that Locke's body might now go where his head and heart had been all summer. On the last point, at least, the father and son were quite of the same mind. And, accordingly, the latter, as the long wished-for period when he could be allowed to give himself wholly to his studies arrived, joyfully packed up his books, and changed the scene of his mental operations from the farm to the school-house. But here again it was his fortune soon to become, though not exactly in the same way as before, the unintentional cause of much uneasiness and perplexity to another personage. That other personage was the schoolmaster, who — his acquirements, as usual with the mass of our district-school teachers, being confined to common arithmetic, grammar, and the like, without the ability to illustrate one half of the principles even of these — viewed with considerable alarm, at the outset, the formidable-looking books which Locke had brought into the school with the avowed intention of pursuing the studies they contained. And he made several attempts to draw the other from his purpose. Common arithmetic, said he, should first be thoroughly studied, and all the sums worked over and over, till they were as familiar as the alphabet. Locke, in reply, said he should like to have a sum pointed out to him in any of the arithmetics which he could not already do; though, if the master would illustrate to him the rules of allegation and double position, he would like to listen, as he did not quite understand all the reasons for the results of these two rules. Not caring to push the matter any farther on that tack, the teacher next recommended geography as a useful and interesting study. In answer to this, Locke proposed to submit himself to an examination; being able, as he believed, to answer every ordinary question that could be raised, either on the maps or in the text-book. The master then mentioned English grammar, advising the other again to commit the grammar book to memory. Here, also, he was met by the obdurate pupil, who, though willing to join the parsing class at their lessons, objected to spending any more time upon his grammar book; and, by the way of furnishing a reason for his objections, he immediately brought forward the book in question, and, handing it to the former, kept him reluctantly looking over till the whole was rattled off at one recitation.

Being foiled in these and every other attempt of the kind, the master concluded to let Locke go on in his chosen pursuits unmolested; and right thankful would he have been for a reciprocation of the favor. This, however, as with reason he had feared, was not granted him by the unconscious object of his dread, who soon called on him for explanations of problems or principles, of which he knew about as much as the man in the moon; but of which he had unwisely determined to conceal his ignorance, lest it should be said in the district, that there were scholars in the school who knew more than their master. And having settled on this course, no other alternative now remained for him, but to meet these calls for instruction in the best way he could. And it would have been amusing enough to a spectator, in the secret, to have witnessed the various shifts to which the poor fellow was driven, to get along with his troublesome pupil, without exposing the ignorance which he was so anxious to conceal. At one time, when thus called on for instruction, he would pretend such a hurry, that he could not attend to the required explanation; at another, when apparently he was about to comply with the request of his pupil, he would suddenly discover some delinquency in the school, which he must immediately attend to, and which would be made to occupy his attention so long, that he would have barely time to hurry through the ordinary duties of school, before the established hour of closing. At another time, he would take the book, look over the difficult passage, and, handing it back to Locke with a knowing smile, advise him to try it again; he would soon see the only difficulty, and it would be better for him to discover it for himself. And at yet another, when hard pressed for assistance, he would read the problem in question several times, and after glancing at the context till he had got the run of the technical terms, proceed with a pretended explanation, for which neither himself, pupil, or any one else, could ever be any the wiser. From this unpleasant predicament, however, the thus sadly annoyed teacher was at length happily relieved. For Locke, finding himself unable to make any thing out of the man, even when he was successful enough to get him to look at his studies, came, after a while, to the conclusion to let him entirely alone, and depend only on himself for mastering the difficulties which he met in his progress. And, with his excellent self-formed habits of thought — that of patient investigation, and of thoroughly understanding every thing, as, step by step, he carefully advanced — he found but little trouble in overcoming every obstacle that presented itself in his course onward. And if ever, as was rarely the case, he was compelled to pass over a difficulty unexplained, he never lost sight of it till it was conquered.

There is nothing, perhaps, upon which the growth of intellect so much depends, as upon habits of thought; nothing which so clearly constitutes the great distinguishing difference, in the present, between a strong intellect and a feeble one; and nothing which so conclusively accounts for the beginning and constant increase of that difference in the past, as the opposite habits of thought that have been contracted in youth, or, at the latest, in the first years of manhood. A glance at the contrasted methods adopted and pursued by two individuals of the two different classes of thinkers to which we have alluded, will show the truth of this position; and, at the same time, explain the causes of their respective intellectual conditions. An individual of one of these classes begins, we will suppose, upon one of the rudiments of education. Before mastering the first elementary principle, he leaves, or is suffered to leave it, for the next. In coming upon this, he has not only to contend with the difficulties he left unmastered in the former lesson, but those likewise of the intrinsically worse one of the present. Both the temptation and excuse are now doubled for sliding superficially over this also. The third, in this way, is found still worse, and consequently is still more imperfectly mastered; and so on, in the particular branch on which he is engaged, or any other, probably, which he shall undertake to learn, to the end of the chapter; at which he will arrive little or none benefited by all that he has acquired. For the knowledge thus gained is imperfect and uncertain, and cannot be relied on as data for reasoning, but is constantly leading to false conclusions. And besides this, he has wholly failed of gaining one of the great objects of study — mental discipline. He has contracted the habit of thinking superficially upon every thing. All his ideas become vague and confused; and all the operations of his mind, are, consequently, imbecile and unsafe, producing no fruits, or but the fruits of error. This intellectual condition, indeed, becomes one that would seem almost to justify the absurd, and without considerable qualification, the false assertion of Pope,

"A little learning is a dangerous thing."

Now for an individual of the other class. Like the former, and with no other advantages, he commences the same rudiments. But, unlike the former, he is induced to make himself completely master of the first principle, and familiar with all its details, before proceeding any farther. This being accomplished, he thus becomes armed with power to encounter the next; which, in this way, he finds but little if any more difficult than the preceding; and which, when equally well perfected, gives him still additional strength to grapple with the third. And so he proceeds, or may proceed, through the whole circle of the sciences, carefully making his way, step by step, onward; never sliding over a difficulty, but often retracing his steps to return to the onset with improved means of overcoming the obstacle in his progress. In this way, as he advances in the path of acquirement, just so much certain knowledge he gains, to be stored away in the chambers of his mind for future appropriation, either to its direct uses, or to the purposes of induction, comparison, or other process of reasoning. In this way, also, his mind acquires method, clearness, and vigor; and he thus becomes enabled to think correctly and thoroughly, and arrive at safe conclusions on whatever subject is presented for his investigation. Now these two individuals will carry the different habits of thought, thus respectively formed by them, into the business and various concerns of life; and the results will there be equally visible, as in the walks of science. The one never thoroughly investigates any subject. His views, as before intimated, are all superficial; and his conclusions, consequently, as often as otherwise, are erroneous, leading him into false movements in business, if guided by his own mind, if not reducing him to a miserable dependence on the opinions of others, by whom he is liable to be equally misled. The other examines every subject presented for his consideration patiently, weighs it carefully, sees it in all its bearings clearly, and thus becomes prepared to decide with confidence and correctness. The one, in short, seeing only part of the bearings of the various questions which are constantly arising in life for his decision, makes bad bargains, or rejects good ones, rushes into uncertain speculations, lives in continued embarrassments and troubles, which he calls misfortunes, but which good habits of thought would have enabled him to avoid, and ends his career, most probably, in poverty and insignificance, or in sudden ruin and disgrace. The other, carrying along with him the means of avoiding the evil, which is brought upon its victim through the causes we have just named, and, at the same time, the means of grasping the good, which, through similar causes, is rejected, goes on increasing in competence, wisdom, and influence, moving quietly through life, and leaving, at his death, a useful example, and an honest fame behind him.

Such are generally the results deducible from good and bad habits of thought; and yet who will say these habits, for good or for evil, are not usually formed through the care or negligence of teachers? Instructors of youth, where rests the responsibility?

But to return to our young hero. For the remainder of the winter school, though left, for the best of reasons, by the master, to work his way unassisted, he pressed forward steadily and rapidly in his chosen course of mathematics. And the school having at length been brought to a close, spring, summer, and autumn again succeeded but to find him, in every moment of his leisure, employed on his studies in the same manner, and with the same untiring perseverance, as in the preceding season. One incident, however, occurred this season to vary the monotony of his secluded life; while, at the same time, it became the means of affording him advantages in his studies, which he never before had been so fortunate as to receive. That was an accidental acquaintance he formed with an old, self-taught land-surveyor, who resided in a different part of the same town; and who, like himself, was a great lover of that strong, but healthy food of the mind — the science of numbers and quantities. Locke and this man, by that sort of intellectual free-masonry which passes among sympathetic minds, were not long, when the opportunity occurred, in finding each other out, and forming a close intimacy. The surveyor, having studied much more than was immediately necessary for the exercise of his calling, and dipped considerably deep into principles, was able to explain to the former many knotty points which he had been puzzled to resolve, besides showing him the practical part of surveying, upon which, having gone through geometry and trigonometry, he had now commenced. Locke, in return, brought the other his books, which, to the extent of more than half of them, at least, he had never seen; and which, being loaned him, he fell to studying with boyish enthusiasm. No sooner was this singular companionship thus fairly established, than our boy-hero was found, every rainy day, and at other times when he had finished his tasks, during the summer and fall, posting off on foot to commune and practise with his gray-headed brother in science. And when met, the two might have been seen intently engaged in surveying fields, measuring heights and distances, or patiently plodding on together in navigation, which they soon jointly commenced.

This pleasing intercourse, however, was at length brought to a close by the stormy weather and bad travelling which immediately preceded the setting-in of winter. And Locke, bidding his old friend farewell, took home his books for the purpose of resuming his studies in the winter school, for the beginning of which the time had now arrived. But in this purpose he was for some time doomed to be disappointed. For, when the usual time for commencing the school came, it was found that no teacher had been engaged. The committee, up to this time, had been waiting for applications for the school, expecting that their only trouble, as usual, would be in deciding upon a selection of the various applicants. But it somehow had unaccountably happened, that not a single application had been made; and the committee were now consequently forced to bestir themselves in going out in search of a teacher. But in this, also, they were without success; for, though they found candidates for teaching in plenty, they could find no one, when they named their particular school, who made not some excuse for not undertaking to instruct it. This they thought very strange, as their school had ever been considered a very orderly one. But as strange and uncommon as the trouble was, they were compelled to yield to it, and reluctantly give up all thought of having a school that winter.

Various were the conjectures formed in the district, by way of accounting for this unexpected failure. Some contended, that the school, after all, must be so unruly that no teacher would engage in it; others, that the masters had not been treated with sufficient attention by the inhabitants of the district; and yet others, that the schoolmasters had combined to strike for higher wages, and had come to the determination not to teach till the punished public should voluntarily come forward, and offer the secretly-fixed prices. Among all these, and other sage conjectures of the cause, however, no one had hit upon the truth. For the true secret of the misfortune at length leaked out; when the discovery was made, that Locke Amsden had, in fact, been the innocent and unconscious cause of the whole of it. He, it appeared, besides annoying his own teacher with questions too hard for him, had also been the means of a similar annoyance to many other teachers of the neighboring districts. He had been in the habit, the preceding winter, of frequently attending the evening spelling-schools, which it was customary for the instructors in that section of the country to appoint and hold at intervals, through the whole term of their engagements. And at each of these evening schools, which he thus went abroad to attend, he was sure to propose to one or two of the best scholars, for answer, some difficult point in grammar, some mathematical question of his own originating, or, as was more generally the case, such as he had met with in his studies, and was anxious to see explained. Nearly all these questions, as had been expected, and, indeed, commonly requested by the mover, were carried for solution to the master; who, too often, was compelled to resort to some pitiful evasion to hide his inability to furnish the required answer. And the same questions, also, besides being agitated in the schools into which they were first introduced, were often communicated to other schools, and thus became a source of trouble to other masters; so that, in this way, there was scarcely a teacher, anywhere in the vicinity, who had not experienced the inconvenience of Locke's scholarship and inquiring disposition; and most of them, though they prudently kept the fact to themselves, fairly wished him out of the country, and secretly resolved never to be caught engaging to instruct any school where he should be a pupil. It appeared, therefore, that the failure of the committee, before mentioned, was occasioned, not by there being bad scholars in the school, but good ones; or rather one, whose aptitude and acquirements had made him so much the dread of the schoolmasters, with whom the country then happened to be favored, as effectually to keep them out of the district.

The disappointment thus occasioned the district, however, as vexatious as it was to Locke at the time, was, like many other disappointments in life, of which we are wont to complain, destined, in a short time, to prove a blessing, not only to him, but to the whole school. For, in a few weeks, an unforeseen occurrence brought them an instructor well qualified for his task. This was a senior collegian, who had returned to spend his last vacation at his father's residence, in a neighboring town; and who, on accidentally learning that the district in question had been unable to supply themselves with a teacher, from the suspected causes we have named, was thereby induced to send them word he would come and instruct their school, if they would give him a dollar per day and board. To be sure, the very unusual price demanded by the young man, threatened, for some days, to prove an insurmountable obstacle to engaging him. The sum asked, contended the committee, was outrageous, unheard of, and it was out of all question that they should give it. But all the larger boys and girls clamored; Locke electioneered as if life and death hung on the event; and his mother, whose influence was generally felt in the neighborhood, when she chose to exert it, went round to see other mothers, who, being either convinced by her arguments in favor of the cause she had espoused, or tired of having their noisy children any longer at home, beset their husbands to beset the committee; and the result was, that the committee, unable to stem the current thus brought to bear against them, started off, and engaged the young gentleman, whose name was Seaver, at his own price. The next Monday morning, to the great joy of Locke, he appeared on the ground, and commenced the duties of his school.

We have said that Mr. Seaver, the instructor now employed, was well qualified for the task he had undertaken; and in so saying, we meant much more than what extensive attainments in science and literature, merely, would necessarily imply. He possessed science, indeed, to an eminent degree; but as is too rarely the case, especially with those fresh from the schools, he possessed it without any of that learned quackery of technical terms and unusual words, which is so often made to shut out knowledge from the common mind as effectually as the monastic walls of the dark ages. His language, indeed, on whatever subject employed, though the most abstruse to be found in the books, was as simple as that of childhood itself; while, at the same time, he had the happy faculty of putting the minds of all he addressed, even to the youngest and weakest, at once into the full possession of his ideas. This, with a good understanding of human nature, — and of human nature, particularly, as developed in the philosophy of the young head and the young heart, to enable him to know how, when, and where to interest, incite, check, and control, — together with a temperament of his own, and a general discrimination to insure a judicious application of his other faculties, combined to make him that invaluable acquisition to society — a good schoolmaster; one who, if adequately rewarded, would do his part in throwing the full light of science, within the gliding years of half a generation, over the mind of a nation.

The instruction of a teacher of the character we have just described, was a new thing to Locke Amsden. And it is needless for us to say, perhaps, how the advantages thus furnished him were improved. The first week he spent in looking up, and obtaining from his teacher, explanations and illustrations of all the knotty points which he had left unmastered in his course of mathematics. When all these were clearly understood and familiarized to his mind, he commenced, in good earnest, his onward progress. Day and night, almost unceasingly, applying every energy of his mind, he soon finished what remained yet to be studied of the ordinary course of mathematics, and thence passed on into and through physics, or natural philosophy, astronomy, and even a considerable portion of fluxions, with a rapidity and comprehension of what he passed over, which perfectly astonished his instructor; who, unwilling to check him in a career where he was accomplishing so much which was important, and which is so often neglected after the pupil is put upon more seductive studies, had thus far suffered him to bestow nearly his undivided attention to the branches we have enumerated. But as the school drew to a close, that instructor began to direct the attention of his favorite scholar to studies which had never, or not so particularly, occupied his mind. After a course of delicate questioning, calculated, with one of his turn, to make him keenly feel his own ignorance, and, at the same time, to furnish incentives to action, the former opened to the wondering and longing view of the latter the necessity and advantage of exploring other departments in the wide field of learning. And, fired with new zeal at the prospect, our young aspirant, as he was thus made to see before him

"Alps on Alps arise,"

now became doubly ambitious to mount their glittering steeps. But the close of the school, which was now at hand, precluded all opportunity, for the present at least, of entering upon this glorious field of exertion; and, with peculiar regret and sorrow, he was compelled to bid adieu to his beloved instructor, relinquish study, and return to the labors of the farm.

After the termination of this school, Locke found himself in a different situation from what he had ever been in before, at least, since he had begun the work of self-education. The books which had been presented him by the kind strangers — around whose fondly-remembered images, fancy, as he grew older, was daily throwing a more romantic interest — had all been studied, and their contents mastered; and, as he was unable to procure others upon those branches which he next wished to peruse, he now found himself without any food for his hungering mind, or at least such as would satisfy a mind like his, whose desires, instead of being appeased, were now tenfold increased. And from this state of unsatisfied longings, without employment for his mental energies in the present, and without hope to encourage him to look forward with certainty to any period when his inclinations could be gratified in the future, fancy began to obtrude her illusive creations into those chambers of thought which before had been devoted to the operations of reason. He became absent, moody, and despondent, and was fast falling a prey to a morbid imagination — a malady than which, for strong and sensitive minds, nothing scarcely is more to be dreaded; for

> " Woe to the youth whom Fancy gains,
> Winning from Reason's hands the reins;
> Pity and woe for such a mind
> Is soft, contemplative, and kind."

In vain did his father attempt to rouse him from his almost continual reverie — in vain attempt to repress those secret desires which he well knew to be the leading cause of his abstraction, and awaken an interest for business. But he little understood the nature of the mind he attempted to control; for as well may we attempt to chain the lightnings of heaven, as the soul really thirsting after knowledge. Such a mind may be thwarted, chilled, ruined; but it can never be so far restrained as to be moulded to other purposes, at least till opportunity be allowed for its ruling desires to become, in some good degree, sated. The father, wholly failing, at length gave up the attempt in vexation and despair; but another, who better understood the nature of the mind thus diseased, and the only remedies which could effect its cure, now undertook the task, and was successful.

One evening, as Locke sat alone in an open window, vacantly, and in moody thoughtfulness, gazing out at the rising moon, or the stars that were fading in her overpowering beams, his mother gently approached, and took a seat by his side.

" Locke," said she, in kind and gentle tones, after sitting a moment without appearing to attract the attention of the other, "Locke, your father complains that you are unusually inattentive to business, this summer."

"Complains? Well, he is always complaining of *me* — *I* can do nothing right; but brother Benjamin — he can do nothing wrong."

"It is possible, indeed, that you may sometimes get more censure than you should, and your brother more praise than he deserves, in the contrast which one of your father's turn would naturally draw between you. But still, Locke, I fear you have given too much cause for these complaints. I have myself often noted your neglect and heedlessness; and I now put it to your own conscience, my son, whether such a course is right, — is justifiable, in you?"

"Perhaps I may sometimes do wrong, in these respects, though it is not because I am unwilling to work — to do right. But you know how anxious I am to study, and may be, I think too much about that, to be as quick and ready as some. Still, I cannot help it; I have almost every thing yet to learn, and I must know, O mother, I must know!"

"I see, Locke, that your whole heart is set on being a great scholar. But scholarship alone, my son, will never make you truly great or happy. It is not the one thing needful; it brings not the pearl of great price. It may, indeed, bring you, as I once read in the works of some poet,

"The world's applause, perhaps the prince's smile,
And flattery's pois'nous potions, smooth as oil;
The poet's laurel, or the victor's palm;
But not one drop of Gilead's precious balm."

"I have often heard you speak of religion, mother, and I have never denied its importance; but I have never before heard you speak in this manner of learning. You surely do not hold it so lightly as one might think from what you have just said, do you?"

"I hold it lightly only, my son, when compared with the things of heaven. It would be my highest ambition to see you, as you enter life, a religious and an educated man."

"Why, then, mother, are you not willing I should be allowed an opportunity to obtain an education?"

"I am, Locke — I am willing — even desirous; but such an education as I fear our means would be sufficient to afford you, would not, I suppose, satisfy you. And yet, seeing how much your mind is set upon it, I have lately been thinking, that something might, and perhaps should now, be done for you. If a year to a good academy would serve your purpose ——"

"A whole year, mother!"

"Yes."

"Oh! if I could go a whole year! But father would never consent to it."

"Judge not too hastily, Locke; perhaps he will consent to it. Your brother has grown to a lusty and active boy, and you might now be much better spared; that is, after the present work-season is over. And that is as soon as I shall be able to fit you out with the necessary clothing. But suppose, Locke, I should try to intercede with your father for you, would you take hold of business as you ought, till after harvesting?"

"I would try, mother; and if you will bring father to the promise, I think — indeed, I know — that neither he or you shall have reason to complain of me any more."

"Well, then, my son, go to your rest now, and get up in the morning with a cheerful look, and go to your business like a man with his senses about him; and, within a few days, we will see what can be done."

Locke did as his mother had advised; and, two days afterwards, his father made the glad announcement of the permission which his mother had encouraged him to hope would be granted him.

From that day, Locke was a new creature. As happy as the lark, with which he rose in the morning, he cheerfully and diligently toiled through the day; giving his undivided attention to any and every kind of work upon which he was requested to engage. So complete a revolution in the business character of his son was the cause of much wonder to Mr. Amsden, who had predicted, that the permission he had given him to go abroad to school in the fall, instead of diminishing, would so increase the faults of which he complained, as entirely to spoil him for business; little dreaming, that his own conduct, in trying to repress his son's overpowering inclinations for study, had more than all else contributed to bring him into that state of mental abstraction and despondency, from which, through his mother's influence, he had been so timely rescued, by the only means, probably, that could ever have proved availing.

In this manner passed away the summer season; and the happy period, which was to reward Locke for his toils, at length approached. As the time drew near, Mr. Amsden, although his strict regard for his word forbade all thought of breaking his promise to his son, began, nevertheless, to feel a great reluctance at parting with him. And when he thought of the efficient help which the boy had rendered him through most of the season, at which he had been both gratified and profited, he could not forbear, by various favorable offers, to try to tempt the other to remain. It was, however, all in vain; for Locke, steady to his unalterable purpose, would listen to nothing short of the promised year's opportunity for study. And when the day fixed for his departure arrived, he packed up his books and scanty wardrobe, and, bidding the family adieu, set out on foot, with a light heart, for the village where the academy at which he proposed to pursue his studies was located. A little more than a day's walk brought him to his destination, when, to his great joy, he found the institution under the charge of his old teacher, Seaver, who, a month or two previous, at the close of his collegiate career, had been engaged as a permanent preceptor.

It is not our purpose to follow our hero in his course of studies through the year that now succeeded. Suffice it to say, that, by the advice of his preceptor, he devoted his time chiefly to the acquisition of the Latin and Greek languages, reserving, however, certain hours of the day, and such times as others generally spent in recreations, to the study of his own language, and such of the higher branches of English education as he had never had an opportunity of acquiring. Having, in his previous course of self-education, been accustomed to depend almost wholly on his own energies for the successful prosecution of his studies, he relaxed nothing from his mental habits here; and the result was, as it will ever be with those who do the like, that although he consulted his teacher, perhaps, less than any one in school, he yet outstripped them all in the rapidity of his progress. And as he was about to leave the institution, at the end of the year, he had the satisfaction of receiving from his venerated instructor the flattering encomium, that he had never known so great an amount of knowledge acquired by any individual in so short a period.

After the close of his year at the academy, young Amsden, who had now shot up into the usual proportions of manhood, returned to his father's with the intention of commencing a vocation to which he had long looked forward with pleasing solicitude — that of imparting to others the knowledge which had afforded him so much happiness in acquiring: For, from his childhood upward, he had heard no one employment so much lauded for honor and usefulness, as that of an instructor of youth; he had seen the same idea reiterated by the most celebrated of authors; and he had not yet learned, that the world too often applaud most what their practice shows they hold in the least estimation.

CHAPTER III.

> "The little knowledge *he* had gain'd,
> Was all from simple nature drain'd."
>
> GAY.

IT was late in the season when our hero returned home; and having inadvertently omitted to apprise his friends of his intention to engage himself as a teacher of some of the winter schools in the vicinity of his father's residence, he found, on his arrival, every situation to which his undoubted qualifications should prompt him to aspire, already occupied by others. He was therefore compelled, unless he relinquished his purpose, to listen to the less eligible offers which came from such smaller and more backward districts or societies as had not engaged their instructors for the winter. One of these he was on the point of deciding to accept, when he received information of a district where the master, from some cause or other, had been dismissed during the first week of his engagement, and where the committee were now in search of another to supply his place. The district from which this information came, was situated in one of the mountain towns about a dozen miles distant, and the particular neighborhood of its location was known in the vicinity, to a considerable extent, by the name of the *Horn of the Moon;* an appellation generally understood to be derived from a peculiar curvature of a mountain that partially enclosed the place. Knowing nothing of the causes which had here led to the recent dismissal of the teacher, nor indeed of the particular character of the school, further than that it was a large one, and one, probably, which, though in rather a new part of the country, would yet furnish something like an adequate remuneration to a good instructor, Locke had no hesitation in deciding to make an immediate application for the situation. Accordingly, the next morning he mounted a horse, and set out for the place in question.

It was a mild December's day; the ground had not yet assumed its winter covering, and the route taken by our hero becoming soon bordered on either side by wild and picturesque mountain scenery, upon which he had ever delighted

"To look from nature up to nature's God,"

the excursion in going was a pleasant one. And occupied by the reflections thus occasioned, together with anticipations of happy results from his expected engagement, he arrived, after a ride of a few hours, at the borders of the romantic-looking place of which he was in quest.

At this point in his journey, he overtook a man on foot, of whom, after discovering him to belong somewhere in the neighborhood, he proceeded to make some inquiries relative to the situation of the school.

"Why," replied the man, "as I live out there in the tip of the Horn, which is, of course, at the outer edge of the district, I know but little about the school affairs; but one thing is certain, they have shipped the master, and want to get another, I suppose."

"For what cause was the master dismissed? For lack of qualifications?"

"Yes, lack of qualifications for our district. The fellow, however, had learning enough, as all agreed, but no spunk; and the young Bunkers, and some others of the big boys, mistrusting this, and being a little riled at some things he had said to them, took it into their heads to train him a little, which they did; when he, instead of showing any grit on the occasion, got frightened and cleared out."

"Why, sir, did his scholars offer him personal violence?"

"O no — not violence. They took him up quite carefully, bound him on to a plank, as I understood, and carried him on their shoulders, in a sort of procession, three times around the schoolhouse, and then, unloosing him, told him to go at his business again."

"And was all this suffered to take place without any interference from your committee?"

"Yes, our committee-man would not interfere in such a case. A master must fight his own way in our district."

"Who is your committee, sir?"

"Captain Bill Bunker is now. They had a meeting after the fracas, and chose a new one."

"Is he a man who is capable of ascertaining for himself the qualifications of a teacher?"

"O yes — at least I had as lief have Bill Bunker's judgment of a man who applied for the school as any other in the district; and yet he is the only man in the whole district but what can read and write, I believe."

"Your school committee not able to read and write?"

"Not a word, and still he does more business than any man in this neighborhood. Why, sir, he keeps a sort of store, sells to A., B., and C., and charges on book in a fashion of his own; and I would as soon trust to his book as that of any regular merchant in the country; though, to be sure, he has got into a jumble, I hear, about some charges against a man at 'tother end of the Horn, and they are having a court about it to-day at Bunker's house, I understand."

"Where does he live?"

"Right on the road, about a mile ahead. You will see his name chalked on a sort of a shop-looking building, which he uses for a store."

The man here turned off from the road, leaving our hero so much surprised and staggered at what he had just heard, not only of the general character of the school of which he had come to propose himself as a teacher, but of the man who now had the control of it, that he drew up the reins, stopped his horse in the road, and sat hesitating some moments whether he would go back or forward. It occurring to him, however, that he could do as he liked about accepting any offer of the place which might be made him, and feeling, moreover, some curiosity to see how a man who could neither read nor write would manage in capacity of an examining school committee, he resolved to go forward, and present himself as a candidate for the school. Accordingly, he rode on, and soon reached a rough-built, but substantial-looking farm-house, with sundry out-buildings, on one of which he read, as he had been told he might, the name of the singular occupant. In the last-named building, he at once perceived that there was a gathering of quite a number of individuals, the nature of which was explained to him by the hint he had received from his informant on the road. And tying his horse, he joined several who were going in, and soon found himself in the midst of the company assembled in the low, unfinished room which constituted the interior, as parties, witnesses, and spectators of a justice's court, the ceremonies of which were about to be commenced. There were no counters, counting-room, or desk; and a few broad shelves, clumsily put up on one side, afforded the only indication, observable in the interior arrangement of the room, of the use to which it was devoted. On these shelves were scattered, at intervals, small bunches of hoes, axes, bed-cords, and such articles as are generally purchased by those who purchase little; while casks of nails, grindstones, quintals of dried salt fish, and the like, arranged round the room on the floor, made up the rest of the owner's merchandise, an annual supply of which, it appeared, he obtained in the cities every winter in exchange for the products of his farm; ever careful, like a good political economist, that the balance of trade should not be against him. The only table and chair in the room were now occupied by the justice; the heads of casks, grindstones, or bunches of rakes, answering for seats for the rest of the company. On the left of the justice sat the defendant, whose composed look, and occasional knowing smile, seemed to indicate his confidence in the strength of his defence, as well as a consciousness of possessing some secret advantage over his opponent. On the other hand sat Bunker, the plaintiff in the suit. Ascertaining from the remarks of the bystanders his identity with the committee-man he had become so curious to see, Locke fell to noting his appearance closely, and the result was, upon the whole, a highly favorable prepossession. He was a remarkably stout, hardy-looking man; and although his features were extremely rough and swarthy, they yet combined to give him an open, honest, and very intelligent countenance. Behind him, as backers, were standing in a group three or four of his sons, of ages varying from fifteen to twenty, and of bodily proportions promising any thing but disparagement to the Herculean stock from which they originated. The parties were now called and sworn; when Bunker, there being no attorneys employed to make two-hour speeches on preliminary questions, proceeded at once to the merits of his case. He produced and spread open his account-book, and then went on to show his manner of charging, which was wholly by hieroglyphics, generally designating the debtor by picturing him out at the top of the page with some peculiarity of his person or calling. In the present case, the debtor, who was a cooper, was designated by the rude picture of a man in the act of hooping a barrel; and the article charged, there being but one item in the account, was placed immediately beneath, and represented by a shaded, circular figure, which the plaintiff said was intended for a cheese, that had been sold to the defendant some years before.

"Now, Mr. Justice," said Bunker, after explaining, in a direct, off-hand manner, his peculiar method of book-keeping, "now, the article here charged the man had — I will, and do swear to it; for here it is in black and white. And I having demanded my pay, and he having not only refused it, but denied ever buying the article in question, I have brought this suit to recover my just due. And now I wish to see if he will get up here in court, and deny the charge under oath. If he will, let him; but may the Lord have mercy on his soul!"

"Well, sir," replied the defendant, promptly rising, "you shall not be kept from having your wish a minute; for I here, under oath, do swear, that I never bought or had a cheese of you in my life."

"Under the oath of God you declare it, do you?" sharply asked Bunker.

"I do, sir," firmly answered the other.

"Well, well!" exclaimed the former, with looks of utter astonishment, "I would not have believed that there was a man in all of the Horn of the Moon who would dare to do that."

After the parties had been indulged in the usual amount of sparring for such occasions, the justice interposed and suggested, that as the oaths of the parties were at complete issue, the evidence of the book itself, which he seemed to think was entitled to credit, would turn the scale in favor of the plaintiff, unless the defendant could produce some rebutting testimony. Upon this hint, the latter called up two of his neighbors, who testified in his behalf, that he himself always made a sufficient supply of cheese for his family; and they were further knowing, that, on the year of the alleged purchase, instead of buying, he actually sold a considerable quantity of the article.

This evidence seemed to settle the question in the mind of the justice; and he now soon announced, that he felt bound to give judgment to the defendant for his costs.

"Judged and sworn out of the whole of it, as I am a sinner!" cried the disconcerted Bunker, after sitting a moment working his rough features in indignant surprise; "yes, fairly sworn out of it, and saddled with a bill of cost to boot! But I can pay it; so reckon it up, Mr. Justice, and we will have it all squared on the spot. And, on the whole, I am not so sure but a dollar or two is well spent, at any time, in finding out a fellow to be a scoundrel who has been passing himself off among people for an honest man," he added, pulling out his purse, and angrily dashing the required amount down upon the table.

"Now, Bill Bunker," said the defendant, after very coolly pocketing his costs, "you have flung out a good deal of your stuff here, and I have bore it without getting riled a hair; for I saw, all the time, that you — correct as folks ginerally think you — that you did n't know what you was about. But now it 's all fixed and settled, I am going jist to convince you that I am not quite the one that has sworn to a perjury in this 'ere business."

"Well, we will see," rejoined Bunker, eying his opponent with a look of mingled doubt and defiance.

"Yes, we *will* see," responded the other, determinedly; "we will see if we can't make you eat your own words. But I want first to tell you where you missed it. When you dunned me, Bunker, for the pay for a cheese, and I said I never had one of you, you went off a little too quick; you called me a liar, before giving me a chance to say another word. And then, I thought I would let you take your own course, till you took that name back. If you had held on a minute, without breaking out so upon me, I should have told you all how it was, and you would have got your pay on the spot; but——"

"Pay!" fiercely interrupted Bunker, "then you admit you had the cheese, do you?"

"No, sir, I admit no sich thing," quickly rejoined the former; "for I still say I never had a cheese of you in the world. But I *did* have a small grindstone of you at the time, and at jest the price you have charged for your supposed cheese; and here is your money for it, sir. Now, Bunker, what do you say to that?"

"Grindstone — cheese — cheese — grindstone!" exclaimed the now evidently nonplussed and doubtful Bunker, taking a few rapid turns about the room, and occasionally stopping at the table to scrutinize anew his hieroglyphical charge; "I must think this matter over again. Grindstone — cheese — cheese — grindstone. Ah! I have it; but may God forgive me for what I have done! It *was* a grindstone, but I forgot to make a hole in the middle for the crank."

Upon this curious development, as will be readily imagined, the opposing parties were not long in effecting an amicable and satisfactory adjustment. And, in a short time, the company broke up and departed, all obviously as much gratified as amused at this singular but happy result of the lawsuit.

As soon as all had left the room but Bunker and his sons, Locke, perceiving that the others now seemed to expect an announcement of his business, at once proceeded to make known the object of his visit.

"Ah, indeed!" said Bunker, in surprise, as he keenly ran his eye over the rather slight proportions of the other. "Why, I had supposed, all the while, that you were some young sprig of the law, who had scented out our foolish little quarrel here from a distance, and had come to see whether the court, like the monkey judge in the fable, would work up all the cheese himself, or leave enough to afford a nibble to a lawyer. But have you really come to offer yourself as a master for such a school as ours?"

"I came for that purpose, sir," replied Locke; "and I trust to be found qualified for the situation. I have brought with me a certificate of qualifications; and further, I am very willing to be examined personally by yourself and others."

"I have been examining you, for some minutes, with my eyes," said the other, "and that is a way of examining masters, for our school at least, which is more necessary than you may imagine. You may have learning enough for us, perhaps; but the question first to be decided is, whether you will be equal to managing our rough boys in the mountains here."

The two largest boys, who had stood in a corner glancing at the person of our hero with a sort of contemptuous twinkling of their eyes, now whispered together, and giggled outright, apparently at the thought that such a fellow should ever attempt to give them a thrashing; for they had always been so accustomed to associate schoolmasters with thrashings, that they never thought of the former without the accompanying idea of the latter.

"Boys," resumed Bunker, "do you know what Josh Bemus intends doing this winter. I have been thinking, for a day or two past, that he probably would have about enough of the tiger in him to make you a very suitable master, if he could be had. You have had king log, and trod upon him; and now, if you don't get king stork, it wont be because you don't deserve it."

"You will hardly get Josh, I think," replied one of the boys. "He told me, at the turkey-shooting last week, that he had engaged to tend horses this winter at the stage-tavern down on Roaring River, because he rather do it than keep school."

"Well, every one for his taste," said Bunker, laughing. "I suppose Josh is not a fellow that would take much pleasure in a thinking life; though, as he has succeeded in subduing one or two unruly schools, I had thought of him for ours. But as that is now out of the question, and as I can hear of no other person who will do, I think we may as well examine into this gentleman's qualifications, now he has applied for the school."

"I have but little hope, sir, that I shall be considered a proper teacher of your district," observed Locke, who had become so much disconcerted by the ominous conduct of the boys, and the remarks of their father of a similar significance, that he now began to think of beating a retreat. "I cannot be the person you want, I think, from what I gather from your observations; and therefore we may as well drop the subject at once, perhaps."

"O, I don't know about that, sir," rejoined Bunker. "You look hardly equal to the task, be sure; but there is considerable snap in those black eyes of yours, I see. I have seen several fellows, in my time, of as little bodily show as you, who turned out to be a match for any thing when called to act. And I should not be surprised if you should prove to be one of the same kidney. Boys," he continued, turning to his sons, "you know how sadly you all got disappointed in that little, feeble-looking master of yours last winter. You calculated, when he began his school, that you should be able to control him as you pleased; but you soon found you had reckoned without your host, I believe."

"Well, he was a mean scamp, for all that," replied the oldest boy; "and we should have shipped him, at one time, if some of the boys had not flummuxed from the agreement. For he deserved it enough, and no mistake. Only think!

He made a rule, that every one who did not get into the school-house as soon as he did, after our play-spell at noon, should take a ferruling. And then what does he do but join us in sliding down hill on a hand-sled; and when we got warm at it, and just as a great load of us, he and all, had got under weigh and could n't stop, off he jumps, gives the sled a kick, and cuts and runs for the school-house, which he reached first, of course; and we had to be ferruled for breaking the rule. Now, you know, father, that was n't a fair shake, and he ought to have been walloped for it; and the boys were sneaks, that they had not stood by us, when we tried, the next day, to turn the tables on him —— "

"As he had first done on you, for some previous trick, eigh?" interrupted the former. "You have generally had strange doings in school, both by scholars and teachers, we all know; but now they have put me in committee, I intend to look after you a little myself. Now, sir," he added, again turning to Locke, "now, sir, we will come back to your case, if you please — what will be your price a month, and boarded?"

"Fifteen dollars."

"We gave but fourteen last winter, and the master could manage such a set of fellows as ours, too. The district will never consent to rise on that price. Can't you fall a dollar?"

"Perhaps I might, if I could make up my mind to undertake your school."

"Make up your mind! why, you offered yourself; and you did not come to trifle with me, did you?"

"Certainly not."

"Well, wait then till we have thought and talked this business all out. Don't get frightened before you are hurt. You may think better of some of us before we get through. But there is another thing: our district require a master to teach all the working days in the month, and not twenty-two days, as you masters generally make a month — would you consent to that?"

"Perhaps I should not be disposed to quarrel with you, even on that point, if I were to take your school."

"Very well. So then we can agree upon the terms, I see," said Bunker. "Now, for the main question — do you know any thing?"

"I trust so, sir," said Locke, hardly knowing yet what to make of the man, "I trust so. Here is a certificate from my late preceptor — will you hear it read?"

"No," replied the other, "I should place no dependence on any thing of that sort. Every one who goes to an academy gets a certificate, if he wants one, I have noticed; while not one in three, who go there, are fit for teachers. So you see, that there is more than an even chance that we get cheated, when we take a man on certificate. Why, how, sir, could a preceptor know whether you could govern a school, when you had never tried it? And how could he certify, that you had a faculty to teach in a school that neither of you had ever seen, where every scholar, perhaps, would require the application of a different method, before he could be brought to learn any thing worth mentioning?"

"I offered the paper only to show my acquirements — that I understood all the sciences taught in common schools," said Locke in reply.

"O, I presume you have gone over enough of what is put down in the books," resumed the other. "But how can I tell, from your recommendation, whether you can think for yourself, independent of your books; and what is more for a teacher, whether you can teach others to think for themselves? Why, sir, I have known many a fellow returned from an academy, and even a college, who had no more ideas of his own than a blue jay. And besides that, his brains were so trammeled by rules, &c. that there was little prospect of his ever bettering his condition. Now, the main object of education should be, in my opinion, to teach men to think, and not depend upon books for every thing to be known. Now, here is the great book of nature open before us, full of every kind of knowledge for those who can think. Then, don't you see the advantage which a man who can read that has over one who can only read the books of men, which are so liable to contain errors?"

"I certainly agree with you in much you have said, sir; but if you intend to say that book learning, as you would term it, is useless, I must wholly dissent," observed Locke.

"I don't say or think so," said Bunker. "No, it gives one great advantages in knowing what others in different parts of the world have found out, and may be, if rightly used and understood, a great help to him in thinking and making discoveries for himself. No, I don't think so of learning; for I am half bothered to death for the want of it myself, as you have to-day seen. And all I want of you is, to find out whether you have it; and, if so, whether it has made you a good thinker, and one who can teach others to be so, as well as to teach them the books."

"Very well, sir," responded the other, "I am quite willing you should satisfy yourself, and in your own way."

"I will," replied Bunker. "And first, let us see how you stand in arithmetic. What will twenty-seven multiplied by twenty-three produce? Don't look round for a slate or paper, but work it out in your head, as I do all my reckoning."

This sum, as soon as the answer was given by the one and pronounced correct by the other, was followed by more questions in each of the other fundamental rules of the science under consideration. Then came questions requiring, first, the aid of two of these rules, then three, then all, each

6

question being more difficult and complex, till the whole ground-work of common arithmetic was passed over by the questioner; in all of which he showed himself a proficient in mental arithmetic to a degree that perfectly astonished our hero, who, though he was, from his former habits of working sums in his head while at work, uncommonly ready at this exercise, was yet often put to his best powers in furnishing answers as soon as they were obtained by the proposer.

"Well, well, young man," said Bunker, with a look of approbation, as he brought his questions in this branch to a close, "it is not every one that can do what you have done. But we will now see if you can do as well in other matters. We will take geography, which I rank next to arithmetic in usefulness. Boys, will one of you step into the house, and bring us my maps?"

The boy despatched soon returned with a full and valuable set of maps, with which, to the surprise of Locke, the owner soon showed himself perfectly familiar; he, it appeared, having purchased them, some years before, for himself and children, with whom he had studied them, always keeping a boy by his side, when thus occupied, to read him the names of rivers, lakes, &c., as, one by one, he traced out each on the map with his finger, till he had mastered the whole.

A thorough and critical examination was now commenced, and, for some time, carried on by Bunker, in a series of novel and ingenious questions, well calculated to detect any deficiency in the examined.

"Very well, very well, sir," said the interrogator, good humoredly, as he finished this part of his examination, "I don't see but what you understand geography nearly as well as a man who can neither read nor write. There is one general question more, however, that I will ask you — which do you call the largest river in the world?"

"The Amazon is so accounted," replied the other.

"Yes, I know it is so laid down in the books; but do you think it so yourself?"

"I had supposed that to be the case, sir."

"Why?"

"Because it discharges the most water in a given time."

"You have got hold of the right manner of testing it, if it was only capable of being reduced to practice; and what you assert of this river may be a fact; but the question is, how it can be ascertained."

"Why, sir, it is the widest river, certainly."

"Widest! There again is one of your book rules, and see where it will land you, sir! Don't these fools of book-makers know, that one river may be twice as deep, and run twice as fast as another; and consequently, that one river of a mile wide may discharge as much water as another of double that width, in the same time?"

"I had concluded that all these circumstances had been taken into the account, when comparing the size of this river with that of the Mississippi, or other large rivers, before the fact in question was put down as established."

"Some guess-work of the kind may have been had on the subject, probably enough. But that is all; for do you suppose anybody has ever measured the depth or swiftness of the currents of these rivers? No! Why, it would take a board of engineers two years, and at the cost of millions, to do this with any accuracy. They would have to go, foot by foot, through the constantly-varying currents from one side to the other; and even then, how would they ascertain whether the water at the surface did not move twice as fast as at the bottom? No, sir, this never was or will be done. We must depend on other methods for ascertaining facts of this kind."

"What other method would you then propose?"

"Why, I have been able to think of no method so good as to ascertain the number of square miles which is drained by a river whose comparative size you wish to know; and when the quantity of surface thus drained is found, take another river, find the surface that drains also, compare the results, and you have the relative size of the two. Now here is a very simple method, which I practise for this purpose," continued the speaker, spreading open the maps of North and South America. "Both these are on the same scale, you see. Now I will place this piece of white paper over that part of South America which is drained by the Amazon, and then cut it down with the scissors, so that its outline shall just cover the extreme points, or sources of all the tributaries of this great river. Then we will cut the paper, thus made to represent the required surface on the same scale with the map, into triangles, or such other figures as can be put together again in some square shape, for measurement in square miles. In this manner, if the map be correct, you get the surface drained by the Amazon. You then can go through the same operation with the Mississippi, obtain your result, compare it with that of the former, and you will have the difference between the sizes of these two king-rivers of the new world. And whenever you do it, you will find that difference much less than is generally supposed; you will find that our Mississippi of a mile wide, when it meets the tide-waters, is more than three-fourths as large as the mighty Amazon, which is put down in the books to be from fifty to one hundred and eighty miles wide at its mouth. And if the maps could be corrected, so as to show the exact truth, I am not so sure but one would be found as large as the other."

"Your method is new to me, Mr. Bunker," observed Locke, "and I shall probably be indebted to you for a new idea. I will think of it."

"Ay, think — that's the way to get true knowledge."

"Have you any questions to ask me in the other branches, sir?"

"Not many. There is reading, writing, grammar, &c., which I know nothing about; and as to them, I must, of course, take you by guess, which will not be much of a guess, after all, if I find you have thought well on all other matters. Do you understand philosophy? It is not often required of our common schoolmasters, I know, but it is a grand thing for them to understand something of it; for then they will naturally, on a thousand occasions, be putting new ideas into the heads of their scholars, and in that way set them to thinking for themselves."

"To what branch of philosophy do you allude, sir?"

"To the only branch there is."

"But you are aware, that philosophy is divided into different kinds, as natural, moral, and intellectual?"

"Nonsense! philosophy is philosophy, and means the study of the reasons and causes of the things which we see, whether it be applied to a crazy man's dreams, or the roasting of potatoes. Have you attended to it?"

"Yes, to a considerable extent, sir."

"I will put a question or two, then, if you please. What is the reason of the fact, for it is a fact, that the damp breath of a person blown on to a good knife, and on to a bad one, will soonest disappear from the well-tempered blade?"

"It may be owing to the difference in the polish of the two blades, perhaps," replied Locke.

"Ah! that is an answer that don't go deeper than the surface," rejoined Bunker, humorously. "As good a thinker as you evidently are, you have not thought of this subject, I suspect. It took me a week, in all, I presume, of hard thinking, and making experiments at a blacksmith's shop, to discover the reason of this. It is not the polish; for take two blades of equal polish, and the breath will disappear from one as much quicker than it does from the other, as the blade is better. It is because the material of the blade is more compact, or less porous, in one case than in the other. In the first place, I ascertained that steel was made more compact by being hammered and tempered, and that the better it was tempered, the more compact it would become; the size of the pores being made, of course, less in the same proportion. Well, then, I saw the reason I was in search of, at once. For we know a wet sponge is longer in drying than a wet piece of green wood, because the pores of the first are bigger. A seasoned or shrunk piece of wood dries quicker than a green one, for the same reason. Or you might bore a piece of wood with large gimblet holes, and another with small ones, fill them both with water, and let them stand till the water evaporated, and the difference of time it would take to do this, would make the case still more plain. So with the blades; the wet or vapor lingers longest on the worst wrought and tempered one, because the pores, being larger, take in more of the wet particles, and require more time in drying."

"Your theory is at least a very ingenious one," observed Locke, "and I am reminded by it of another of the natural phenomena, of the true explanation of which I have not been able to satisfy myself. It is this: what makes the earth freeze harder and deeper under a trodden path than the untrodden earth around it. All that I have asked, say it is because the trodden earth is more compact. But is that reason a sufficient one?"

"No," said Bunker, "but I will tell you what the reason is; for I thought that out long ago. You know that, in the freezing months, much of the warmth we get is given out by the earth, from which, at intervals, if not constantly, to some extent, ascend the warm vapors to mingle with and moderate the cold atmosphere above. Now those ascending streams of warm air would be almost wholly obstructed by the compactness of a trodden path, and they would naturally divide at some distance below it, and pass up through the loose earth on each side, leaving the ground along the line of the path, to a great depth beneath it, a cold, dead mass, through which the frost would continue to penetrate, unchecked by the internal heat, which, in its unobstructed ascent on each side, would be continually checking or overcoming the frost in its action on the earth around. That, sir, is the true philosophy of the case, you may depend upon it. But now let me ask you a question — and it shall be the last one — a question which, perhaps, you may think a trifling one, but which, for all that, is full of meaning. What is the truest sign by which you can judge of the coming weather?"

"The quantity of dew that has fallen the night before, or that is then falling, if it be evening and the prognostic is required for the next day," replied the other. "At least I have never noticed any better criterion."

"That is an old rule, and a good one, I grant you," remarked Bunker; "but not so curious and unfailing as another which I, some time ago, began to observe."

"What may that be, sir?"

"Why, this, when you wish to know what the weather is going to be, just go out, and select the smallest cloud you can see, keep your eye upon it, and if it decreases and disappears, it shows a state of the air which will be sure to be followed by fair weather; but if it increases, you may as well take your great coat with you, if you are going from home, for falling weather will not be far off."

"That is, indeed, a curious and interesting fact in meteorology," responded Locke, "and I can readily see the reason why the indication should generally, at least, hold good."

"And what is that reason?" asked Bunker, with interest.

"Why, it is resolvable into electric phenomenon, I suspect," answered the former. "Whenever the air is becoming charged with electricity, you will see every cloud attracting all less ones towards it, till it gathers into a shower. And, on the contrary, when this fluid is passing off, or diffusing itself, even a large cloud will be seen breaking to pieces and dissolving."

"Right, sir!" cried Bunker; "you are a thinker, and no mistake. And let me tell you, there's more depending on that same electricity than your book philosophers dream of. I am pretty well satisfied, that not only our dry seasons and our wet ones, our cold seasons and our warm ones, are caused by some variation in the state of the electric fluid, but that our epidemical diseases, and a thousand other things that we cannot account for, are to be attributed to the same cause. But we will now drop the discussion of these matters; for I am abundantly satisfied, that you have not only knowledge enough, but that you can think for yourself. And now, sir, all I wish to know further about you is, whether you can teach others to think, which is half the battle with a teacher. But as I have had an eye on this point, while attending to the others, probably one experiment, which I will put upon you to make on one of the boys here, will be all I shall want."

"Proceed, sir," said the other.

"Ay, sir," rejoined Bunker, turning to the open fire-place, in which the burning wood was sending up a column of smoke; "there you see that smoke rising, don't you? Well, you and I know the reason why smoke goes upward, but my youngest boy don't, I rather think. Now take your own way, and see if you can make him clearly understand it."

Locke, after a moment's reflection and a glance round the room for something to serve for apparatus, took from a shelf, where he had espied a number of the articles, the smallest of a set of cast-iron cart-boxes, as is usually termed the round, hollow tubes, in which the axletree of a carriage turns. Then selecting a tin cup, that would just take in the box, and turning into the cup as much water as he judged, with the box, would fill it, he presented them separately to the boy, and said,

"There, my lad, tell me which of these is the heaviest?"

"Why, the cart-box, to be sure," replied the boy, taking the cup half-filled with water in one hand, and the hollow iron in the other.

"Then you think this iron is heavier than as much water as would fill the place of it, do you?" resumed Locke.

"Why, yes, as heavy again, and more too — I know 't is," promptly said the boy.

"Well, sir, now mark what I do," proceeded the former, dropping into the cup the iron box, through the hollow of which the water instantly rose to the brim of the vessel.

"There, you saw that water rise to the top of the cup, did you?"

"Yes, I did."

"Very well, what caused it to do so?"

"Why, I know well enough, if I could think; why, it is because the iron is the heaviest, and as it comes all round the water so it can't get away sideways, it is forced up."

"That is right; and now I want you to tell me what makes that smoke rise up the chimney."

"Why, I guess," replied the boy, scratching his head, "I guess — I guess I don't know."

"Did you ever get up in a chair to look on some high shelf, so that your head was brought near the ceiling of a heated room, in winter? and, if so, did you notice any difference between the air up there and the air near the floor below?"

"Yes, I remember — I have, and found the air up there as warm as mustard; and when I got down, and bent my head near the floor to pick up something, I found it as cold as tunket."

"That is ever the case; but I wish you to tell me how the cold air always happens to settle down to the lower part of the room, while the warm air, some how, at the same time, gets above."

"Why, why, heavy things settle down, and the cold air — yes, that's it, an't it? — the cold air is heaviest, and so settles down, and crowds up the warm air, that is lightest."

"Very good. You then understand that cold air is heavier than the heated air, as that iron is heavier than the water; so we now will go back to the main question — what makes the smoke go upwards?"

"Oh! I see it now as plain as day; the cold air settles down all round, like the iron box, and drives up the hot air, as fast as the fire heats it in the middle, like the water; and so the hot air carries the smoke along up with it, same as feathers and things in a whirlwind. Gorry! I have found out what makes smoke go up — it is curious, though, an't it, you?"

"Done like a philosopher!" cried Bunker. "The thing is settled. I will give up that you are an academician of a thousand. You can not only think for yourself, but can teach others to think; and I therefore pronounce you well qualified for a schoolmaster, in every thing except government, about which we will hope for the best, and run the risk; so you may call it a bargain as quick as you please."

"You offer to make it so on your part, I suppose you mean to be understood," said Locke; "for on mine, you remember I told you, some time ago, that I feel unwilling to undertake to govern a school of the character I have discovered yours to be."

"What, back out now?" exclaimed the other, with a disappointed air. "Why, I was beginning to have a first-rate opinion of you, and thought, of course, you would have spunk enough to make a trial, at least. Surely, you an't such a coward as to be afraid to do that, are you?"

These last remarks of Bunker, as taunting as they were in import, were yet made in such a half-reproachful, half-respectful manner, that they might not have brought our hero to any decision, but for the low, deriding laugh which the two larger boys set up on the occasion, and which fell upon his ears with such an exasperating effect, that it brought him to an instant determination, and he replied, with unwonted spirit,

"I will come on, sir; and with your permission, we will see whether pupil or teacher shall be the master of the school for the remainder of the winter."

"Good! that sounds like something," said Bunker, with returning good humor. "Boys," he continued, nodding significantly to his two oldest sons, "boys, did you hear that? Ah! all will come out well enough, I imagine. But come, sir, now we have settled the contract, we will walk into the house for a little refreshment before we let you go home; and while taking it, we will fix on the day of beginning the school, first boarding place, &c. Come, sir, come on; and if you have a good appetite, I will promise you a good dinner."

The decisive answer, which bound our hero to engage in this school, had now been given, and he had too much pride to make any attempts to recede from it; although, it must be confessed, that as soon as the momentary impulse, under which he had thus consummated the bargain, had died away, he more than half regretted the step he had taken. As it was, however, he soon determined to throw aside, as far as possible, both fears and regrets, and, arming himself with the rectitude of his purposes, proceed boldly and decidedly upon the task now before him. He at once saw, that, in this school, as in many others in our country, especially in the newer parts of it, a false standard of honor had, from some peculiar combination of circumstances, sprung up among the scholars; that instead of intellectual attainments, physical prowess, or mere brute force, had unfortunately been made the subject of predominating applause; and that this, as a very natural consequence, had led to the insubordination, and the frequent attempts of bullying the master, of which he had heard. And he justly reasoned, that, if he could break down this false standard, and set up the true one, as he was resolved, as far as practicable, to do, it would not only insure his own success, but prove the greatest of blessings to the school. He could not expect, however, to effect this object, at once; and the greatest difficulties, therefore, he would have to encounter, would be likely to occur during the first weeks of his school. It was this which had caused him so long to hesitate. But having, at length, been spurred into the undertaking, in the manner above mentioned, he now made up his mind to face the dangers manfully; and, if acts of moral courage would not serve, physical force, according to the best of his ability, should be employed to complete the conquest, till his contemplated reformation, in this objectionable feature of the school, could be effected. It was with these feelings, that, after an interesting hour spent in general conversation, during the preparing and partaking of the substantial meal provided on the occasion, Locke Amsden took leave of his singular host and employer, and departed.

On his way homeward, young Amsden fell to revolving over in mind the occurrences of the day, dwelling on the unexpected manner in which he had been received and examined, and on the still more unexpected intelligence of the man with whom he had thus come in contact, with the interested and curious feelings of one to whom some new leaf in the book of human nature has been presented for contemplation and study. He had been taken by complete surprise by the character of Bunker. Like many other students, whose intercourse is yet mainly confined to their fellows and instructors of the high schools, he had been led to underrate the strength and compass of the uneducated mind;

and he had expected to find, in the person in question, when he understood him to be ignorant of even the simplest rudiments of learning, one of a corresponding ignorance of principles and lack of ideas. But, instead of this, he had found a wholly unlettered man, who had grasped and mastered all the leading principles of several of the most important sciences; and who, by his own unassisted thought and observation, had stored his mind with a fund of original ideas more ample, perhaps, than that of many a scholar who had trod the whole round of the sciences. Some of Bunker's notions, it is true — such, for instance, as his opinion of book-learning, and the views he apparently entertained relative to a dependence on force for governing a school — our hero believed to be entirely erroneous; but the greater part of the man's ideas had struck him as not only new, but generally as forcible and just. And now, as he again called them to mind, and thought of the disadvantages under which they had been acquired, he could not forbear mentally exclaiming, "What might not such a mind become by the assistance of a well-applied education?"

Such were the reflections of our young aspirant, who, ever eager for knowledge, from whatever source it might come, felt himself instructed by what he had that day heard and witnessed. And well and wisely had he acted, in listening, in the spirit of candid inquiry, to the suggestions of one whose ideas were so entirely the fruits of his own independent thought and discriminating observation; for among people of such minds, however obscure or illiterate they may be, will be found, for those who can separate truth from the errors with which it may there occasionally be intermixed, the most productive fields for gleaning knowledge.

It was a favorite theory of the self-taught mountaineer whom we have introduced, it will be recollected, that every thing depended on being able to think. It would be well, perhaps, for the cause of science, if there were among those claiming to be friends to her advancement, more who held to the same opinion — who were at the same pains to enforce, by precept and example, this theory in its true meaning, as they are to remould, amplify, and bring out in new dresses, the thoughts which those old strong thinkers of gone-by days have wrought out for the appropriation of the intellectual idlers and surface-skimming book-makers of the present. This may be, and doubtless is, a reading age; but with all its advantages, we see not what claim it has to be called a thinking age. The cause of this may, in some measure, perhaps, be attributable to the prevailing utilitarian spirit of the times, which is more likely to lead only to the lighter investigations required in turning to account what is already known in science, than to laborious thinking, and those profound researches by which the scholars of past times were accustomed to push their way in the field of discovery; and which, by inviting and turning, through superior inducement, the greater proportion of the talents of the day into one channel, may have a tendency to circumscribe, impede, and weaken the operations of mind, and unfit it for the free, bold, and vigorous action which ever characterizes a thinking age. Another cause for this intellectual characteristic of our times may, perhaps, be found in the great comparative ease with which knowledge is now acquired. The sciences, as now taught in our schools, are simplified to the utmost. Besides this, a great proportion of our textbooks are prepared with questions involving most of what is essential to be learned on the subject matter therein contained. The answers to these questions, we fear, are quite too often obtained at an easier rate than by investigations of the lessons from which they alone should be gathered, and consequently without a full understanding of the subject. What is still worse in this system, as usually conducted, it naturally fixes in the mind of the pupil a limit beyond which he conceives he need not push his investigations; and when that limit, which embraces all the questions propounded, is gained, he thinks his task perfected. In this manner he is deterred from extending his inquiries on many different points which might otherwise occur to his mind, and from examining many bearings of the subject which he otherwise would do. But whatever may be the cause of the fact, if fact it be, as we believe, the existence of that fact is an evil which is as unnecessary as it is ominous to the progress of scientific discovery; and it should awaken the attention of the friends of science to the adoption of a course of measures that shall have a tendency to supply a remedy, without infringing upon the advantages to be derived from any real improvements which have been made.

We will now return from our digression. After a long and tedious ride, during which a dark and squally night had shut down over the desolate landscape, our hero's eyes were at length greeted with the cheering light that issued from the blazing logs, which, as usual on nights of the wintry character of the present, were liberally piled on the hearth of his father's kitchen. On reaching the house, he put his horse into the stable, and joined the family group within, whom, for the last hour, he had been envying, as he truly pictured them sitting in comfort around the social fireside. Having done good justice to a choice repast which maternal solicitude had prepared and kept in readiness for his expected return, he related the adventures of his excursion and the result, and paused to hear the comments which his parents and brother might make on the occasion.

"They must be strange people," remarked Mrs. Amsden; "and as parents, singular, indeed, must be their notions, which permit them thus to sanction the conduct of their boys, in such treatment of their instructors. Why, I am sorry you engaged in such a place, Locke."

"O, I don't know," said Mr. Amsden; "they seem rather rough, according to Locke's story, to be sure; but it may do him good to place him among folks that will wake him up a little. There's spunk enough in him, if you could get it to the surface, I rather guess. At all events, now he has engaged, I would do my best to carry it out, if I was he."

"So would I," promptly responded Ben. "Why, I've seen those Horn-of-the-Moon boys often enough at the wrestling rings at the muster trainings. Some of 'em, particularly the Bunkers, are as strong as mooses, sure enough; but, in any case that takes real grit to carry it out, I don't believe they are any great scratch. I saw a little *up-and-coming* sort of a fellow, from Sodom corner, in a fracas that a lot of 'em got into at the last muster, fairly scare from the ground a fellow of the Horn gang as big as two of him; and then stumped all the rest to come on, one at a time, and there was n't a soul of the whole boodle that dared go it. Concern 'em! I could contrive a way to manage 'em."

"And what would be the general features of your plan of operations, my learned brother?" said Locke, smiling good-naturedly at the thought of the other turning adviser in matters of school-keeping.

"I am learned enough to know what is the best way of getting along with such a pack as the Horn-of-the-Moon boys, at any rate, I think," replied Ben, slightly nettled; "and that is more than you know, or can do, without help, I fear. But if you want to know my plan, I will tell you: — In the first place, I would give out, in some way, that I was most furious quick-tempered, and so unfortunate bad and ructious, that from a child, when any one crossed and disputed me, I would fly all to pieces, and, without knowing what I did, lay hold of the first thing I could find, and knock him down. Now, don't you think they would be rather careful what they did, after they believed that?"

"I shall go on and endeavor to do my duty in a proper and decided manner," said Locke, in reply; "but to adopt your plan, though it might have its effect for a while, would yet be practising a deception to which I could never condescend."

"That is right, my son," said Mrs. Amsden: "I approve your determination to practise no deception; I would not, whatever the result."

"Why, mother," said Ben, "to fight Old Nick with Old Nick's play, if we must fight him at all, I thought was right, the world over."

"No, Benjamin," rejoined the mother seriously, but kindly, "that is a bad principle to act upon. Deception never long prospers; and, by its destructive effect on the morals of him who begins to practise it, generally ends in the ruin of him and all his plans."

Ben did not attempt to controvert his mother's general position, but still manifested a disposition to adhere to his opinion respecting the right and expediency of adopting the particular project he had advanced; and muttering, "Well, Locke must be helped for all that," fell to musing and devising some means by which his plan might be carried into effect without his brother's agency; but, not seeing fit to make known any of his conclusions, his remarks were soon forgotten, and the whole subject being at length dropped, the family retired for the night.

CHAPTER IV.

"Delightful task to rear the tender thought—
To teach the young idea how to shoot!"
THOMSON.

THOSE who have had much experience in the business of school-keeping, before yielding their unqualified assent to the oft-quoted sentiment of the great rural poet which we have placed over this chapter, would generally, we apprehend, wish to offer, as legislators say, an amendment to the proposition, in the shape of a proviso, something like the following: — *Provided always,* that the teacher can have the privilege of selecting his pupils. Such, at all events, were the feelings of our hero, as, with many misgivings, he set out, on the appointed day, for the place where he was to establish a government, in which (since the understood failure of Mr. Jefferson's experiment of introducing self-government, on the principles of a republic, into the college of which he was the founder) the golden mean between absolute monarchy and anarchy is wholly wanting — a government over what, he had reason to believe, would prove, in the present instance, as rebellious a set of subjects as were ever brought to order beneath the birchen sceptre of a pedagogue. But however mild his disposition, or unassuming his general demeanor, Locke Amsden was by no means wanting in resolution. He possessed, indeed, one of those seemingly paradoxical characters, so often to be found in the world, and yet almost as often misunderstood, in which great diffidence of manner is united with great firmness of purpose, and a full confidence in the ability to execute. And, consequently, whatever his fears and misgivings, he bravely combated them, and endeavored to fortify his mind against the approaching hour of trial. In this, he was much aided by his resolute little brother, Ben; who, for some secret reason, had contrived to defeat a previously-made different arrangement for the present journey, that he might himself attend the former, in whose success his pride and interest seemed to be wonderfully awakened.

On reaching the district where he had been engaged, Locke repaired at once to the residence of his employer, at whose house, it had been before arranged, he should first take up his lodgings, as the beginning of that round of boarding through the district, which here, as in many other places, was made to add variety, to say the least of it, to the monotonous life of the schoolmaster. He was received with much rough cordiality by Bunker, and with some show of respect by his mastiff-mannered boys. The good dame of the house soon began to bestir herself in preparation for a meal for the "new master" and his brother, the latter of whom, it was understood, after obtaining refreshment for himself and horse, was to return home that evening.

While the dinner was preparing, Ben, having departed for the stables, to see to his horse, in company with the boys, with whom he seemed determined to scrape acquaintance, Locke and his host soon became engaged in conversation on those topics in which they had previously discovered themselves to feel a mutual interest.

"I have felt considerable curiosity, since I became acquainted with you, the other day," observed our hero, at a point in the conversation when the remark might seem appropriately introduced, "to know how it could have happened, that so thinking a man as yourself had never learned to read?"

"Are you quite certain I should have been so much of a thinker as I am, if I had received a book-education?" said Bunker, in reply.

"Your knowledge would have been more extensive, in that case, doubtless, sir; and if you had been the worse thinker for it, the fault would have been your own, I imagine," replied the other.

"All that may be," remarked Bunker, musingly, "and perhaps it is so — perhaps it is with learning, as it is with property, which we never keep and improve so well when given to us, or get easily, as when it is obtained by our own exertions — by hard knocks and long digging. But whether this is so or not, one thing to my mind is certain, and that is, that more than half of your great book-men are, after all, but very shallow thinkers; though the way they dress up a subject with language, generally procures them the credit of being otherwise; for it is curious enough to see what a deal of real ignorance a few long words and learned terms are made to conceal."

"Ay," said Locke, "but does not your argument run against the abuse of learning, rather than its use?"

"Possibly," replied Bunker; "but, at any rate, I have often thought, that if I had received an education equal to some of your great scholars, I should have found out rather more than most of them appear to have done."

"Your impressions," rejoined Locke, "are, I suspect, by no means uncommon. I formerly thought so myself; but the more I study, the more I am convinced, that the unlearned are accustomed to expect much more from the learned than they should do. Scholars, however profound, can never discover what God has purposely hidden from the human mind."

"There may be something in your remarks," observed the

other, "and I will think over the subject again. But now, to return to your first question — What was the reason I had never learned to read, was it?"

"It was."

"Well, I will tell you honestly: it was, first, total want of opportunity, and then pride, till I had got to be so old a dog, that I thought I would not attempt to learn any new tricks."

"Those are rather unusual reasons, for this country, at least, are they not?"

"They are the true ones, in my case, nevertheless. My father was a trapper, and pitched his cabin at the very outskirts of civilization, on one of the great rivers in Canada, where schools were wholly out of the question; — even books were so rare, that I don't recollect of ever seeing but one during the whole of my boyhood. That one was my mother's old worn and torn bible, which, at last, a gray squirrel, that came in through the roof of our cabin, one day when we were all out, knocked down from a shelf into the fire, as we concluded, because we saw him escaping with a leaf in his mouth, to help make his nest. This, as I said, was the only book I remember to have seen; and this I should not recollect, probably, but for the singular manner in which it was destroyed, and the fact also that my mother, when she discovered her loss, sat down and cried like a child — God bless her memory! — if she had lived, she would have got another, and most likely have taught me to read it. But she died soon after, leaving me, at the age of about five, to the care of an ignorant hussy, that my father, in due time, married. Well, there I remained till I was twenty; when I left, and found my way into this part of the country, among people, who, to my surprise, could all read and write. I was not long, however, in discovering, that I was about as ignorant a heathen as ever came out of the bush. But, instead of going to school as I might and should have done, I felt ashamed to let people know my condition, and so let pride deprive me of a blessing which I could have easily obtained. And so it continued with me, till I married and settled down here on a new farm; when, if the pride I spoke of died away, its place was soon supplied by business cares and a lot of little squallers, that took away all chance or thought of learning to read. But, though not able to read myself, I can easily get others to do this for me. And, late years, having bought a good many books of different kinds for my wife or boys to read to me, I have got, in this way, and by talking with book-men both round home and abroad, a pretty tolerable good run of most that has been printed. And the result has been, that I have been sadly disappointed in what I used to suppose the mighty wisdom of books. To be sure, there are many books that are full of information and true philosophy; but let me tell you, sir, there is a prodigious sight of nonsense bound up together in the shape of books."

The dinner being now announced as in readiness, Locke went out to call in his brother, whom he at length espied in the yard of a grist-mill belonging to Bunker, and situated at no great distance from his house. Ben had here collected round him not only the young Bunkers, but several other boys who had come to mill from different parts of the district; and he was apparently making some communications to them, to which they were very evidently listening with considerable interest and surprise. What might be the nature of his communication, however, Locke, at that time, neither suspected nor ascertained, as he did not go near enough to hear what was said, and as Ben, when questioned on the subject, after joining the other, refused or evaded any direct answer.

As soon as the brothers had finished the repast which had been prepared for them, Ben got up his team, and, bidding his brother "to remember to put on a stiff upper lip when he went into his school," cracked his whip and started off for home.

The next morning, after breakfast, as Locke was about to leave for the school-house, for the commencement of his task, Bunker took him aside: —

"I should like to ask you one question, master," he said; "and if you answer it at all, which you can do as you like about, I hope you will do it candidly."

"Certainly, I will, Mr. Bunker," replied the other, in some surprise.

"Well, I overheard my boys saying last night, that your brother, who came with you, told them and some others down at the mill, that you had such a fiery and ungovernable temper, that your family, as well as all the boys in your neighborhood, always run from you, when you get offended (as you often do at almost nothing), lest you should seize an axe and split their brains out; and he begged of them, with tears in his eyes, not to cross you in school, or break any of your orders; for if they did, you would be almost certain to seize the shovel or a cleft of wood, and kill one of them on the spot; and then he should have to see his brother hung for doing only what was natural to him, and what he could n't help. Now, though I have said nothing, yet I think I see through the object of this story; and I want to ask you, not whether it is true — for I think it must be all humbug — but whether you put your brother up to this little plot, or whether it was one of his own hatching?"

"It was one solely of his own contriving, and used without my knowledge or consent," replied Locke, promptly.

"I am glad of it," rejoined Bunker; "for, though there would have been nothing very criminal in such a course, yet, I confess, it would have lowered you in my opinion. It was well enough in such a chick as I suspect your brother to be and I have concluded to have it go, for the present, just as he left it; for there is no knowing how much it may help you in keeping the boys under. So I advise you to keep your own counsel, go to your school, be decided, but treat your scholars like men and women, and not like slaves or senseless puppets, as some of our masters have done, to their own sorrow, I think. Do this, and I presume you will have no trouble in managing them. But whatever method you may take to govern them, be sure that you make them good thinkers."

On reaching the school-house, where he found most of the pupils assembled, Locke soon saw indications, which convinced him, that Ben's bugbear representations, which had been made with so much address and apparent honesty that the truth of them seems not to have been doubted, were already known to every individual in school; and that, in consequence, he had become, with the younger portion of them especially, the object of a terror which he little thought it would ever be his lot to inspire. This, indeed, was plainly discoverable the first moment he entered the house; for coming among them somewhat unexpectedly, while his fancied traits of character were under discussion, they scattered for their seats with nearly as much haste and trepidation, as they would have shown had a dangerous wild beast walked into the room. And, in two minutes, all was so still, that not a sound, unless it was the beating of the hearts of the more timid, could be heard in the apartment. Nor did the vivid impressions of their new master's severity, which had thus oddly been received by the scholars, and which had fairly frightened them into such unwonted stillness, prove of so temporary a character as he expected. And often during the day, while arranging his classes or attending to the ordinary duties of the school, he scarcely knew whether he felt most secret amusement or pity at the evident sensations of many around him, as he observed with what trembling anxiety his movements were watched, and saw how many furtive and expressive glances were cast at his face, in which, as their excited imaginations then pictured him, they appeared to read that which put all thoughts of roguery or misbehavior to instant flight. All this, to be sure, had reference mainly to the younger portion of the pupils. The older part, it is true, though their demeanor was marked by a respectful quietness, appeared rather to be debating in their minds the expediency of taking their former courses, than entertaining any particular alarms for themselves, while their behavior should be, to a decent degree, orderly. And during the intermissions of the first two or three days, little groups of the usually insubordinate might have been seen engaged in discussing the momentous question, how far it might be safe or feasible to attempt to subjugate the master, in the same way they had several of his predecessors. In all these consultations, however, Tom Bunker, whom his father had secretly engaged to take Locke's part in case of trouble, unexpectedly hung back, telling them they could do as they pleased; but perhaps they would find out, that they had better let the man alone. This coming, as it did, from their acknowledged champion, and one who had generally acted as ringleader in their former outbreaks against their teachers, not a little dampened the ardor of the advocates of rebellion. And after a few idle threats and expressions of defiance, thrown out by the way of warding off any imputations which might be made on their courage for retreating from their position, they finally relinquished their designs on the master, and concluded to submit to his authority, at least till he became the aggressor, in those acts of tyranny that they expected he would ere long exhibit towards them. The movements of the latter, therefore, were watched with no less silent suspicion by the larger, than with fear by the smaller pupils, during the first week of his school. Perceiving all this, he very wisely shaped his course for establishing his authority on a more permanent foundation than can ever be raised in feelings where fear alone is the governing principle. While dignity and decision of manner marked his conduct in enforcing good order in school, he yet made kindness and courtesy to characterize his general demeanor towards all his scholars. This course he adopted no less from the suggestions of his own mind, drawn from the remembrance of the effect which kindness and respect in a teacher always produced on his feelings when he himself was a pupil, than from the recommendation of Bunker, "to treat his scholars like men and women."

The sentiment of the last-named person on this subject is indeed one well deserving of the consideration of all instructors of youth. Few teachers seem to be aware what a just estimate children put upon manners — how quickly they pass a sentence of condemnation on all that is coarse, contemptuous, or unfeeling, and how soon they appreciate every thing that denotes respect and kindness towards them. If teachers would properly consider this, they would find less difficulty, perhaps, in accounting for the little influence which they often find themselves capable of exercising over the minds of their pupils: for almost as certain as one pursues the first-named course of conduct towards them, will his precepts be rejected; while the precepts of him who exhibits the last-mentioned conduct will be readily received, and treasured up for improvement.

And such was the effect of the kind and judicious manner which Locke displayed among the rough and uncultured pupils he had undertaken to control. When they saw, that, instead of turning out the cruel and capricious tyrant they had expected, he wanted nothing of them but what their own consciences told them was just and reasonable, and especially when they found themselves uniformly treated with such respectful courtesy, when their behavior was not exceptionable, all the mingled feelings of hatred, fear, and suspicion, with which they had armed themselves in anticipation of an opposite treatment, rapidly melted into an affectionate reverence, that not only destroyed, in most of them, all inclination for insubordinate conduct, but made them anxious to gain his approbation; the more particularly so, doubtless, from the belief they still entertained, that his displeasure would be attended with fearful consequences to themselves.

The first object of our instructor, that of gaining willing ears for what he wished to impart, was now, to a good degree, accomplished. And no sooner had he made sure of this important point, than he began to redouble his exertions to rouse their minds from that cold and listless intellectual condition in which they were unconsciously sunk, and which caused them to look upon learning and all attempts at mental excellence as a mere matter of secondary concern. This he did, not so much by general exhortation (for he well knew that scholars generally hate preaching masters), as by what logicians call arguments *ad hominem*, addressing the self-love of one, the vanity of another, the curiosity of a third, and so on; the dispositions of each having been previously studied for the purpose. In fine, he adopted almost as many expedients as he had pupils, in inciting them to push forward in their particular studies, and in awakening in their bosoms a love of learning. And, in doing this, he also labored incessantly, with argument, ridicule, and such familiar illustrations as they could best understand and appreciate, in showing them the superiority of mind over matter, or mere physical powers; and in setting up the true standard of excellence among them, instead of the false one, to attain to which seemed hitherto to have been the only object of their emulation. The happy results of these well-directed exertions were soon apparent. The exploits of the wrestling ring, the leaping match, and other of the rough athletics, in which it had been their chief pride to excel, were no longer the main topic of conversation; and the feats of bullies and hectoring blades, exercised upon schoolmasters, ministers, and deacons, were no longer considered a matter of boasting. The keen interest formerly manifested on all these subjects, indeed, had so sensibly declined, that they were now seldom mentioned. But in their place were heard, both during the intermissions of school, and the evenings spent at home, almost nothing but talk of studies, anecdotes of the school, or the discussion of the arithmetical puzzles, and the various interesting and curious questions relative to the phenomena of nature, which the teacher was in the habit of putting out, with which to exercise the minds of his pupils. The parents of the district witnessed this change in their children with no less surprise than pleasure, and wondered by what magic it could have been effected. Bunker, the committee-man, daily grew proud of his selection of a teacher, and declared he had already done more towards making good thinkers of his scholars than any of their former instructors had done in a whole winter. In short, before two weeks had elapsed, the whole Horn-of-the-Moon was ringing with praises of the new master.

But although young Amsden's school was fast becoming what he had so sedulously labored to make it, and although his pupils had generally, since the expiration of the first half week of their attendance, so far shown themselves disposed to obedience and propriety of behavior, as led him to believe that no attempt would now be made to resist his orders, yet it was not long before he found he should not be permitted to avoid the test to which a master's firmness and discretion are almost invariably put, in maintaining his authority, at some period or other of his school.

This period, which forms a sort of crisis in the teacher's government, resulting either in its overthrow, or in its establishment on a permanent basis, generally occurs about the third week of the school. After the first few days of the school, during which the restraints which scholars feel under a new master, or the fears they may entertain of his yet untried spirit and promptitude in administering punishment, usually keep them quiet and orderly, they begin to take liberties; though at first of so trivial a character, that a teacher, not finding in them any particular cause of complaint, suffers them to pass unnoticed. From this, the more evil-disposed go on crowding, crowding a little, and a little more, upon his authority, till they get so bold that he finds the most decisive measures will alone save his dominion from a total overthrow.

Something like this was the process which Locke had perceived going on in his school, without knowing exactly where to interpose his authority; when one, a boy of about fourteen, who had been more forward than others in the course, one day grew so bold as to place his orders at absolute defiance. Perceiving at once that his government was at an end, unless the offender was conquered, and indignant at his unexpected audacity, our hero, under the impulse of the moment, was about to chastise him on the spot. A second thought, however, told him that he was too much irritated to do this now with the best effect on the offender, or on others inclined to become so; and he accordingly apprised the boy of the reason for deferring his punishment, but promised him, at the same time, that punishment would certainly follow. Although this act of disobedience was not instigated by any one, even by those from whom he had most reason to apprehend difficulties, yet either that, or the threatened chastisement, seemed to produce considerable sensation among them, by awakening, perhaps, remembrances of their old fracases in resisting their teachers on similar occasions, and in exciting in some degree their sleeping inclinations to take some such part when the punishment of the present offender should be inflicted. In addition to these suspicious appearances, he noticed, after his school was dismissed for the day, considerable mysterious whispering among two or three of those just mentioned, and overheard one of them, a relative of the offender, trying to excite the others to join him in preventing the threatened punishment, which they supposed would take place on the opening of the school the next morning. But our hero, unmoved by these unexpected and somewhat ominous demonstrations, resolved to go resolutely forward and do his duty, whatever might be the consequences to himself. On his way homeward, however, while reflecting upon the subject of school-punishment, its object, and the most effective manner of administering it to obtain that object, he began seriously to doubt the wisdom and expediency of the custom which he had always witnessed, and which he had proposed to follow in the present case,— that of inflicting chastisements in open school. He reasoned, and from a just notion of the human heart too, that the presence of companions, whom the delinquent knew to be looking on to see with what spirit he bore up under the operation, that they might afterwards praise him for the *spunk* he exhibited, or taunt him for his weakness if he was seen to succumb, would in most instances have a tendency to arm him with feelings of pride and obstinacy, which would not only destroy all the beneficial effects to be gained from the punishment, but often make him more obdurate than before. So strongly, indeed, did these considerations weigh on the mind of Locke, that he at length determined to adopt a different mode of punishing the boy in question; and after trying to judge of his own feelings, were he placed in the offender's situation, as to what course would most conduce to that penitence and humility best calculated for amendment, and calling to mind all he had ever observed of the effects of punishment on others, he at last hit on a plan which he determined to carry into immediate execution. Accordingly, after obtaining his supper, he repaired at once to the culprit's residence, and, taking his father aside, made known the boy's conduct, the absolute necessity of his punishment, and gave his reasons for wishing to inflict that punishment in private; ending with a request, that the other should call out his boy, and that they all three should repair together to the school-house for the purpose he had mentioned.

"Why, the boy deserves a basting richly enough, no doubt," observed the father; "yes, and a good one too. And, if I was you, I would give it to him. But what on earth do you want my help in flogging him for? Why, that is part of what we are paying you for, I take it, master."

"I wish for no help in the mere chastisement," replied Locke; "but I think your presence would add much to its beneficial effects, and it is only for your son's good that I request you to go."

"Well, well," rejoined the former, "if you think it will do the boy any good,—and I don't know but you are half right about it; for I think if I was a boy, I should dislike most confoundedly to be licked by a schoolmaster before my father—if you think this, why, I will go with you; but I kinder hate to, that's a fact."

His reluctance having been thus wisely overcome, the father promptly called out his boy, who, not daring to disobey the command which was then given him, followed the two others, in dogged silence, to the school-house. On reaching the house, which, as expected and desired, was entirely solitary, Locke raised a light, and proceeded to the painful task before him. He first kindly addressed the offender; and, in a manner calculated to humble without irritating, set forth the probable consequences, both to him and the school, of suffering his offence to pass without punishment, which he had been called there to receive, and then administered a chastisement of adequate severity. After this, he was again addressed by his teacher, the father occasionally putting in a word, for nearly an hour, before the expiration of which he gave unequivocal evidence of not only being deeply penitent for the past, but resolved on good behavior for the future.

While so many alterations and improvements have been made in the education and management of children and youth at school, it is somewhat remarkable, that so little variation has taken place in the mode and character of school punishments, which, with some slight abatement, perhaps, in degree and frequency, have remained nearly the same since the days of King Solomon, who had a wondrous high opinion, it will be recollected, of the virtues of the rod. From nearly all our civil codes, instituted for the government of men, whipping, for the punishment of offences, has been repudiated, as not only barbarous, but calculated to harden rather than amend; and confinement in prison, or other punishment, substituted. Is the distinction which is thus kept up between the government of men and children, made because the young are more obdurate than the old? Certainly not; for the reverse of this is acknowledged to be the fact. Is it, then, because a similar change in the government of schools is impracticable? We understand not why this should be; since, if expulsions or degradations would not effect the object, rooms for solitary confinement might easily be provided for every school-house, and the delinquent imprisoned till he would be glad to purchase liberty by amendment. There may be sound reasons for the distinction we have mentioned, but we confess we are unable to discover them.

But suppose we admit, that the punishment of whipping is sometimes indispensable for insuring obedience and order in school, is there not room for improvement both in the frequency and manner of its application? Nothing has a greater tendency to brutalize the feelings, to deaden all the best sensibilities of the heart, than frequent repetitions of this questionable practice. If it must be resorted to, let it be seldom; and then, for reasons before suggested, let it be done in private, and, if possible, in the presence of a parent. If thus done, unless we have read in vain the young heart, its restraining fears, and its keen and overpowering sense of guilt and shame, when conscious that there is no one present to uphold and countenance it in error, rare indeed will be the cases in which a repetition of the punishment will ever be found necessary.

The scholars, the next morning, assembled under the expectation that the business of the day would be opened by the promised punishment of the culprit of yesterday. But when they perceived that no movement of the kind was likely to be made, and especially when they noticed the altered demeanor of the boy, whose whole appearance, instead of the brazen looks which he wore on leaving school the preceding evening, now indicated the deepest humility, their disappointment was equalled only by their surprise. It was evident enough to them, that something had occurred to effect this unexpected alteration of circumstances. But what this was, they were wholly at a loss to conjecture. And, as the boy, when they went out, either avoided them or evaded their questions, the mystery was not solved till one of the boys, who had been home for his dinner, accidentally got hold of the truth, and hastened back to impart the important news to his companions.

"Hurra! boys," he exclaimed, as he came puffing up to a group assembled in the school-house yard to discuss the subject anew before entering the school for the afternoon, "hurra! boys, I have found out all about it, now."

"How was it, — how was it?" asked a dozen eager voices at once.

"I'll tell ye," replied the boy, lowering his voice, and assuming a look of awe, as he thought of what he was about to relate. "They took him — that is, his father and the master — they took him last night here to the school-house — only think of that, all alone in the night! — and then the master gave him, I do spose, one of the terriblest hidings that ever was heard of."

"What! right afore his father?" exclaimed several of the older boys, evidently surprised and disconcerted to hear of this new mode of punishment, which might soon be adopted in their own cases.

"Yes," replied the former, "and then kept him half the night, forzino, talking to him like a minister, till he most cried himself to death, they said. How awful! wa'nt it, now?"

"Why, I rather he 'd a killed me," responded one of the former, in which he seemed to be joined by both old and young; all of whom, for different reasons, saw much to dislike and dread in the picture.

"Well, I give in beat," observed the young bully, who, as before intimated, was meditating resistance to the punishment in question; "somehow, I can't get the hang of this new master. He does every thing so different from what a fellow is looking for; and I have about concluded we may as well mind our own business, and let him alone."

"So, Mike, you have come to my opinion at last, have you?" said Tom Bunker, who had been listening in silence. "Now I have said but little about this affair, from first to last; and if you had had a chance to go on with the shine you was thinking of, I can't say what part I should have taken, if the master had needed help; but I want to tell you I think he has used us all like a gentleman, and I would fight for him. And now, Mike, what do you say to backing him up in keeping order, and using him as he wants to use us, for the rest of the winter?"

"That is what I have been thinking of myself—I am agreed," answered Mike.

"Well, then, boys," rejoined Tom, "let us all hands now into the house for our books; and the one that learns the most, and behaves the best, shall be the best fellow."

The crisis had passed. In the defeat of this last and impotent attempt to break down the authority of our schoolmaster, his triumph was completed. All seemed to understand this; and, for the remainder of the season, no school could have been more distinguished for good order and obedience.

All troubles in regard to government being now at an end, and no others being anticipated by Locke, he urged his pupils forward in their studies with all the incitements he could command. But even this may sometimes, perhaps, be carried too far. At all events, he was accused of so doing, in connection with an event which soon occurred, and which came near breaking up his school. But the relation of this unexpected and painful incident, we will reserve for a new chapter.

CHAPTER V.

"So swift the ill — of *such mysterious* kind,
That fear with pity mingled in each mind.'"

CRABBE.

IT was near the middle of the dark and dreary season which characterizes our northern clime. Old Winter had taken his January nap. And having protracted longer than usual his cold, sweaty slumbers, he had now, as if to make amends for his remissness, aroused himself with a rage and fury which seemed to show his determination to expel the last vestige of his antagonistic element, heat, that had thus invaded and for a while disarmed him, for ever from his dominions. The whole season, indeed, to drop the metaphorical for plain language, had been one of uncommon mildness. A warm and broken December had been succeeded by a still warmer and more thawy January. And so little had people been made aware of the presence of winter thus far, that their doors were often left open, and small fires only were either used or required. But the cold weather now set in with intense severity, and compelled all to keep tightly closed doors and roaring fires.

The school-house, which we have been for some time making the scene of action, had been built the preceding fall; and the interior, consequently, had been freshly plastered; while the wood-work of the doors and windows, already tight before from its newness, had been swollen by the recent thawy weather; so that the whole room, by this, and the finishing operation of the frost in closing up the remaining interstices, had been made almost wholly impervious to the admission of any fresh air from without. From this, however, no evil consequences, owing to the mildness of the season, and the attendant circumstances we have mentioned, had resulted to the school. But scarcely a week had elapsed, after the change of weather just described, before the scholars, though apparently much enjoying the contrasted comforts of their tight, stove-heated room, while the cold, savage blasts could be heard raging and howling without, became very visibly affected. A livid paleness overspread their features; while their every appearance and movement indicated great and increasing languor and feebleness. The general health of the school, in short, including that of the master, seemed to be rapidly failing. These indications were soon followed by several instances of so great illness as to confine its victims to their homes, and even to their beds. Among the latter was the case of the only son and child of a poor, but pious and intelligent widow, by the name of Marvin, which excited in the bosom of Locke feelings of the deepest sorrow for the misfortune of the boy, and sympathy in the affliction of his doating parent. And it was not without reason that both teacher and parent were touched with peculiar grief on the occasion; for the boy, who was about ten years old, was not only kind and amiable in disposition, but a very excellent scholar. And now, almost for the first time, having the advantages of good instruction, and his ambition and natural love of learning having been kindled into enthusiasm by the various incitements held out to him by his instructor, with whom he had become a secret favorite, he pursued his studies with an ardor and assiduity which knew no relaxation. And having made surprising progress in grammar, during the few weeks the school had kept, he had recently solicited and obtained leave to commence arithmetic, to which he was giving his whole heart and soul, when he was thus snatched from his engrossing pursuit by the hand of sickness.

These cases of sickness, and especially the more serious one of the good and studious little Henry, the boy we have particularized, produced much sensation in the neighborhood. And the cause, not only of these instances of absolute illness, but of the altered and sickly appearance of the whole school, which now excited observation and uneasiness, began to be generally discussed. As no epidemic was prevailing in the country, and as all other schools in the vicinity, as far as could be heard from, were even unusually healthy, it was soon concluded that the present unhealthiness must be occasioned by something wrong about the school-house, or in the manner of conducting the school. And as nothing amiss could possibly be perceived in the school-house, which all pronounced warm and comfortable, it was settled that the fault, of course, must be looked for in the master. Some averred that the latter, by undue severity, or by some other means, had broken down the spirit of his scholars, which had caused them to become melancholy, drooping, and sickly. Others said that he had made the scholars study so hard, that it had caused their health to give way under the tasks which they were induced, through fear, or some mysterious influence he had obtained over their minds, to perform. And there were yet others who carried still farther the idea thrown out by those last named, and contended that the master must have resorted to some unlawful art or power, which he had exercised upon his pupils, not only to subjugate them, but somehow to give them an unnatural thirst for their studies, and as unnatural a power of mastering them. In proof of this, one man cited the instance of his son, who, having become half-crazed on his arithmetic, and having worked all one evening on a sum which he could not do, went to bed, leaving his slate upon the table, but rose some time in the night in his sleep, actually worked out the answer, returned to bed, wholly unconscious of what he had done, and slept till morning, when he found, to his surprise, the whole process, in his own figures, upon the slate.* This incident, however little it might have had to do, in the minds of others, in proving the position it was cited to sustain, seemed to go far with these people in confirming the strange notion they were beginning to conceive, that the master had brought some unnatural influence to bear upon his pupils. And when they compared the wild, thoughtless, and unstudious conduct which had ever characterized the scholars before, with their present greatly altered behavior, and the eager diligence with which many of them, both day and night, pursued their studies, particularly mathematical studies, they mysteriously shook their heads, and said "they did n't know about these things; such a change might have come in a natural way, but they could n't understand it." It was agreed on all hands, they further argued, that the master was deep in figures. Capt. Bunker, who was considered the best natural reckoner in those parts, had confessed that he could n't hold a candle to him in that respect. They had always heard that strange things could be done with figures, if a person sought to do so. Indeed, there was a certain point in figures, they supposed, beyond which, if a person persisted in going, he was sure to have help from one who should be nameless, but who always exacted his pay for his assistance. They hoped this was not the case with their master; but if it was, and he was trying to lead his scholars into the same forbidden paths, it was no wonder that they had such strange, blue looks; nor was it at all surprising that sickness should come upon

* This incident, improbable as it may appear to some, is a true one, having occurred within the knowledge of the author, who otherwise would not have ventured on relating it.

them, as a judgment. And they again shook their heads, and said "it was high time that something should be done."

Let it not be inferred, that we would convey the idea, that the people of the country in which our scene is laid were generally as superstitious as some of the circumstances here represented to have taken place might seem to imply. They certainly were not so. And comparatively few locations, we presume, could have been found, where such arguments as we have put into the mouths of some of the good people of this uncultured district, would have been listened to a moment. But our observations, made during considerable travel and intercourse among the common classes of people in the Middle and Northern States, have apprised us, that instances of the prevalence of notions similar to those just mentioned are still to be found, and much oftener, too, than we had formerly supposed. We have often come across isolated neighborhoods, even in the heart of intelligent communities, where, to our surprise, we found all the exploded notions of witchcraft, sorcery, divination, and the like, still entertained; and to an extent, indeed, that led us almost to doubt whether we had not, by some miracle or other, been carried back a century and a half, and set down among a clan of the immediate disciples of old Cotton Mather, who spent so much time and learning in making mystery and mischief about things which have no existence, except in imagination. Such a neighborhood, with a few honorable exceptions, we are constrained to say, was that of the *Horn-of-the-Moon.*

On the day following that during which the singular surmises and discussions, to which we have alluded, were started, two more members of the school were taken down; and the situation of Henry Marvin had become so alarming, that his agonized mother, some time in the preceding night, had despatched a man for a physician of high reputation, residing in a large village, known by the name of *Cartersville*, nearly thirty miles distant; though she was compelled to pledge her only cow to defray the expenses of the man, and induce him to become answerable to the doctor for his pay. All this, as may be supposed, much increased the alarm in the district, and quickened into action those who had busied themselves in getting up an excitement against the master. Meanwhile, the innocent victim of these absurd imputations remained at his post, wholly ignorant of the stir that was going on about him, and thinking only of the misfortune which threatened his school. On the evening of the day last mentioned, he dismissed his school early, and with a heavy heart repaired to the residence of the distressed widow, to visit his sick little favorite. On reaching the house, he entered the room ordinarily occupied by the family; when he was introduced, by a woman in attendance, to Dr. Lincoln, the physician before named, who, having arrived a short time before, was now taking some refreshment.

"Our little patient here is a pupil of yours, sir?" inquiringly said the doctor, who was a small, unostentatious, but a highly intellectual man.

"He is," replied Locke; "and I can hardly express how much anxiety I feel for his situation, which I fear you will pronounce dangerous."

"Your apprehensions, I regret to say, are but too well grounded, sir."

"What do you consider the true character of his disease?"

"Whatever it may have been at first, it is now a brain fever, threatening congestion."

"Are you prepared to assign any particular cause?"

"Of his first attack, I am not. In regard to the form the disease has now assumed, I may be better prepared, perhaps, to give an opinion after asking you a few questions. What are the boy's habits of study and scholarship?"

"He is a bright scholar — uncommonly so — very industrious and anxious to learn."

"I suspected so. And you have held up to him what to others, perhaps, would scarcely be an inducement sufficient to move them, but what, to his sensitive mind, has incited him to unwonted exertions?"

"As you say, sir, I may have said that which had the effect to incite *him;* although, I am sure, I have used more exertions with many others."

"I presume so. It does not require a timber-chain to draw a miser to a supposed bed of gold. A bare glimpse of the loved treasure is enough to kindle his whole soul for the eager grasp. So with the youthful intellect, if bright, and united with a strong love of learning. And let me caution you, my dear sir, how you spur on such a mind, in one of tender years. The body must be permitted to grow, as well as the mind. Very bright children are said always to die first, and though the cause generally assigned for this may be false, there is yet much truth in the saying; the true cause of the fact being, that the minds of such children, by the injudiciously applied incitements of parents and teachers, are often so over-wrought, that disease, at every slight attack on other parts of the system, is prone to fly to the enfeebled brain, and, oftener than otherwise, destroy its victim. In these remarks you will read the opinion to which I incline respecting the present case."

"Ay; but are you aware that several others of my school have been taken ill, and those, too, that would be the last to whom you would think of imputing injury from undue mental exertion?"

"I have so understood, sir. There may have been some local cause for these, as well as the first attack of the poor little fellow here. Has any such cause suggested itself to your mind?"

"No! unless it be the late sudden and great change in the weather."

"That will hardly account for the manner in which your school, almost the whole of it, in some degree, as I understand, has been affected, in a time of such general health. There must be other causes, which I feel some curiosity to ascertain before I return."

The conversation was here interrupted by the entrance of a woman of the neighborhood, one of that valuable class of society who retail news, with comments.

"Do you attend the school-meeting to-night, Mr. Amsden?" she soon asked; for she did not appear very bashful in claiming her right to a share in the conversation.

"School-meeting, madam!" said Locke, in surprise; I was not aware that there was to be one."

"O yes, there is; why, everybody is going, they say. I supposed you, *of course*, knew it."

"This is the first I have heard of it. But what is the object of the meeting?"

"O, to see what's to be done about the scholars being in this sickly and malagantly way, to be sure. Some say the school won't keep any more, at any rate. But I tell 'em, like enough the master will clear it up, after all 's said and done."

"Clear up what, pray, madam? Of what can I possibly be accused, in connection with this misfortune to my school?"

"O, do n't ask me now — I let it pass into one ear and out the other, what I hear; because I never mean to be one of those who go about telling things to breed mischief and ill-will among people." And here the good and scrupulous lady struck off in a tangent, and asked the doctor, now while she thought of it, as she said, seeing she had heard a great many disputes about it, "whether saffron or camomile tea was, upon the whole, the best for the measles?"

As soon as the doctor, who was a man of much sly but caustic humor, had gravely delivered himself of a very learned answer, which, he said, *upon the whole*, all things carefully considered, he must conclude in the language of the great Dr. Pope,

> "For forms of *diet drinks* let fools contest:
> That which is best administered is best."

As soon as he had done this, Locke, whose mind was still running upon the inexplicable news he had just heard from the woman, again turned to her, and asked if she knew whether Mr. Bunker had returned from the journey on which he had been for the last fortnight absent."

"Why, we do n't certainly know yet," replied the news-mongress; "but we kinder 'spect he got home this very afternoon. Jim Walker, who was to our house about a nour ago, to borrow a sassage-filler for his wife, said he thought he saw, from his house, a creter over there, that looked like the captain's old black hoss, going to water, and rolling in the snow as if he 'd jest been onharnessed after a journey."

"Well, I am thankful for that, if he has indeed arrived," replied Locke, who felt anxious for the presence of his friend at the approaching meeting.

"Come, Mr. Amsden," said the doctor, rising, "you will of course attend the school-meeting; and I will go with you, if I can be spared; but we will now walk into the sick room, if you please. We cannot admit much company," he continued, as he saw the gossip turn a longing eye upon the opening door, as if waiting for an invitation to accompany them; "but Mr. Amsden is the boy's teacher, whose presence may be a benefit, by recalling his wandering mind."

When they entered the sick chamber, a scene of silent but touching woe presented itself. The grief-stricken mother, who scarcely heeded their approach, sat bending over the pillowed couch, intensely gazing, with fixed, glazed, and watery eyes, upon the face of the little sufferer, as he lay nervously moving his restless limbs, and rolling his swathed head, in the deep and troubled slumbers which exhausted nature seemed to be strongly claiming on the one hand, and grappling disease fiercely disputing and constantly disturbing on the other. The doctor took the patient's hand, and attentively examined his pulse; when some movement, in restoring the limb to its place, awoke him. As his dim and slowly wandering eyes fell upon the face of his beloved teacher, a single glance of intelligence slightly illumined them; and the semblance of an affectionate smile played faintly, an instant, over his sunken and livid features, vanishing away like some struggling sunbeam that has partially burst through a stormy cloud. The mother saw the glance, with the recognition it evinced. And the association, as her thoughts flew back to the happy days of her darling boy's health and friendly intercourse with his teacher, of which that look had so plainly spoken, and reverted to what he now was, and probably soon would be, the association thus called up was too much for her bursting heart. She groaned aloud from the inmost recesses of her troubled spirit. Her whole frame became deeply agitated, and her bosom shook with the convulsive throes of her agony, as with indistinct, quick, whispered ejaculations, she seemed eagerly snatching for the hand of mercy from above, to save her from sinking under the insupportable weight of her own feelings. Her prayers were so far answered as to bring her the temporary relief of tears, which now gushed and fell like rain from their opening fountains of bitterness.

"I am glad to see that," observed Lincoln, brushing away a tear that had started out upon his knitting brows. "It will relieve you, madam. And now let me persuade you to go out, bathe your face, and otherwise refresh yourself. We will remain, and take care of your son."

"Our profession," resumed the doctor, after the widow had retired, as she did, in silence, on the suggestion just made to her, "our profession, Mr. Amsden, is one which brings along with it many pains, but which, at the same time, is not without its gratifications. A case now, like this, an almost hopelessly sick child, with a distracted parent hanging over it — and we are daily pained with witnessing such scenes — draws hard, hard, I confess, upon my sympathies. But again, on the other hand, if this boy should recover through my means, I shall lay up in the bosom of that mother, whether I deserve it or not, a store of gratitude which will, perhaps, often find utterance in blessings at the bare mention of my name! Yes, if he recover," continued the speaker, musingly, as he rose at some new appearance he noticed in the patient, and went to the bedside, "if he recover — and all that I can do shall be done, and that too with no charge to the poor woman, even if I knew I had got to beg my next meal. But it is a fierce and unmanageable disease, and I tremble for the crisis of this night. Here, step here, Mr. Amsden, and listen to the confused mutterings of broken thoughts and images that are whirling in the chaos of that perplexed and laboring brain."

Locke immediately complied with the request; and as he turned his ear towards the rapidly-moving lips of the delirious boy, he could soon distinguish "*six times six are thirty-six — seven times six are forty-two — eight times six are forty-eight*," and so on. Sometimes he would follow one figure in this manner through all its successive multipliers, in the usual table, and then take up another, follow it awhile, and suddenly drop it for a third, which in turn, perhaps, would be relinquished for some attempted process in subtraction or division; in all of which he seemed to be constantly meeting with troubles and perplexities, with which he would appear to contend awhile, and then return to his old starting point in the multiplication table, and with freshened impulse hurry on with "*six times six are thirty-six — seven times six are forty-two*," &c. &c., till something again occurred to turn his bewildered mind from the course it was mechanically pursuing.

"Poor, poor boy!" exclaimed Locke, as, with a sigh and starting tear, he turned away from the affecting spectacle.

The time having arrived for our hero's departure for the school-meeting, and the widow now coming in, the doctor apprised her of his intention of accompanying the former, and, giving his directions for the next hour, requested her to send for him should any considerable change occur in the patient, when they both set off together for the school-house.

On reaching the place of destination, they found, with the exception of Bunker and one or two others, all the men, together with several of the older scholars of the district, already assembled, and on the point of proceeding to business. As soon as Locke had helped his friend, the doctor, to a seat, and taken one near by for himself, he cast a leisurely look round the assembly. It required neither much time nor closeness of observation to apprise him that there was a great deal of suppressed, excited feeling prevailing generally among the company. Nor was he much longer in satisfying himself, from the words which occasionally reached his ears, from little knots of eager whisperers around him, and from the many cold and suspicious glances he encountered, that a great portion of this feeling was unfavorably directed against himself, the cause of which he was still unable to conjecture.

"I motion Deacon Gilchrist be Moderator of this meeting," said one, bobbing half-way up, and hastily squatting back to his seat, before the sentence was fairly out of his mouth.

"I am not so sure but they will need a *moderator* before they get through," whispered the doctor to Locke, emphasizing the word so as to give it a literal signification.

The vote having been taken, and the chairman, a short, sluggish man, whose wisdom and sanctity lay principally in his face, being duly installed in his seat, he pronounced the meeting open, and invited those present "to offer."

"I motion," again said the person who had first spoken, "I motion, Mr. Moderator, that this school come to an eend. And I 've got my reasons for 't."

The motion was eagerly seconded by two or three others, all speaking at once, and demanding the question, in a manner that plainly showed that a considerable portion of those present were acting in concert, and with the intention of having the vote taken before any debate could be had on the subject. And the chairman, who was evidently a secret favorer of the project, jumped up to put the question; when Locke, who had witnessed the movement with the utmost surprise, rose and demanded the reasons which the mover asserted he had for his proposed measure.

"I call for the vote — put it to vote!" was the only reply which Locke received to his reasonable demand.

"Look here now, Mr. Moderator," cried a tall, rough-looking young fellow, who rose in a different part of the room from that occupied by the combined party, "I have neither chick or child to send to school, to be sure; but I'm a voter here, and I must say I think you are for pushing the master rather hard, to vote him out without giving him your reasons, so as to allow him a chance to clear it up, if he can. And as to any blame for the sickness resting on him, I an't so sure but what he can; for I can 't say I think much of this *black art* business, or of its having any thing to do in bringing on the trouble. I would n't give much for all the help the master or any body else ever got that way. Now you may think as you 're a mind to; but I never thought the old boy was half so much of a critter as he 's cracked up to be. And I do n't believe he 's any great scratch at cipherin' himself neither, much less to teach it to others."

The sensibilities of the good deacon received a very visible shock from this strange and irreverent speech, as it was deemed; and his zealous supporter, whom we have mentioned as taking the lead in motions thus far made, was so much outraged in his feelings, either by the sentiments of the speaker, or the opposition they implied to his plans, that he rose, and said he thought the young man ought to be rebuked for such loose discourse, in a meeting like this, where folks had so much reason to be solemn. "I wonder if he believes," continued the zealot, warming up, "what the scripture says about the power of sorcerers' getting unlawful help to do what other folks could n't do? And I should like to ask him where he thinks the help come from, when young John Mugridge, that the master had got along so unnatural fast in figures, did a hard sum in his sleep. I want to know, too, what he thinks about widow Marvin's boy being taken sick — in mercy, perhaps — the very next week after the master put him to ciphering. And then I wish he 'd tell us what makes the whole school look so blue and ghastly, if there a n't any thing wrong in the master's doings. And I call on the master himself to say whether he can deny that he understands the black art."

Locke could hardly bring himself to reply to this ridiculous charge, or even to answer the particular question that he had been thus publicly called on to answer. He did so, however, by briefly stating that he knew of no such art. He had heard, indeed, that the faculty of foretelling events, fortunes, and the like, was supposed to be attainable by figures. And he recollected, as he commenced arithmetic when a mere boy, indulging a sort of vague expectation that he should come across this art, if he went far enough. But the further he advanced, the more did he see the impossibility of acquiring any such faculty by the use of figures, which, more peculiarly than any other science, discarded all suppositions, and had to do only with certain demonstrable facts. And now, having studied or examined, as he believed, nearly all of that science that had been published, he was fully prepared to say that the belief in the faculty in question was wholly a delusion.

"I do n't blame him for denying it," said the superstitious spokesman before named. "I think I should, if I was wicked enough to tamper with sich forbidden things. But I should like to hear Deacon Gilchrist the Moderator's views on this subject."

The Moderator, after sundry hems and haws, by way of getting his apparatus of speech in motion, assumed a look of wise solemnity, and observed, —

"It appears to me, my beloved friends, that there 's an awful responsibility on us. Duty is duty. I do think so. I do n't know, nor want to, much about the hidden things of figures, except they are thought to be the instruments that Satan works by sometimes. We know there were sorcerers and workers in hidden mysteries, in the days of the apostles; and the scripter says they shall be multiplied in the latter days, which now is. I once read a book by a great and deep divine — I 've eeny most forgot his name, but I think it was Woollen Marther, or some sich oncommon crissen name — who had seen, with his own eyes, a great deal of the awful doings of Satan. And he speaks of the strange looks of those that were buffeted by the adversary, and the divers maladies and sore evils that befell those who were led by his emissaries into unlawful ways. And I do think, my friends, there's something very mysterious in this 'ere school. I do think we have seen a token of displeasure, that seems to say to us, in a loud voice — yea, the voice of many thunders — *Come out, and be separate from him that bringeth the evil upon you.*"

This speech was triumphantly echoed by several of the deacon's supporters, as an unanswerable argument for the measure they were so intent on carrying. There were others, however, who were so obtuse as not to perceive the force of the argument, or the justice of its application. Among these were the intended victim of this combination, and his newly-found friend, the tall fellow, whose speech had so scandalized his opponents; both of whom made a reply to the oracular speech of our modern Solomon — the one by denying both premises and conclusions, and the other by drolly asking pardon of the old boy, the deacon, or any of their friends, if he had underrated or offended them in his former speech, and by contending that the master had cleared himself, to his mind, of the charge of ciphering his scholars into fevers, and their parents into fidgets. These replies led to a good deal of scattering debate, in which nearly all, by speech, word thrown in, or other manifestation, participated; and by which it became apparent that there were strictly three parties in the assembly: first, the deacon's trained followers, who, numbering about one third of the district, were for breaking up the school, for reasons before given; second, another portion, of about the same number, who had been induced to come into the plan of the former, through their secret fears that some contagious disease was about to break out in the school, which their children would be more likely to take, if the school continued; and last, the other third, who believed the master in no way chargeable for the condition of the school, which they wished might be still continued.

The deacon's party, perceiving, by this time, that they could safely count on strength enough to carry their measure, clamored more loudly than ever for a decision of the question. Locke gave himself up as lost, and a few minutes more would, indeed, have been decisive of his doom, but for the unexpected arrival of a new personage. This was Bunker, who having reached home only a few hours before, had not heard what was in train till the evening was considerably advanced; when, accidentally learning something of the facts, he came post haste to the scene of action. This arrival very visibly disconcerted the deacon's party, and produced a dead pause in their proceedings, during which the former marched boldly up to Locke, and gave him one of those hearty and cordial shakes of the hand, which send assurance to the desponding heart, and are more gratefully felt, on some emergencies, than a thousand expressed pledges of friendship, on others. After being introduced to Dr. Lincoln, Bunker, taking a conspicuous stand before the company, immediately demanded the object of the meeting, and, by a series of sharp and rapid questions, addressed first to one, then another, soon succeeded in drawing out the whole truth, with all that had transpired.

"O ye miserable thinkers!" he exclaimed, as soon as he had satisfied himself of the true situation of affairs, "what, in the name of common sense, could have put ye up to such nonsense and folly as this? Three decent efforts for a correct idea should have told you that the master would not be caught teaching, for nothing, so valuable a secret as the black art, if that art is all you suppose it to be. Why, by foretelling the rise in the markets, or the lucky number of the ticket that is to draw the highest prize in the next lottery, he can make an independent fortune in six months, if he will keep his secret to himself; but if he goes and imparts this faculty to others, they will get away all his chances for such luck, and his art won't be worth a farthing to him. Do you believe he would do such a foolish thing? No! not a soul of you. There is thought number one for you.

"Again — what could make you think that the teaching of this art ever did, or could, bring ill-health, either upon the teacher or the taught? This was never a fact. Is there any thing said in the Bible about the magicians, witches, or diviners, or their followers, being taken sickly for their practices? Did Simon Magus make anybody sick? Did the sorceress, or black-art girl, that St. Paul converted, carry disease in her train? No; for she had brought her master a good deal of money by telling folk's fortunes; when, if she had brought sickness and judgments upon them, they would have given him more money to have kept her away. Nor was there any such misfortunes connected with the witchcraft in the old Bay State. Doctor Mather, even in his book, do n't say so; for I have heard it read. The bewitched, according to his story, only acted and appeared a little wild and devilish. But, if his book had said this, it would amount to nothing; for I do n't believe, if the old Nick himself should turn book-maker to-day, and sit down, with his old yellow, brimstone-tempered steel pen, and do his best, for a month, he could get more of the real essence of falsehood between the two lids of a book, than can be found in the book I've mentioned. And if ever that learned doctor — for he was accounted pious — gets within the walls of the New Jerusalem, he will find, I fear, when he comes to see what suffering, death, and crime, were brought about through his influence and example, as well as he might mean — that heaven will be rather an uneasy place for him. But, supposing the judgments of sickness, and so on, did attend such doings, what then? How would it stand in the present case? Why, the master, by the very art that was to produce the misfortune, would know that the misfortune would follow his attempt to teach it.

And do you think he would try it, when he knew it would bring sickness and trouble on his school, that must break it up, cost him the loss of all his wages, and, what is more, send him off with a character that would for ever prevent his getting another school? Would he be such a stupid fool as to do this? Never! and you all now see and know it. There is thought number two for you.

"Once more. In what I have said, I have taken you wholly on your own ground; so that you should not say I could meet you only on my own dunghill. I will now make you come on to my ground, and see if you can stand fire any better there. And this is my ground: — I say that this black art, as you understand it, the faculty of foretelling events, together with sorcery, magic, or witchery, and every other art that lays claim to any such faculty by the aid of figures, or any thing else, is all moonshine, imposition, and falsehood. And I do n't want to set before you but one single idea to make you know and feel the truth of my assertion. Now follow me. Did you ever know or hear of a rich fortune-teller, black-art-worker, or conjuror? Speak out, if you ever did. A single one that was *rich*, I say. You do n't speak? No; for you can 't say you ever did hear of such an one. You all well know that they are a set of poor, beggarly rascals from beginning to end. Well now, what prevents them, as I said of our master here, if they have this faculty of looking or figuring into futurity, from seeing and seizing upon every lottery ticket that is to draw a good prize; from buying every article in the markets that is about to rise greatly in price? What prevents them from doing this, and making their fortunes at a blow? Tell me, you, or you, or you. This is thought number three for you.

"Now my number first pinned an argument upon you — even allowing you your own false premises — with nothing but a wooden pin, that you could not break. My number second, still giving you the same advantage, put in a board nail, that, with or without the pin, not one of you could twist or move. And my number third puts a double ten clincher upon the whole, that all of you together can never start. Now stand forth and gainsay it, ye persecutors of the best teacher we ever had in the district, or for ever hold your peace! No one speaks; and I pronounce the master guiltless, and acquitted of your foolish charge.

"But although the master is no way blameable, yet that an unusual number of the scholars are sick, and nearly all drooping, if I am rightly informed, I am not going to deny. And there is some cause for it, which we must try to discover, that we may stop the evil. If it is not the starting point of some epidemic disease that is about to spread over the country, why, then it must be owing to something wrong about the school-house. By taking up the possibilities, one after another, I probably could think it out myself within twenty-four hours. But here is a man," continued the speaker, turning towards the doctor, "who has been in the way of thinking of such things half of his life. Let us have his opinion. Dr. Lincoln, will you favor us with your views on the subject of inquiry?"

The doctor, who had attentively listened to the whole debate, much of which he had appeared to enjoy with the highest zest, now rose, and observed that he had already made up his mind to offer his opinion on the matter in question, before called on; and he would now proceed to do so. He had some secret suspicion of the cause of the general unhealthiness of the school, on first learning the fact; and having come to the meeting, mainly with the view of satisfying himself in relation to the matter, his attention, during the time he had been here, had been particularly directed to the subject; and he was now prepared to say, that what was before a mere suspicion with him was now a confirmed opinion. The cause, and sole cause, of this unhealthiness was the want of ventilation; and, from what he had suffered himself since in the room, although the door had been frequently opened, he was only surprised that the condition of the scholars was not infinitely worse than he understood it was. Though not wishing it to strengthen his own convictions, yet, as it might better convince others, he would proceed to set the matter in a stronger light before them.

The doctor, then, while every ear and eye were regarding his words and movements with intense interest, called on Locke to ascertain the number of cubic feet contained in the empty space of the room. A carpenter present, who happened to have a bundle of his tools with him, having called into the meeting while on his way home from some finished job, produced a rule, and took the different dimensions of the apartment with great exactness; when Locke, from the data thus furnished, quickly ascertained and told off the number of cubic feet, as required. This number, owing to the ill-advised construction of the school-room, in which the floor rose from one side at so great at angle as to take up about one sixth part of what would have been the space with a level floor, amounted only, with proper deductions for stove, seats, &c., to sixteen hundred cubic feet.

"Now let me observe," said the doctor, "that, from the latest and most accurate experiments of chemists and medical men, it has been ascertained that one person, by respiration from the lungs alone, destroys all the oxygen, or vital principle, in thirteen cubic feet of space per hour. How many scholars have you, Mr. Amsden?"

"Sixty, upon the average, perhaps more, say sixty-four."

"Ascertain, then, how many cubic feet of vital air these all will destroy in one hour."

"Both Locke and Bunker, the latter of whom now began

to be in his element, almost the next instant gave the same answer — eight hundred and thirty-two feet.

"How long do you generally keep them in without intermission, in which the doors would necessarily remain open a moment while they were passing out?"

"Generally an hour and a half, sometimes two."

"Then, gentlemen," said the doctor, "the true, but greatly misconceived, cause of your trouble and just alarm is now plainly before you. You see, by our calculation, that, in less than two hours, all the air that can sustain life a moment would be, in this new and almost bottle-tight room, if not renovated by opening the doors or windows, entirely consumed. And, taking into the account the quantity of this vital principle inhaled by the pores of so many persons, and the probably greater portion destroyed by the fire and reflecting surface of the stove and pipe, I presume one hour is sufficient to render the air extremely unhealthy; an hour and a half, absolutely poisonous; and two hours, so fatally so as to cause your children to drop dead on the floor."

"Thunder!" exclaimed Bunker, "can this be so? I long since knew that we were put upon our allowance, when in close rooms, for the right kind of breathing air; but I never supposed there was so much death in the pot as that comes to. But that fact which you build upon — the amount of vital air a person destroys an hour — I am afraid, doctor, you got it only out of the books, which I am rather shy in trusting for what I call gospel."

"Both from books and my own imperfect experiments," replied Lincoln, "and I am satisfied that the proportion is not rated too highly. But I have not quite done all that I proposed in this case. We have now been in the room, I perceive by my watch, but three quarters of an hour, while there are not probably over thirty persons present. And yet, even in this time, and with this number, I will ask you all, if you do not feel oppressed and uneasy from the impurity of the air here?"

"I do — and I — and I too," responded several; while others, as the case was thus now brought home to their own senses, which plainly spoke in the affirmative, sprang forward in alarm to throw open the doors.

"Not yet — not yet," said the doctor, interposing. "We can live awhile longer; and I wish in some degree to satisfy you, and particularly Captain Bunker here, whose thorough mode of coming at results I much admire, that what I have said is not altogether incapable of proof, even with the means at hand. Cannot our carpenter here, with a few minutes' work, so alter the casings, that the upper sashes of these windows can be lowered some few inches?"

Locke — who felt both pained and chagrined, that his inattention to this matter, in which he so well knew all the principles involved, should have so nearly led to disastrous consequences, and whose active mind, having seen through the whole subject at a glance, the moment the doctor put him on the track, had long since been engaged in devising a ready remedy for the discovered evil — here interposed, and suggested that an opening made in the centre of the ceiling, would best effect the object in view.

"If it can be done?" inquiringly said the doctor.

"Be done!" said Bunker, "yes, it can. Here, carpenter, up in this chair with your tools, and make a hole through there, in no time. This business is just beginning to get through my hair."

A few moments sufficed to make an aperture about eight inches square, opening into the attic story above; the square form being adopted, as best comporting with the simple contrivance with which it was proposed to cover it — that of a mere board slide, supported by cleats, in which it would play back and forth, as the aperture required to be opened for ventilation, or shut to preserve the warmth of the room. Scarcely had the workman time to adjust the slide in its place, before every particle of impure air had apparently escaped through the opening, to pass off by the crevices in the roof. All felt and acknowledged the change, with astonishment and delight. The sensations of languor and oppression, that had begun to weigh heavily on the feelings and spirits of the company, had left them almost as unexpectedly and suddenly as fell the bundle of sins from the back of Bunyan's Pilgrim.

"Well, gentlemen," said Doctor Lincoln, as he looked round, and saw in the speaking countenances of the company, that all were as well satisfied as they were gratified at the result; "I believe the mystery is now solved. At all events, I'll agree to cure, for nothing, all the scholars that are hereafter made sick from any thing about the school-house, or in the conduct of their master."

"Yes, the room is as clear as a horn, by George!" exclaimed Bunker, "and the thing is done — proved out as square as a brick, right in our face and eyes; and there 's no getting away from it. But what sticks in my crop is, that we must have a man — and a book man, too, though he plainly do n't swallow books whole, without chewing, as most of 'em do — have a man come thirty miles to think it out for us! Master, you and I ought to be trounced."

"Well, Mr. Moderator," said the deacon's tormenter, the rustic humorist, we mean, who was the first to take up for Locke in the debate, and who now seemed greatly to enjoy the triumph of the latter over the little clique of his chop-fallen foes — "Well, Mr. Moderator, how is it about the old boy and his little blue influences, now? Do n't you think they 've pretty much all cleared out through that hole up yonder? Ah! I was about right, deacon: if the old chap had been any great affair, he could n't have crept out through so small a hole as that comes to, quite so quick, you may depend on 't."

But the deacon, who suddenly recollected a promise he had made to carry, that night, some thorough-wort to a jaundery neighbor, was in too much of a hurry to reply to such scoffing questions; and he, with one or two of his most zealous supporters, immediately quitted the house, leaving the rest of the vanquished party, whether superstitionists or alarmists, to join the master and his increasing number of friends, acknowledge their error, and reciprocate congratulations on the unexpectedly happy result of the whole of this singular affair. We say the whole; for, before the company broke up, word was brought by one of the larger scholars, who had gone over to Widow Marvin's during the meeting, and just returned, that the sick boy there had fallen into a quiet sleep, attended by gentle perspiration;—symptoms which the gratified doctor at once pronounced to be a plain indication that the disease was going off, by what he technically termed resolution. And the result, in this case at least, went to prove the doctor's skill in prognostics. The boy, after that night, was consigned, by his departing physician, to the care only of his grateful mother, who, within a fortnight, had the unspeakable happiness of seeing her darling son restored to health, and his still loved, but now more temperately pursued studies.

Of the remainder of young Amsden's career in this district, little more need be added. Compared with the trials, vexations, and labors of the past, he now found but a path of flowers. The recent misfortune in his school, and the consequent infatuated movement to overthrow him, operating as all overwrought persecutions usually do, instead of injuring him, were the means of turning the popular current strongly in his favor, and of giving him a place in the estimation of nearly all around him, which he otherwise would have failed to obtain. Being no further troubled with the injudicious interference of parents, or the misbehavior of their children,—those two evils which too often require the best part of a teacher's time and attention to meet and overcome them,—he had nothing to do but instruct his pupils. And by no means unprofitably did the latter use the opportunity thus afforded them. From a rough, wild, unthinking set of creatures, who could appreciate nothing but animal pleasures or physical prowess, they became rational beings, ambitious for the acquisition of knowledge, and capable of intellectual pleasures. A new standard of taste and merit, in short, had been imperceptibly raised among them; and the winter that Locke Amsden kept school became an era in the district, from which commenced a visible and happy change in the whole moral and intellectual tone of its society.

Nor were the advantages which attended his exertions in this place wholly on one side. In teaching others, the master himself was often taught. Questions were daily put to him, even by children in their abs, which led him to reflection, research, and discoveries of truths, which, thorough scholar as he was, he found, to his surprise, he had before overlooked, and which otherwise might never have occurred to him;—discoveries, we repeat, of important truths, in almost every study of his school, and particularly in those of orthography, orthoepy, and etymology, those sadly neglected branches which require a philosopher to teach them understandingly, but which are yet, oftener than otherwise, entrusted to the teaching of an ignoramus!

In what is termed a physical education, also, he here received hints, which led him to the adoption of much more correct and enlarged views than any he had before entertained. His attention, indeed, had never been directed to the subject; and he had therefore continued to look upon it as did others around him, either as a matter of little importance, or, at best, as one which had no legitimate connection with popular education. But the painful and alarming occurrences which we have described, as arising from the want of ventilation in his school-house, taught him a lesson which could not be disregarded or easily forgotten; caused him to give an earnest consideration to this subject in all its bearings, whether in relation to ventilation, length of confinement to study, or ease of position; and forced upon his mind the conviction, that physical education, or an observance of those laws of life which can only insure the health of the body, and the consequent health of the mind, is, as truly as any other, a part of an instructor's duty, for the performance of which, before high Heaven, he will be held responsible.

CHAPTER VI.

"Low in the world, because he scorns its arts;
A man of letters, manners, morals, parts;
Unpatronized, and therefore little known;
Wise for himself and his few friends alone."

COWPER.

HAVING fulfilled his engagement in the *Horn-of-the-Moon*, and bid a regretful adieu to the many friends he had there made, among the stanchest of whom was the straight-going and strong-minded Bunker, young Amsden returned to his family, with the intention of negociating, on some terms, with his father, for his time, during the remainder of his minority, that he might resume his studies. On naming the subject to his parents, his father gave him the choice of serving out his time, and receiving in return a portion of the homestead or a new lot of land when he should become of age, or of going now with nothing. Locke thanked him for the option, and instantly decided to depart. His decision, however, was not grounded on any dislike to an agricultural life; for, on the contrary, he ever thought highly of that healthful and noble avocation, which so early received the signal sanction of Heaven. And ever since that charmed hour in which he listened to the glowing picture of the life of the scientific farmer, drawn by the stranger gentleman, whose visit, with that of his bright-eyed daughter, was still secretly cherished in remembrance, as an event which first fairly apprised him he had a mind to be expanded, and a heart to be affected, he had determined eventually to return to that life. But he must first have knowledge, more knowledge, a little more knowledge; and all the temptations of earth should not divert him from his purpose. To gain this, he had, as we have just mentioned, freely relinquished, for aught he knew, his whole birthright; and so, with as little hesitation, would he have done, had its value been tenfold greater than it was, even had he been compelled to go forth as penniless as the beggar of the streets. He was not finally permitted, however, to depart wholly unprovided. His good mother, who had heard him reject the offers of his father, and dropped a silent tear, — drawn forth, not at witnessing the sacrifice, but the self-sacrificing and noble motive which had prompted it, — again exerted her influence in his behalf, and not altogether in vain. On the morning of his departure, he was furnished with an outfit, which, with the limited amount of his winter's wages, was sufficient to ensure his support for another year, in his favorite pursuits. And with this little fund, and a light heart, he was soon on his way to the public seminary he had quitted the fall previous. On reaching his destination, he was cordially received by his old friend Seaver, who still remained the successful head of the institution, to which he was proud to welcome one whom, the year before, he had esteemed its brightest ornament.

Hitherto, our hero had entertained no thought of entering any higher institution of learning, than the one at which he had been pursuing his studies. But, although he cared nothing for the honors of a college diploma, he yet was certainly ambitious to be deserving of one. And, having long since informed himself of the course of studies required to complete a collegiate education, he had, during the latter part of the preceding year, secretly directed his own studies with a view of eventually mastering, in their order, all those sciences embraced in the course thus required. In pursuing this object, he soon discovered how much his labors would be shortened by the unusual extent of his acquirements in mathematics, which, with those branches immediately founded on them, composed nearly half of the course in question. Feeling conscious that, with the proficiency he had already made, it would require but very little exertion to make him master of the branches last mentioned, he had devoted his time and energies almost wholly to the acquisition of the dead languages. And such had been his progress, that he now soon found himself rapidly passing over the studies of the second year of the prescribed course. For all this, however, he had thus far, as before stated, formed no design of transferring the scene of his labors to a college. But Seaver, who felt a pride in the thought of furnishing the institution of which he was a graduate, with a scholar of Locke's excellence, and believing, moreover, that he should be promoting the best interests of the latter, now began to beset him to make up his mind to leave the academy and enter college, by joining, if he preferred, such of the upper classes as his qualifications should be found to warrant.

"Have you yet concluded," said the friendly preceptor, coming to repeat his advice one day, some two or three months from his pupil's return to the academy, — "have you yet concluded, Mr. Amsden, to follow my suggestions with regard to entering college?"

"No," replied Locke, "my means are too limited; and were it otherwise, your academy furnishes me with all the advantages which I at present desire, and more than I can fully improve. Great advantages do not always make great scholars."

"True, too true," rejoined Seaver; "but yet you, probably, as do many others, greatly misapprehend the character of the peculiar advantages of a college education. The sciences, indeed, may be equally well acquired elsewhere — even more rapidly and perfectly, sometimes, perhaps, as may be seen in the case of yourself, who, uninterrupted by the multiplicity of exercises into which the student's time is cut up in these institutions, have swept on, till you are already master of more science, I doubt not, than many of those who pass from the walls of college with diplomas in their pockets. And still you have not had the opportunity of profiting by the advantages I have named."

"In what do these distinguishing advantages consist, let me ask?"

"In this: — In the first place, you soon learn, in your intercourse and collision with so many intellects of all grades and of all degrees of erudition, the exact measure of your own mind — its weakness and its strength. This, in the walks of life, must always be of incalculable advantage: it will teach one what his self-esteem had before entirely concealed from him — the certainty of a failure in many an aim which the same blinding principle would have otherwise led him to attempt. And it will teach another that he possesses capabilities of which he was, perhaps, before wholly unconscious, and thus lead him successfully to essay some noble goal, to which, but for that, he would never have aspired or attained. And, in the second place, among this congregation of talent, consisting of the many hundreds of the votaries of learning, with whom you will be constantly associated, you will hear, during your collegiate career, almost every possible subject, pertaining not only to science, but all else that has ever exercised the thoughts of men, discussed — discussed with all the lights that can be thrown upon it, and settled, as far as may be, by reference to professors, or other good authorities; so that you will be thus enabled to enter the mingled world of men, who are too bustling and busy to think much themselves, or allow others much time to do so, with a ready store of sifted knowledge, which he who has acquired his education in comparative solitude will rarely ever obtain. And there is yet another consideration which will be important, especially to you, who intend becoming a professional teacher. You will receive a diploma of the graduate's degree, which perhaps may be indispensable in obtaining the preceptorship of an academy — or, at least, so eligible a one as your merits should command."

"Ay; but I propose to become a teacher of common schools — "

"Till you can do better — is it not so, my friend?"

"No, Mr. Seaver, no. Both experience and observation have shown me the sadly defective condition of our common schools — those first nurseries of science, upon the management of which, as it appears to me, almost all that we prize depends. They must not only foster and bring forward all the germs that are transplanted into our higher institutions of learning, which will flourish or decline according to the numbers and quality of the supply thus furnished; but they are the radiating points of intelligence to the great mass of the community, that will become enlightened in proportion as the light emitted from these points is strong or feeble. But how can either of the two great objects I have named be expected from schools conducted, as most of our common schools now are, by those who need the very instruction they are employed to impart to others? Men do not thus manage the objects of their care in the physical world. There the greatest skill and attention are always bestowed on the youngest plant, till it is nursed, moulded, and brought forward into a shape and condition in which it will push up rightly of itself, or require less skilful hands to attend it. And yet the parallel between the young plant and the young mind is in every body's mouth! My own wants and troubles in obtaining good instruction, when a boy, have led me to think much, and feel deeply on this subject. And I have long since resolved that my feeble powers, as far as they may go, shall be contributed to the object of remedying the existing evil; for there I think they will do the most good, and there I am very sure they are the most needed."

"There is much force in your remarks, Mr. Amsden. The condition of our common schools is indeed deplorable. And the people of this country appear to be strangely blind on the subject. They either do not see it in the just light in which you have placed it, or they expect what they will never see — men qualified for the task engaging as teachers of common schools, for wages which will not pay the interest of the money and time — estimated at its worth in money — spent by them in obtaining their qualifications. But why should you, who are poor, be the first to make the sacrifice, which you must make, if you engage in this employment?"

"And why should I not? I am satisfied that examples of the kind must be set, and sacrifices be made, before the eyes of the community will be opened to the difference between what now is done, and what may be done, with our common schools. And why, I repeat, should not I be the first to go forward? The pecuniary sacrifice which I may be compelled to make, will, with my present feelings, cause no abridgment of my happiness; and I shall rest content with the pleasure of my employment, and the consciousness of doing good for my reward."

"The purpose is indeed a high and noble one, Mr. Amsden; and my conscience will not permit me to say another word in dissuasion. But, allowing that you persist in your determination, does that — to return to the point from which we started — does that circumstance furnish any answer to the main part of the argument I have advanced as the ground on which I advised you to change the present scene of your studies to that of a college?"

"Perhaps not. Your views, Mr. Seaver, were certainly new to me; and they have had sufficient weight on my mind to determine me to reconsider the matter in question. But

I must reflect before I can permit myself to decide. It is possible that your arguments, as far as opinion is concerned, may prevail."

And the arguments of Seaver did prevail. The objected want of pecuniary means having been obviated by the proffered assistance of the generous and high-minded friend who had induced him to take the step, — Amsden, after a few days spent in preparation, and in writing to apprise his friends of his change of purpose, set out for the college to which he had been recommended by his preceptor, and for which his course of studies more particularly fitted him. Reaching the institution, after little more than a day's journey, he immediately presented himself for examination; when, having been found amply qualified, he was permitted to unite himself with the Sophomores, at a time when they had been nearly two years in college. And, within a fortnight from the time of the conversation above detailed, he might have been found within the classic walls of his newly adopted *Alma Mater*, burning, in his eager pursuit of knowledge, the midnight oil, where

——— "around the lamp that o'er
His chamber shed its lonely beam,
Was widely spread the varied lore
Which feeds, in youth, our feverish dream."

But alike vain and thankless would be the attempt to interest the general reader in a description of the seemingly dull and unvaried routine of a life of study. The student's world is all within his own mind. There he finds enough to engage, enough to interest him. Others, however, think not of this, nor take note of the treasures he is silently hoarding up for the rich and glorious appropriation of the future. They can see nothing to admire in his listless, abstracted appearance; and when, in after times, he comes forth into the active scenes of life, which call for an exhibition of his treasured knowledge and wisdom, and in which the results of years of toil are seen perhaps in a day, they are astonished at his unexpected display of intellectual power, and wonder why they had never heard or thought any thing of that man before.

For nearly a year and a half, through vacations and all, our hero applied himself, with all the enthusiasm and mental energy with which he was so unusually gifted, in unremitting labor to the grateful task before him, not only perfecting the particular sciences required of him, but extending his researches into the broad and widening fields of general knowledge. At the end of this period, however, having gone over, in advance of his class, the little of actual study that now remained to complete the whole course prescribed by the rules of the institution to entitle him to a degree, he asked, and very readily obtained, leave of a discretionary term of absence, to enable him to replenish his pecuniary resources, by resuming the avocation of teaching, which it was still his unaltered purpose, in despite of all probable sacrifices, to make the business of his life.

CHAPTER VII.

> "'What differ more,' you cry, 'than crown and cowl?'"
> I tell you, friend, — a wise man and a fool."
>
> POPE.

THE year was again drawing towards its close; and the usual season for beginning winter schools had nearly arrived. In his journeys to and from college, at the time of his matriculation, and afterwards on his occasional brief visits to his family, young Amsden had passed through a thriving little village, which was generally known by the name of Mill Town, but which its ambitious inhabitants had recently thought to dignify, by re-christening it by the more sonorous and classical appellation of Mill Town Emporium. The village, numbering perhaps two hundred souls, contained a store, a tavern, a cluster of mills, and several very spruce-looking dwelling-houses, among which the newly-painted two-story house of the merchant glared in conspicuous whiteness. And, as our hero was now on his way homeward, and in search of some good situation in a winter's school, which he had neglected to secure, — though many eligible ones had been offered him, which he had declined on account of their location, — he concluded to call at this place, in order to ascertain whether he might not here obtain a situation, which for him might prove a desirable one, as the village was pleasantly located on the main road leading to, and within half a day's ride from, the residence of his family, with whom he wished to keep up a personal intercourse. Upon inquiry of the bustling keeper of the inn where he stopped, Locke was told that the village school had not yet been supplied with a teacher; and that the managing committee, consisting of the merchant of the place, the tailor, and the newspaper editor (for a political newspaper, called *The Blazing Star*, had just been established in this miniature city), "were now on the look-out to engage a man of those splendidest qualifications which the growing importance of the place demanded." Though somewhat startled at this pompous announcement, our candidate yet took directions to the house of the merchant, who, it was said, would probably exercise a rather controlling influence among this able board of managers. A few steps brought him to the showy white house before named, as belonging to the popular personage — as an only merchant of a little village generally is — of whom he was in quest. On applying the knocker, the door was opened by the merchant himself, who appeared with a pen behind his ear, and invited the other into his sitting room, where it appeared he had been posting his books. He was a youngerly man, of an affectedly brisk and courteous manner. Supposing his visiter had called for the purposes of trade, he received him with all the smirks and bows of a practised salesman, and began to talk rapidly about nothing — i. e. the state of the weather, and the condition of the roads for travelling. As soon, however, as Locke announced his name and business, he suddenly became much less profuse of his bows and smiles, and, assuming a consequential air, observed, —

"Why, sir, we are not over-anxious to engage a teacher just now — though, to be sure, we have so many applications pressing upon us, that we shall be compelled to decide soon. But you see, sir, we have a flourishing village here. It is thought we shall have an academy soon. There are many public-spirited and genteel people in the place; and they will not be suited with any thing short of a teacher of the most superfine qualifications."

"I trust to be able to answer all reasonable expectations, in that respect," remarked Amsden, scarcely able to repress a smile at the other's singular application of terms.

"Presume it — presume it — that is, can't say to the contrary. But do you bring any letters of credit with you?"

"Credentials? I have something of the kind about me, I believe; but having seen how easily they are obtained, and how little reliance the public place upon them, I thought not of offering them, preferring to be examined, and not doubting that your committee would be abundantly able to satisfy yourselves of my qualifications by such a course much better than by a dependence on the certificates of others."

"That 's fair — that 's fair, sir. Why, to be sure, I profess to know something myself about education, having been to an academy a quarter before entering business; and the gentlemen who are committee with me, one the editor of the *Blazing Star*, and the other the merchant tailor of our village, are both men of some parts — especially our editor, whom I consider to be a man of splendid talents. I will send for them, sir."

So saying, the merchant committee-man went out and despatched a boy for his colleagues, who soon made their appearance, and were thereupon introduced, in due form, to our candidate for the throne of a village school. The new-comers also were both men below the middle age. He of the goose (we mean no disrespect to that honest calling, who take all the jokes and get all the money) was a man of a fair, feminine appearance, of pert, jaunty manners, and of showy dress, done in the very extremes of last year's city fashions, though recently made, and now worn as a sort of sign-board sample to display constantly before the great public of Mill Town Emporium, and its tributaries, convincing proof of his signal ability to make good the glowing professions of his standing advertisement in the *Blazing Star*, "to be always prepared to cut and make to order after the very latest New York and London fashions." The editor was a personage of quite a different appearance. He was grave and severe of look, his countenance plainly indicating how deeply he was conscious of the important responsibilities of his position, as conductor of the *Blazing Star*, on which the political destinies of the country so much depended.

The sage trio, who were to decide on our hero's qualifications in the sciences, being thus brought together, the merchant announced to his colleagues the cause of the convocation, and the progress already made in the business on hand.

"Do you teach after the latest style and fashion of teaching, sir?" commenced the tailor, "there must be much in that, I think. There is nothing like keeping up with the improvements and latest style of the times, if one calculates to succeed, in almost any thing, at this day."

"As far as I could see changes to be improvements, I certainly should follow them," replied Locke.

"Do you teach book-keeping?" asked the merchant: "I consider that to be of the last importance."

"Literally, so do I, sir. An understanding, and mechanical skill of execution, of the principles of penmanship, I consider of the first importance; and, these attained, it may be be lastly important that the pupil be instructed in book-keeping," answered Locke, without observing the air of pique which became visible in the countenance of the interrogator at this answer.

"I feel impelled by my sense of duty to my country," said the editor, "to make a preliminary question. And I trust the gentleman will excuse my desire to know which of the two great political parties of the day he supports. This I would not consider a *sine qua non*, or even very important, at some periods in our public affairs; but when, as now, I see an obnoxious party power stalking through the land, like the besom of destruction, to overthrow the sacred liberties of the country, I do hold it an imperious duty to know the principles of those we encourage; not because I should fear that one of that party, whose further increase I so much deprecate, could exercise a pernicious influence in our intelligent village, where, since the establishment of the *Blazing Star*, the political views of the people, I am proud to say, are so generally correct — no, not at all on that account, but for the inherent principle of the thing."

"I have never," replied Locke, utterly surprised that a test-question of this kind should be put to him, "I have never, till within the present year, been qualified by age for a voter. I have examined the leading principles of our government, it is true, and I much admire them; but, supposing that the opposing parties of the day were all mainly agreed in their aims to sustain those principles, and were, after all, only disputing about men, or at the worst, the different means of gaining the same end, I have so little interested myself in party questions, that I have as yet formed no decided preferences for either side."

"You are mistaken, sir," rejoined the editor. "If you suppose that both parties are for sustaining the same principles, you are most" —

The speaker was here interrupted by a smart rap of the knocker without. The merchant sprang to the door, and soon ushered into the room a personage alike unexpected and unknown to all present. His appearance at once showed him to be a person of many airs, with no lack of confidence in himself. He carried a tasselled cane, and wore a showy safety-chain, with an abundance of watch-seals, to say the least, dangling from his pocket, while his dress was what has significantly been termed the shabby-genteel. After inquiring if the gentlemen present were the school committee, he announced his business, which, to the surprise, and, it must be confessed, somewhat to the uneasiness of our hero, proved to be the same that had prompted his own call. The committee, however, seemed very far from looking upon the visit of the stranger as an intrusion; and, apprising him that they had just commenced the examination of one candidate, they told him "the more the merrier," as it would afford them a better chance for selection, and invited him to make number two; which being assented to, they proceeded with the examination.

"What are your views, Mr. Blake — for that, I think, you told me was your name" — said the editor, whose mind was still running on the subject on which he was about to be eloquent, when interrupted by the entrance of the new candidate; "What are your views of the propriety of instilling correct political principles into the minds of your pupils, who are the rising generation, and soon to wield the destinies of our glorious republic?"

"I hold, sir," replied Blake, who, it appeared, had cunningly inquired out the calling, politics, &c., of each of the committee, before coming near them, — "I do hold, though others may disagree with me, that it is rather important to attend to the particular you have instigated, sir. I'm always open in my politics. I read several articles in a newspaper over at the tavern, just now, while waiting for my dinner, that speaks my sentiments on that head exactly."

"What paper was it?" eagerly asked the editor.

"I did n't mind particularly," replied the other, with affected carelessness; "but I think it was the Star, or some such title."

"The Blazing Star?" said the former, with a complaisant bow.

"The same," rejoined Blake, "the very same; I now recall it."

"That is the paper, sir, which I have the honor of conducting," said the other, with another bow, and a gracious smile.

"Indeed! Why, sir," said Blake, with pretended embarrassment, "why, sir, had I supposed — but I was so struck with the able — I hope you will pardon me, sir, for introducing" —

"O certainly, certainly, sir," interrupted the editor. "I feel myself both flattered and gratified by your opinions. There, gentlemen," he continued, turning with a triumphant air to his two associates, "I have done what I considered my duty with the candidates, on the point in which I feel a deep interest. I am now willing to turn them over to you, for examination in the sciences."

"I should like to hear what Mr. Blake thinks about teaching book-keeping in a school, since I have the misfortune to disagree with the other gentleman here," said the merchant.

"Book-keeping?" said Blake, instantly catching a hint from the last part of the other's observation. "O, book-keeping is quite essential — quite, sir, quite; I always learn it to my pupils."

"I think so; I think it's an important item in the account," responded the merchant, glancing round at his colleagues, significantly, as he threw himself back with a self-satisfied air.

"I have a boy," said the tailor, "whom is pretty cute in grammar, as all allow; and I would be pleased to hear the gentlemen explain on that department, and tell whether their mode and manner of teaching it is of the latest style?"

Mr. Blake here being not so prompt as usual in taking the lead, Amsden briefly but clearly explained the first principles of English Grammar, the object and uses of that branch, and his manner of teaching it by the text-books of Murray and others. The other candidate, after waiting till pressed to give his views in so pointed a manner, that he saw no way to avoid saying something on the subject — with some hesitation observed,

"Well, gentlemen, my notions about grammar may be different from others, perhaps yours. Now my sentiments is something like this: — the true use of grammar is to learn 'em sense. Well, in what the gentleman here calls parsing Syntax, *I*, now, should make my scholars find out the sense of a piece. And if they can do that, it is all I should require; because the only use of grammar being to learn 'em the sense, as I said, why, the work is done, a n't it? I take it so, gentlemen. But suppose they can't do this, then I should take the piece in hand myself; and if I could not make sense out of it, then I should call it false grammar, that's all. So when I have my scholars write compositions, I square the grammar of their pieces upon the sense they contain; for where there's sense, there must, in course, be grammar; and visy versy. Now that's my system, gentlemen. For I have no notion of spoiling sense to make it fay in with book rules; but I make the grammar come down to the sense, not the sense give up to the grammar."

"Just my sentiments, to a shaving!" exclaimed the merchant. I used to study grammar when at the academy, and bothered and bothered to parse by the rules; but I never could see the use of it. And now, in my business letters, I never think of trying to write by any of the rules I learnt; and yet I write grammar, because I write sense, as he says. Yes, them's my sentiments about grammar."

"Well, it does look kinder reasonable," said the tailor, "though my boy learnt the rules, syntax, and catemology, and all; and I do n't know what he would say to leaving 'em off. But perhaps this way of teaching grammar the gentleman speaks of is some new imported fashion, that's soon to be all the style?" he added, inquiringly looking at the patent grammarian who had just before spoken.

"Precisely," answered the other, with a conciliating nod; "it is indeed, sir, a new system, of the very latest cut."

"I am satisfied, then, sir," rejoined the other.

"Which is the most useful rule in arithmetic, Mr. Amsden?" asked the merchant. "I profess to know something about that, myself."

"Why, that would be nearly as difficult to tell, I imagine, as regards all the fundamental rules, as it would be to point out the most useful wheel of a watch, in which all the wheels are required to keep the whole in motion," replied Locke.

"Now I don't think so," said the questioner; "but I'll ask Mr. Blake?"

"O, I say the rule that helps a man most to do business by, and you know quite well what that is, I fancy; for you tell what the articles you sell come to by that," observed Blake, obsequiously bowing to the merchant.

"Ay; I see you are a practical man, Mr. Blake," here chimed in the editor; "and such men are the very nerves and sinews of our republic."

"I care less about that," rejoined the merchant; "but I must say I approve the gentleman's views of grammar and arithmetic. But suppose we now pass on to geography —

"How do you bound the Polar Sea, Mr. Amsden?"

"Which Polar Sea?" asked Locke, quite innocently.

"Why, the Frozen Sea, to be sure," said the other.

"I must still ask to which Polar or Frozen Sea you refer, sir, before I can answer your question," said the former; "the Northern or Southern?"

"Well, that beats me," observed the erudite dealer; "I had supposed the Frozen Ocean was, of course, in the north; for we all know that the farther we go north, the colder it is;

and the farther we go south, the warmer it is. Do n't you think so, Mr. Blake?"

"Why, I had thought so, certainly," responded Blake, glancing at Amsden with a supercilious smile — "not that I have any wish to expose any body's ignorance, by any means; but being appealed to in the matter, so, it 's but civil to answer the question. And, now I am speaking on the subject of geographical literature, I may as well, gentlemen," he continued — deeming it now a favorable time to press the advantage he supposed he had gained over his rival, by an extra display of his erudition — "I may as well tell you at once, that I rather pride myself on my knowledge of terrestrial geography, and my improved modes of teaching it. I teach it almost entirely by maps, and the map-making process. And it would astonish you to see how quick scholars, in this way, will become accomplished geographians. I learn 'em, in a very short time, also, to make the most splendid maps, equal, nearly, to the printed ones, of all sorts and sizes, both on Mercator's project, as they call it, and on the principle of circular latitudes. Nor is this but a small part of the embellishments I teach my scholars, when they have the proper instruments to work with. There 's the problems and the circles, the squares, triangular geometry, ovals, perspective configurations, and a thousand curious things, I could teach, if I only had the instruments; such as Gunter's dividers, circumflutors, and the like. And then I would teach musical psalmody, of evenings, for nothing, which, as I see you are about building a new church here, might be an object. In short, gentlemen, I should be very happy to add my best powers in accomplishing your children, and helping to build up your flourishing village. But I leave the decision to you, gentlemen, with the greatest pleasure; because I have discovered you to be men of the most ecstatic discernment."

As soon as the speaker had fairly delivered himself of this

learned harangue, Amsden, who knew not which most to admire, the effrontery and ignorance of the fellow, or the ignorance and blindness of the committee, who seemed so readily to swallow all he said — inquired if there was not some man of science in the place, who could be called in to conduct the examination, and assist the committee in deciding upon the merits of the applicants now before them. This inquiry, as reasonable and fair as was its obvious object, produced, as a close observer might have easily seen, considerable sensation in the before well-assured mind of Locke's exulting competitor; and his uneasiness was the next moment increased into downright apprehension, by a remark of the tailor, who, in a rather hesitating manner, said, —

"Why, there 's the minister that preaches half the time here — and he 's now in the place, I guess. He 's a college-learnt man, they say, and would be willing to come in, perhaps, if — "

"Why, if these gentlemen," interrupted Blake, rising in visible agitation, "if these gentlemen do n't consider themselves capable of deciding on our qualifications and embellishments, then, I say, I am willing — perfectly willing, I say, to" —

"Well, I am not," interposed the luminous head of the *Blazing Star*, with much decision. "I shall most pointedly object to that measure. I should consider it as no less than involving an approach to a sanction of that never-to-be-enough reprobated doctrine of the union of church and state. And I should raise my voice" —

"Ah! I think we can get along," said the merchant, breaking in on the latter, and now rising and looking at his watch with an impatient and irritated air, "I think we can get along without the help of the minister in this business. And if the two gentlemen," he continued, with rather a discriminating gesture, "will step into the other room, or over to the tavern, we can probably come to a decision of the case without much trouble, I think."

The two candidates accordingly retired, — Blake into the adjoining room, and Amsden, as was doubtless intended, to the tavern, — to give to the astute trio of examiners an opportunity for private deliberation.

"Shall we mark, gentlemen?" said the merchant, cutting three separate slips of paper, and passing two of them to his colleagues, with a pencil, that each might write the name of the candidate he would select, and present it for comparison with those of the others, after the manner of appraising a horse.

"Well, if I was fully satisfied about Mr. Blake's grammar" — said the tailor, doubtingly, holding his pencil over his paper.

"I am satisfied about it well enough for my case," observed the merchant, dashing down the chosen name with a decisive sweep of the hand.

"And so am I," responded the editor; "and what is more, he is sound in political principles, to the core.

"O, I an't strenuous, gentlemen," said the tailor, following the example of the others in filling his blank.

The three slips, with the written sides downward, were then held up together, and turned over, bringing the name on each to view. And it was *Blake — Blake — Blake!*

"As I supposed," said the merchant; "just as I knew it must be. Boy," he continued, opening the door leading into the kitchen, "you may step over to the tavern, and say to the gentleman who just went from here, that he need n't trouble himself to call again. And, here! take this decanter, and get it filled with the best wine at the store. We will call in Mr. Blake, and settle the terms with him, over a bottle of my nice Madeira; for I feel like taking a bumper on the occasion."

Meanwhile Locke, who was travelling horseback, but too well anticipating the result of the deliberation just described, had ordered his horse to the door, and stood impatiently waiting for some sign or message from the white house, which should apprise him of the decision of the committee. The message came even sooner than he expected, and was delivered by the boy literally, and no less cavalierly than it was indited by his master. The next instant our rejected candidate was in his saddle, and leaving Mill-Town Emporium at a pace which his sober steed appeared to wonder should be required by one who before had shown himself so moderate and gentle a rider.

As soon as his feelings, smarting with chagrin and vexation at his mortifying defeat, and the folly and ignorance which, he believed, alone had occasioned it, — as soon as his excited feelings had sufficiently subsided to permit of connected thought, he reined his thankful horse into a walk, to try to review the novel occurrences he had just witnessed, and bestow upon them something like sober reflection.

"What does education avail me?" he despondingly soliloquized, as he thought over his recent reception, and how he had been set aside for an ignorant coxcomb, or at best a pitiful smatterer. "The more I study, the worse I succeed. Yes, what avails all this intellectual toil, if my acquirements thereby are to be thus rewarded?" And as he pondered upon these discouraging circumstances, he almost resolved to abandon for ever all thought of that noble employment to which he had so often declared his intention to devote himself. Locke had, thus far, had no acquaintance with aught but country life, with which he had been accustomed to associate ideas of comparative ignorance and degradation, while his mind had been directed to villages and cities, as the exclusive seats of intelligence and refinement. Like many another modest country lad of merit, he would have bowed in deference to the pert dashing villager or citizen, as his supposed superior, when the latter, probably, possessed not a tithe of his own worth in all that should constitute true excellence of character. For he had not learned that the people of cities and villages, as a mass, are, generally, less thinking, and often, less reading communities, than those formed of the residents of the country, who, finding themselves outshone by the former in external appearance, are thus driven to depend more on intrinsic qualities on which to base a reputation, leaving the others to dazzle by show, and, too often only,

> "To measure their worth by the cloth of their coats."

It was not very strange, therefore, that with impressions and views like those just named, contracted through a limited knowledge of the world, young Amsden should have presented himself at Mill-Town with a high opinion of the intelligence of its inhabitants, or that his disappointment should be great at finding things so exactly the reverse of what he had anticipated. A knowledge of the world as it is would have taught him that what he had witnessed was no miracle, even in the most favored parts of our land of boasted intelligence; and it might have taught him also, that he who would succeed must always, in some measure, adapt the means he employs to the compass of the minds of those with whom he desires success.

As Locke was slowly jogging onward, deeply engrossed in reflections which grew out of the occasion, and no less deeply dejected in spirits at the dark and discouraging prospects before him, he met a man in a sulky, who, in passing him, suddenly halted, and pronounced his name. Looking up at the traveller, now for the first time, the former at once recognized him to be no other than Dr. Lincoln, the kind and gifted physician, with whom he had formed so interesting an acquaintance at his school in the Horn-of-the-Moon.

"Why, this is a singular affair, this meeting you just at this time and place," said the doctor, gaily, after the usual salutations had been exchanged. "I am almost minded to quote a homely old proverb; for I have not travelled forty rods since I was thinking of you, and really wishing that I knew where you might be found. But more of that anon. How has the world used you since I parted with you, Mr. Amsden?"

"Mainly well — quite so, indeed, if I except a little vexation of to-day's occurrence."

"And what has crossed your path to-day of an unpleasant nature? I perceived at the first glance that your countenance wore a look of dejection that did not formerly belong to it."

"O, it is nothing of consequence, sir."

"In one sense, it may be. I have long since observed, sir, that there is no way in which a disturbed mind can be sooner restored to its natural equilibrium, than by a disclosure of its burden to others; even though it receive no sympathy in return. We are made social beings; and the law of our nature cannot be contravened with impunity here, any more than in more important matters. The cause of your trouble is none of my business to be sure; but a communication of it, I will venture to say, will lighten your heart. And it is best to enjoy all the happiness we can get, you know. So let us have your story."

Struck with the kind interest which the other seemed to take in his concerns, Locke proceeded to give him a minute detail of all the circumstances attending his application for the school in the village he had just left, his examination, and the result of the whole affair.

"And what opinion did you form of your successful rival?"

asked the doctor, after indulging in a hearty laugh at some parts of the story.

"Why, that he was a pitiful ignoramus, to be sure."

"Undoubtedly; but yet a fellow of considerable tact, and a pretty keen insight into the weaknesses of men, and the unworthy passions and selfish motives that too often govern them. And all this he had need of, to succeed upon pretensions so ridiculous; but with it, you see, he did succeed, and that too, at fearful odds against him. With what low cunning he first inquired the characters of the committee! — for such, as you suppose, was probably the case. And then how eagerly he seized on the first opportunity to bedaub them with flattery, rightly judging that, in this instance, the words of the poet would hold good,

—— "flattery never seems absurd —
The flattered always take your word."

And having thus secured the feelings and prejudices of the committee for himself, he appears fairly to have exemplified, with them, the truth of another line of the same writer, by making

"Impossibilities seem just."

Indeed, sir, I think the fellow, who may be a broken-down pedler, or possibly a discarded subscription agent of catchpenny books or periodicals, managed his slender stock in trade to pretty good advantage. I see but one blunder that need at all to have endangered him with his learned examiners, — that was his mention of "*circumflutors*," meaning, probably, to have hit on *circumferentors*, of which he might have heard from some students or surveyors with whom he chanced to fall in company, perhaps. But even that blunder, it seems, passed unnoticed. O, yes," continued the doctor, with an ironical smile, "this fellow managed his part to admiration. But what shall we say of that committee, who, both through ignorance and will, have thus betrayed their trust? And, furthermore, what shall we say of the people of that village, who so blindly conferred that important trust on such men? But we may spare words; for the employment of this imposter will fall as a judgment on their children, in the shape of errors imbibed, that will sufficiently punish these people for their unpardonable blindness and folly. And I will here tell you, Mr. Amsden, we have more to do in improving the condition of our common schools than to increase the number of qualified teachers. We have got to appoint managing committees who are qualified to discover and appreciate them. But enough of this; where do you think of looking for a school now, my dear sir?"

"I know not where to look, or what to do," replied Locke, despondingly. "I am poor, and need, particularly at this time, the amount of what would be respectable wages. But our country schools afford so little remuneration; and as for the villages, you see what my success is with them."

"Do n't despair quite so soon, sir," said Lincoln, a little roguishly; "you may find some men in other villages of a little larger pattern than that of the learned trio you just encountered. What say you to coming to Cartersville, and taking the school in the district where I live?"

"I would," replied Locke, "if you were to be the examining committee."

"Well, I shall be," rejoined the doctor, "for all the examination I shall want of you."

"How am I to take you, sir?" asked the former, with a doubtful air.

"Why, that, as it strangely happens, I am sole committee myself," answered the doctor.

"Indeed! is it possible?" exclaimed Locke, unable to conceal the pleasure that this unexpected announcement occasioned him.

"It happens, for once, to be so," said the other. "About a week since, being at home, and at leisure, I, for the first time for years, attended our annual school-meeting, and was, partly out of sport, I do believe, voted in sole committee-man, nobody believing I would accept the office. I, however, after giving them my views as to the kind of teacher we needed, his compensation, &c., told the meeting I would accept, if they would allow me to do exactly as I chose, without grumbling. And, they finally consenting, I took upon myself the really important duties of that post. And it was with a view of faithfully discharging them, that I was just thinking of you, as a teacher who would do much towards raising the low condition of our school. You shall name your own wages, if within any reasonable sum, and the length of your engagement for any period short of six months. What say you to all this, my friend?"

It is needless to say how gladly these proposals were accepted by our hero. And, having settled the details of the bargain, he bade adieu, for the present, to his kind friend, and with a countenance as grateful and sunny, as, one half hour before, it had been gloomy and dejected, resumed his journey homewards, to spend a happy week with his family, before entering on his new engagement.

CHAPTER VIII.

"Not long the house so raised, so prop'd, can stand;
For, like the fool's, 't is built upon the sand."

PARNEL.

THE place to which we will now repair, as the seat of the future operations of our schoolmaster, was a thriving interior village, with a population of something over a thousand. Its name, Cartersville, was derived from that of its founder, a Mr. Carter, an enterprising individual, who, some forty or fifty years before the period of our story, here established himself, erected several kinds of mills, and opened a store, which, with the natural advantages of the location, soon drew around them the buildings and shops of other settlers, till the place swelled, at length, into a village of considerable importance, with, perhaps, even more than the usual complement of mechanics' shops, taverns, stores, churches, and fine dwelling houses. At the time of which we are writing, the first Carter, whom we have named as the principal founder of this village, had been dead many years. He had amassed, during a prosperous and active life, an amount of property, which, for a country merchant, was considered very large. This he had left to three sons and a daughter. Two of the sons became spendthrifts, soon squandered their portions, and left the country. The daughter, who was now dead, had married a man that had lost her portion also, and gone abroad, but little better than bankrupt. The remaining son, who alone inherited any of his father's talents for business, or attempted to improve on the property left him, continued in the trade to which he had been brought up, that of merchandise, and was now accounted the rich man of the place, being extensively engaged in business, and still a man of industry and good calculations in traffic, though otherwise a person of rather contracted notions. His family, however, consisting of a wife and three daughters, were of small advantage to him, either in improving his property, or in elevating his character, — at least not to any correct standard of moral action. For his wife was a woman of false tastes, and of affectedly fashionable habits; and accordingly she had brought up her daughters, who, as might be expected under such maternal guidance, had little to boast, of which they had reason to be proud, being vain, empty-headed, wrong-hearted girls, fond of expensive display, priding themselves upon their father's wealth, talking much about family distinction, and only ambitious to be looked up to — as they unfortunately were by the young society of the place — as a sort of inapproachable standard in dress, and all matters pertaining to what they deemed stylish life, and to be considered, as they considered themselves, the very

"Glass of fashion and the mould of form."

This family belonged to the school district in which Locke Amsden was now engaged as a teacher for the ensuing winter; but, being above patronizing a common school for the purposes of educating their children, Mr. and Mrs. Carter, or rather Mrs. Carter, in conjunction with two or three other wealthy families of similar views, had established a private school, or select academy, as they called it, which was designed to afford the means of what they chose to term a genteel education, leaving the district schools of the village to be attended by the children of less distinguished families, and all those who had tastes for nothing better. At the head of this establishment was, at present, a fellow whose mind, manners, qualifications, and general character, admirably fitted him for such a station. He wrote himself *Manlius C. W. Tilden, Professor of Elegant Literature;* and taught crow-quill penmanship, drawing sundry problems in geometry, French, fashionable pronunciation, and the whole round of what he designated belles-lettres accomplishments, including music upon the piano, flagelet, &c., if required. The tendency of this school had been, as might be expected, to create envy, as little as there was reason for it, towards the favored few who attended it, and to cause the common schools to be neglected and looked upon with contempt. And Dr. Lincoln, who was a man of science, and an abominator of every thing of the tinsel order, was the first man to whom it occurred that it was a matter of importance to attempt to elevate the character of the common schools of the place, both to counteract the influence we have named, which he considered in all respects baneful, and to make those schools what they should be for public benefit.

Towards night on the day previous to the one appointed for entering upon his engagement, young Amsden arrived in the village to which we have just introduced the reader, and immediately repaired to the residence of his employer, Dr. Lincoln.

"Your arrival just now is most opportune, Mr. Amsden," said Lincoln, shaking the other heartily by the hand; "for I hope to have the remainder of the afternoon to myself, uninterrupted by professional calls, to enable me to spend a little time with you, in introducing you at your boarding place (for we have concluded to board you at one place), visiting with you our school-house, and in apprising you, in some measure, of the difficulties you will have to encounter, if you earn your money, as I intend you shall. But, come, sir, walk into the house first — you will stay with us through the night, and we will talk over these matters at our leisure."

The doctor then ushered the other into his house, and introduced him to his wife, a highly intelligent and agreeable lady, who, with her husband, — they having no children, — and a domestic of each sex, constituted the whole family.

After a pleasant half-hour spent in general conversation, the doctor and his guest set forth to visit the school-house, as the former had proposed.

"You have rather a large proportion of fine dwelling-houses in your village, have you not, doctor?" said Amsden, as they gained the street, and proceeded on their way.

"It may be so," replied the doctor. "Some ambitious people, in times past, erected several expensive buildings; since which many others, having imbibed the idea that social happiness is dependent on the size of the house where it is to be enjoyed, have followed the example; less for their own good, in some instances, I believe, than the good appearance of the village."

"Quite possible. But to whom belongs that large house, up yonder, observed Locke, pointing to a castle-like building, standing on an eminence, a little aloof from all others.

"O, that is the residence of the Carter family," answered the other. "This village took its name from the father of the owner of that house. The old gentleman was a stirring man, in his day, and died very wealthy. And his son, who built that fabric, is esteemed by some to be now equally rich; though he built, as some shrewd ones would have it, not so much according to his own judgment, as on his wife's somewhat different scale of greatness."

"It is a showy thing, indeed," rejoined the former; "but still I fancy it less than that much smaller, but more truly elegant house, as I should esteem it, standing within the borders of that beautiful farm, lying to the east of the Carter establishment."

"Ah! that was built by a man of true taste, and one of the finest of gentlemen," said the doctor, warmly. "He married the daughter of the elder Carter, and received that farm as her dowry. But he got entangled by his profligate brothers-in-law, and lost the whole establishment, which went into the hands of city creditors, while the unfortunate debtor was left to shift for himself, and, finally, to go to foreign lands, and there die, as is now generally supposed."

By this time they reached the school-house, which was situated in a noisy business corner, about ten paces from the street, with a blacksmith's shop on one side, and a cooper's on the other.

"Here is your palace, my lord of the birchen sceptre," said Lincoln, giving the other a good-natured slap on the shoulder.

"Ay, but it is rather near the street here; is it not, doctor?" remarked Amsden.

"True," replied the former, ironically; "but do n't you perceive the wise design of that? It is to inure the children to the danger of being run over, and horses to the danger of being frightened, to the peril of the necks and limbs of their drivers."

"You succeed so well in reasons," observed the other, laughing, "that I will hear you tell why the house is made to stand between two such noisy shops."

"O, the idea," answered Lincoln, in the same strain, "the idea must have been taken from the classics; as you scholars, I think, should at once perceive. Demosthenes, you know, practised oratory amid the roar and racket of waterfalls. And who knows how much the future orators, that shall have been educated in this school, will be indebted for their good articulation to the clinking of these hammers, of which you appear so disposed to complain?"

They then entered the house for an inspection of the interior, whose miserable construction and arrangement were the same as are still a greater part, perhaps, of common schoolhouses at the present day.

"I had looked to see things different here," remarked Locke, glancing round the room, as they entered it. But you have the same construction of seats as is seen so generally elsewhere — close, narrow, and all of an equal height; so that, while the limbs of the larger pupils are cramped up, and otherwise rendered uncomfortable, the feet of the little ones are left dangling in the air."

"Why, the object of that plan doubtless is," said the doctor, "to train the legs of the large ones to occupy a modest space in this world, and to cause those of the little ones to become so benumbed by hanging over the corners of the seats, which will thus impede the circulation of the blood in the arteries and veins, as to take away the troublesome desire of the restless creatures to run about, and go out of doors. And is not the custom sanctioned by that old and refined nation, the Chinese, who cramp the feet, &c., of their children? And are not the modern corsets of the intelligent and fashionable ladies of our own enlightened land, used on the same principle?"

"And then these seats," resumed the former, without replying to the comments of the other, whose ironical meaning he perfectly understood; "these seats, as usual, rise from the front here, where we stand, like the seats of an old amphitheatre — rise one above another, till the last one, yonder, is nearly half way up to the ceiling; so that the pupils on the upper tiers of the seats will be uncomfortably warm, in the heated air which always occupies the upper portion of the room, while the pupils on the lower seats will be, at the same time, perhaps, as uncomfortably cold."

"Very true," rejoined Lincoln, "very true; but then the object in this, also, is perfectly plain — it is to have the softest heads in the school placed up there to be baked over, so that they may be on a par with the others."

"Well, I wonder," remarked Locke, now laughing heartily at the satirical hit of the other, "I wonder, in view of the other conveniences of the house, how the matter of ventilation came ever here to be thought of, as it appears to have been, by that contrivance for lowering the upper sashes of the windows?"

"You remember the lesson you formerly received, I see," replied the doctor, assuming a serious air. "These windows were altered to admit of ventilation, at my own suggestion, some years ago. An opening might be made in the ceiling, as was done in your school-house, if thought necessary; but as this building is so old, and full of crevices for the admission of fresh air, perhaps it will be hardly worth the while to do this."

"Perhaps not, in this old house," said Locke; "but in a new one, which you will build here soon, I conclude, you will probably have this attended to, as well as several other improvements, which should be made in the interior of most of our school rooms; for I think you must agree with me, doctor, in the opinion that our school-houses are, generally, but illy adapted to the purposes for which they are, or should be intended."

"I certainly do, Mr. Amsden," answered the other. "And the reason I treated the defects you have here pointed out, in the manner I did, was because I thought with old Horace,

——"Ridiculum acri
Fortius ac melius, plerumque secat res,"—

"that ridicule sometimes is more sharply effective than direct denunciation;" and I felt like seizing on the sharpest weapon I could find for cutting up the faults and defects in question. Yes, sir, I have noticed the inattention of the public to this subject for years; and I have the more wondered at it when I saw that improvements were going on in all other kinds of buildings. The people now are getting to have convenient and healthy houses for themselves. They also build very warm and well-contrived stables for their horses and other cattle. They have even, lately, built houses for their hogs, on new plans, which are well adapted to their purposes. But the houses for educating their children in — they are never thought of!"

"Will your school prove a troublesome one to govern?" asked Amsden, as they now left the house on their return.

"O no," answered the other; "at least, I suspect not. You will find the scholars mischievous and noisy enough, no doubt, but not disposed to dispute your authority, I think. The difficulties you will have to encounter, before making any thing of your school, will be of a different, and, I really fear, of a worse character to overcome. You will find the school at the lowest ebb, flat, dead — dead to all ambition, all inclination to study and learn. We have gone on the cheap-teacher system till our school has completely run down. And I have employed you to elevate it, Mr. Amsden."

After Lincoln had taken Locke to the quarters he had engaged for him, and introduced him there, the two returned to the house of the former, where they found waiting for them an excellent supper, that was partaken with a keen appetite, and enlivened by a conversation of that easy, elevated, and sparkling character, which persons of intellect and attainments can always so easily get up, and which such only know how to appreciate and enjoy.

"If you, Mrs. Lincoln," said the doctor, rising from the

table and looking at his watch, as they finished their repast, "if you will entertain Mr. Amsden in my absence, I will now go out for an hour or two."

"Certainly," replied the lady; "but where do you think of going, husband? You know you may have urgent calls, when it will be necessary that you be found."

"True," answered the former. "Well, I have my poor patient at the corner, up here, to visit; and then I think of calling at Carter's."

"Mr. Carter's family are not sick, are they?"

"No, wife; but I am going to make an effort to get some of those girls into Mr. Amsden's school. It would be not only for their own good, but it would be a triumph over their Professor of Gimcracks, which I should enjoy."

"You will hardly prevail on Mrs. Carter to listen to any thing of that kind, I fancy, sir."

"As respects her own daughters, possibly not; but recollect there is a sprout there of a different stock, who has sense enough to see the difference between science and syllabubs."

"Ay; but to expect her to take such a course in despite the ridicule and sneers she would have to withstand from so many there, would be expecting considerable in a young lady of eighteen, you must remember."

"In an ordinary young lady it might be so. But she is not an ordinary young lady, and as I am well acquainted with her" —

"What vanity, now!"

"Vanity or no vanity, I shall talk with her on the subject."

"And in vain."

"We shall see."

The lady playfully shook her head, and the doctor departed on his destination. But, instead of following, we will precede the latter, a few moments, in his proposed visit, and introduce the reader to the family which had been the subject of the above discussion.

In a showily furnished apartment in the large house which we have before mentioned, sat a starchy-looking woman of perhaps forty, surrounded by four young ladies — three of them her daughters, the other her husband's niece. One of the daughters was thrumming a guitar. The other two sat nearly facing each other, at the opposite ends of a large sofa, lazily lolling their heads and shoulders over the cushioned arms, while their feet met and intermingled in the middle. One was reading, with an occasional sigh, a fashionable English novel; the other, a volume of Byron's poems. By the side of a stand, which had been drawn up near the sofa to furnish light to the two readers, sat the niece, darning stockings. The daughters, all looking much alike, were of delicate forms and quite fair complexions, but they were leaden-eyed beauties; and their trained countenances were sadly lacking in natural expression. The niece was a different looking person. Instead of the dawdling negligence exhibited in the ill-fitting, ill-matched, and gaudy apparel of the others, every article of her plain, but extremely neat dress, seemed exactly fitted, both by its color and fashion, to grace her small, compact, and elegantly turned figure. It was said by those who had noted her face at church, or when she sat listless, that her features were beautifully regular, and well shapen; but those with whom she had ever conversed, could never remember how that was; for the expression of her clear, wholesome, and smile-lit countenance so instantly caught and arrested the scanning eye, and called up the heart to blind it, that they either could never think to make the examination, or sufficiently succeed, if they attempted it, to enable them afterwards to say any thing decisive of the question. Her character, also, was as different from that of her cousins just named, as was her appearance. Whenever she appeared abroad, she was greeted by all persons most noted for understanding, with recognitions of the most marked respect; and the eyes of the poor and lowly, as they followed her, spoke blessings. But still she did not dress like her cousins. She was not the daughter of the stylish Mrs. and the rich Mr. Carter, and the fashionable world said but little about her.

Presently the sharp jingle of the door-bell announced a visiter. The mother pulled up her high-starched ruff still higher. The daughter at the guitar stopped short in her thrumming, and assumed a graceful leaning attitude over her instrument; while the other two daughters suddenly righted themselves on the sofa, and fell to adjusting their deranged false curls with most commendable diligence. The less cumbered niece, who had none of these important duties to perform, at once laid down her work, rose, and was approaching the door with the view of ushering in the new comer, when her step was arrested by the interposing gesture and words of Mrs. Carter,—

"No, no! let the servant do that—it's decidedly the most fashionable."

The other then quietly returned to her place, and fearlessly resumed her ungenteel employment.

In a moment the inner door was thrown open by the servant girl, and Dr. Lincoln entered, and made his compliments to the ladies.

"Why, you have made quite a mistake, doctor," said Miss Ann Lucretia, the elder Miss Carter, with a pretty simper, as she lightly tapped her white finger on a string of her guitar; "we are not sick, only a little *en dishabille*, as you perceive."

"Well, I felt quite endishable myself, an hour ago; but a

chance at a good dish of wife's toast for supper has overcome the feeling," said the doctor, with apparent honesty of manner.

"Now how can you pretend to be so ignorant of elegant literature, doctor?" exclaimed Miss Angeline Louisa, gracefully flirting her novel in her delicate hands.

"Perhaps the doctor do n't appreciate us, sister," lisped Miss Matilda Mandeville, the youngest of the three, a girl of about fifteen — "few do, you know; at least Professor Tilden says so."

"O! indeed I do," replied the doctor, with a bow and deprecating smile. "I am always just so blundering. But now for business: I called to say to you, Mrs. Carter," he continued, turning to that lady — "that I have supplied with a good teacher our district school, which commences to-morrow" —

The speaker paused, and the lady stared with a look which seemed plainly to say, "well, I wonder what I have to do with that?" — "and I did not know but you would feel like patronizing the school a little," at length added the speaker.

"We do patronize it by paying half the taxes that support it, for aught I know; for I never troubled my head to inquire about the district school, I am sure — not but what it may be very useful for the lower classes," replied the lady, with great dignity.

"Certainly," said the other; "and I have sometimes known good families turn in their sons and daughters with good advantage to them. And I thought it possible that some of the young ladies here might be disposed to attend, for the sake of looking a little into the common sciences."

"No, I thank you, doctor," replied the elder sister, with an ineffable toss of the head, "we are quite satisfied with our present instructor, whose select academy, I believe, is allowed to be very *distingué*."

"La, me!" cried Miss Angeline Louisa, "I wonder what Professor Tilden would say to our attending a district school! Come, what do you say to turning in with the ragged urchins of the *canaille*, Matilda Mandeville?" she added, giggling outright at the thought.

"O, dear me! how could one be so very vulgar?" exclaimed the fair sprig of gentility to whom the question was put.

"And what does Miss Maverick think of this matter?" said the doctor, who, finding himself repulsed, as he had been forewarned, with the mother and daughters, now turned confidently to the niece before described; "what does Miss Maverick think?" he repeated with an expression which he intended and believed she alone would rightly interpret,—"perhaps *she* is not so erudite but that she might attend our school awhile, with some benefit."

The young lady thus addressed lifted her clear blue eyes to the shrewd interrogator, and turned upon him, as he concluded, a look of the most searching scrutiny. The next instant, however, that look lost all its severity, and melted into a sweet, appreciating smile, that told that she had read a compliment instead of disparagement, in the doubly significant words of the speaker.

"I am quite conscious of my deficiencies in the solid sciences, sir," she replied; "and I confess I have sometimes wished for an opportunity to study them more. If you have a well-qualified instructor, I have but little doubt that it might be more profitable for *me*"—

"Now you are not in earnest, surely, are you, Mary?" interposed Miss Ann Lucretia; "why, where can be your taste? What! leave our Academy of Elegant Literature, so very *recherché*, for a common district school, filled up with the mere rabble, and headed by a country rustic, no doubt, who perhaps never trod on a carpet in his life?"

"Why, our notions vary a little in these particulars, you know, cousin Ann," modestly replied the former. "But, were they alike, I know not but I ought to be willing to attend oui district school, for the purpose of lessening the burden of expense to uncle Carter, who has so kindly paid the high tuition which your instructor asks, that I might have the same privilege with his own daughters.

"I suppose Mary wishes to keep in our circle of society?" significantly remarked the old lady.

"Why, who could think of such a thing as going to a district school?" said Miss Angeline Louisa; "I should be ashamed to have people know I thought of the thing."

"Indeed, so should I," chimed in the delicate lisper, Miss Matilda Mandeville; "for common schoolmasters are nothing but pedagogues, and they are the ones, you know, that Professor Tilden laughs so much about."

The conversation was here interrupted by another peal of the bell; and, in a moment more, the notable personage to whom the young ladies had so often alluded in the foregoing discussion, was shown into the apartment. He was a man something under thirty, dressed in the extremes of fashion, and of manners which he evidently considered very Chesterfieldian. He bowed with an attitude on entering; and, as soon as he had disengaged himself from the three besieging sisters, who all sprang forward to meet him at the door, he advanced to a proffered seat, with a patronizing nod to the doctor, a distant "how d'ye do" to the still seated Mary, and a superb double congee to Mrs. Carter."

In the black-bird chit-chat that now sprang up between the sisters and their elegant professor, Lincoln found opportunity to speak with Miss Maverick alone.

"Now for your decision, Miss Maverick," he said.

"On the subject you were speaking of when he entered?" she asked; O, I have come to no decision, sir."

"What would your father have advised in such a case, Miss Maverick?" persisted the former.

"You are quite a skilful pleader, doctor," replied the other, with a melancholy, yet arch smile; "are you sure you did not mistake your profession?"

"No," said the doctor, smiling in surprise and admiration; "but what other girl would have taken that view of the drift of my question? If, however, you think I am appealing to what I might well suppose would be, with you, unanswerable authority, for the purpose of carrying some selfish point only, you are mistaken. I will therefore press the question."

"My father," said Mary, "as perhaps you may know, sir, was very anxious that I should first secure the solid sciences, and kept me at those schools where he thought I could study such of them as suited my age, to the best advantage. He even taught me in them, a part of the time, himself."

"Then I have your opinion in this matter — have I not?"

"Perhaps not; for, as unsuitable as I have felt my late course of study to be, for me at least, I have seen but little chance of pursuing any other with the hope of good instruction in your school, with the instructors you have lately had."

"There is something in your observation, doubtless, Miss Maverick; but we shall have a different instructor this winter."

"Do you know him personally, that you can answer for his qualifications?"

"I do. He is a scholar and a gentleman. Now shall I not have your decision? I know it will require some nerve to stem certain currents. But, as your father's friend, let me advise you to do it."

"I know," rejoined Mary, with a moistened eye, and other evidences of tender emotion, "I know you were my good father's friend, and he yours. And I thank you kindly, Dr. Lincoln, for the interest you take in me. But I cannot now answer your question. I must first consult uncle Carter. I am too much indebted to him to take any step which he might disapprove, whatever my own opinion should happen to be."

The doctor now took his leave of the family, and, after seeking out Mr. Carter at his store, and saying a few words to him in private, returned to his own happy abode.

CHAPTER IX.

> "There in his noisy mansion skill'd to rule,
> The village master taught his little school."
>
> GOLDSMITH.

On repairing to his school-house, the next morning, for the purpose of commencing his winter's task, Amsden unexpectedly found, among the pupils there assembled, and awaiting his coming, one whose appearance instantly attracted his attention, and awakened in his bosom a lively and peculiar interest. This was no other than Mary Maverick, the dependent orphan, who, on Dr. Lincoln's warrant of having a qualified teacher, had nobly braved the ridicule of her fashionable cousins, and the sneers of their arrogant professor, and come here to pursue those studies and receive that instruction which her own excellent judgment told her would most truly accomplish her, not only for the duties, but for the elegancies of life. Often did the former, during the forenoon, while engaged in ascertaining the intended studies of the different portions of his school, and arranging his classes, detect his attracted vision stealing in half-involuntary glances to the face of his fair pupil. He felt a vague though deepening impression that he had seen that remarkable countenance before; but it was rather a sensation of the heart than a recollection of the mind; for where or when he could have seen her, his taxed memory refused to inform him. And every effort he made to form a conclusion on the subject but added to his perplexity. Nor did the object of his mental inquiry herself seem wholly at ease in her posi tion. There was a sort of tell-tale consciousness about her looks that bespoke either an actual recognition, or a dilemma no less pleasant than his own. Could it be that this was the sprightly little daughter of the interesting stranger, whose call at his father's, in former years, had left such an impression on his mind, and given such a turn to his destinies? He thought it not probable; for between that fairy little being, whose image, as she then in her child-like simplicity appeared, had ever been brightly pictured on his mind — and the sweetly dignified young lady before him, his thoughts could find no resemblance which would warrant him in determining on their identity. And yet, though his mind dared not entertain the pleasing thought, his heart continued to whisper, that, however great the transformation, they were one and the same. In this state of delicate embarrassment, he suffered himself to remain through the day. He might, as he well knew, have easily resolved his doubts, by conversing with her, and making some allusions to former circumstances. But, absurd as it may appear, the very solicitude he felt on the subject prevented him from doing this, or even going so far, in this respect, as his duties as her teacher perhaps required. And when he dismissed his school at night, he was not only ignorant of what he was most anxious to know respecting his interesting pupil, but he had not even ascertained her name.

After taking supper at his boarding-house, at which he had now taken up his quarters, our hero took occasion, with what secret motives we will not pretend to decide, to call at the house of Dr. Lincoln.

"Ah, ha! my friend," exclaimed the doctor, gaily, as the other entered; "I am glad to see you; for I wish to ask you what you think of the condition of your numerous family."

"Rather low, as you intimated yesterday, but by no means hopeless, I trust, doctor," replied Amsden, in the same strain.

"Well, I am gratified to hear you say even so much. But did my phœnix make her appearance there to-day?"

"Who, sir?"

"O, the young lady at Carter's — his niece, whom you heard me mention last night as likely to attend."

"There was a young lady at school to-day, who I thought might be the one to whom you alluded; but I did not learn her name."

"Not learn her name!"

"No; you did not mention it, and a teacher cannot often ascertain all the names of his pupils in one day. But who is she?"

"It is rather curious that a young gentleman should let a whole day pass, under such circumstances, without ascertaining who such a girl as Mary Maverick is," replied the doctor with a surprised and somewhat incredulous look; "but I will tell you. She is the only child of Col. Maverick, the gentleman who, as I was naming to you yesterday, married the present Mr. Carter's only sister, lost his wife, failed, and finally went to South America by my advice, to repair his shattered health and fortunes — particularly the former; as I thought I detected, in his ill-health, indications of an approaching consumption, which another winter's residence in our climate, I was fearful, would develope. It was ascertained that he left the port at which he arrived, for the interior of Brazil, since which he has never been heard from. He doubtless there fell a prey to disease, or perished in the civil wars by which that country was then distracted."

"How many years ago was this?" asked the other, with assumed indifference.

"Six years, the coming May, I believe — yes, it was in May that he left here. He had been the superintendent of a factory, in a village about an hundred miles to the south of this, where the year previous he had resided, having taken his daughter with him to attend a school in the place. He returned with her early in the spring, and, leaving her in the care of her uncle, departed, never to return."

"Where she has ever since remained, I suppose?" said Locke, who, though now satisfied of the identity he had been secretly trying to establish, was yet reluctant to let the subject drop.

"Yes, to be sure," replied Lincoln, throwing an inquiring look at the other; "yes, she has remained in that family, it is true; but she has not been spoiled for all that, — if such is an answer to what I take to be the drift of your question. No, the father was a man of high qualities, both of head and heart; and the daughter — but I shall leave you to find that out, Amsden, as you soon will — unless," he banteringly added, "unless the progress you have made in her acquaintance to-day is to be taken as a fair sample of the future."

Amsden now was quite willing to let the subject rest; and, after some further conversation on indifferent topics, he bade the other good night, and departed.

On entering his school-room the next morning, a little before the usual time of opening his school, Amsden was agreeably surprised to find the fair object of his yesterday's solicitude already there, engaged upon her studies. Feeling himself now, by the discoveries he had made last evening, measurably relieved from the embarrassment which had kept him aloof the day before, he no longer hesitated to approach her, pay his respects, and make inquiries respecting the studies she proposed to pursue. His advances being here met with unaffected kindness and respectful courtesy, he soon ventured to allude to the circumstance of their former meeting, at his father's; and he felt not a little gratified and flattered to find that all the little incidents connected with that brief visit were fresh in her recollection. She had even learned his subsequent history, almost to the present time, from a mutual acquaintance of both, who had formerly attended Seaver's academy. An understanding being thus effected between them, not only as regarded the relations of teacher and pupil, but in the more delicate ties of a friendship based on reciprocal respect, and the kindly remembrances and prepossessions of the past, it were, perhaps, almost needless to say how happy our hero became in his situation. His duties, as arduous as they were, seemed light and pleasant in the bright presence in which they were continually performed. And if her presence alone could thus sweeten his labors with others, how delightful the task of imparting instruction to her, — to her whose mind, as he soon found, was fully capable of appreciating his own, and whose proficiency in the sciences awakened his admiration! And with what pleasure did he, each day, look forward to the peaceful, intellectual hour, which, after the dismissal of the main part of his scholars, he usually devoted to her, and a few others, whom her noble example soon brought into school! To him this duty became a privilege, and a privilege which afforded him all the happiness his heart desired.

With regard to the general character and condition of the school of which he had taken charge, Amsden found matters much as his employer had represented. In the government of his school — so far, at least, as respected a disposition to acknowledge and obey his authority generally — he experienced, it is true, no difficulty with his pupils. For it having not been any part of their ambition to bully their masters, and having been accustomed to the discipline of those whose chief object seemed to have been to govern rather than to instruct, they appeared to expect, with all their trifling and restlessness, that order would be enforced, and they must yield to its requisitions. But with this negative virtue ended all that was promising or commendable in the appearance of the school. The scholars, though they had been kept at school, perhaps two thirds of the time, for years, were yet extremely deficient — in any correct knowledge, at least — of the most common rudiments of learning. They had, many of them, gone over much ground, indeed; but they had acquired but little correctly, and less understandingly. And it was still with the utmost difficulty that they were restrained from running over whole pages for a lesson, when perhaps as many sentences would be more than they would have thoroughly mastered. Besides this, the common vice of our schools, especially village schools, the scholars seemed to have little or no relish for their studies, and as little ambition to excel in them.

Although this unpromising condition of the school was, as before intimated, directly attributable to the mismanagement of unqualified or unfaithful teachers, there was yet another circumstance, which had not only, in a great measure, probably, remotely caused the whole evil, by leading to the employing of such teachers in the first place, but which continued to operate with the most unfavorable effect on the advancement of the pupils. This was the total neglect with which the whole subject was treated by the inhabitants of the district, who, as is too often the case, rarely troubled their heads even to inquire about the school, much less to visit it.

With all these obstacles before him, it was some time before Amsden, with all his tact and perseverance, could succeed in confining his pupils to methods of study which promised any real improvement. And if he succeeded in doing that, he found it no less difficult to excite in them an interest in their studies sufficient to insure an application productive of any important results.

At length, however, by extraordinary exertions, he so far overcame the difficulties with which he had to contend, as to command the attention of his pupils, and to raise, in most of them, some little ambition to press forward in the path of improvement. But, aware that much remained to be done, and being sensible at the same time that but few scholars will long persevere in attempts which the exertions of a teacher, only, have induced them to make, unless they expect their labors will be rewarded by the encouragement and approbation of those to whom they are in the habit of looking for every thing else in life, his next step was to enlist the interest of the parents in his school, and thus secure their coöperation in bringing about the desired object. With this end in view, he at first made an effort to induce the parents and guardians of the district to make individual visits to his school. But, meeting with no other success in this attempt than what consisted of promises, reluctantly given and invariably broken, he next determined to appoint a particular day for the reception of visiters, and to prepare his scholars for going through such interesting exercises on the occasion, as should furnish an additional inducement for the invited, at least, to attend. In pursuance of this plan, he fixed on a future day for what he concluded to call a public examination of his school. And, having caused information of the appointment to be spread through the neighborhood, he began to make arrangements for the purpose among his pupils, and to exhort them to the use of such diligence in their studies as should enable them to acquit themselves creditably before the expected assemblage. Incited afresh by the thought of displaying their acquisitions before their parents and others, or fearful of exposing their deficiences, the scholars, with almost one accord, betook themselves eagerly to their respective studies. And, in the two weeks that intervened before the day of the proposed examination, they had made such progress that their teacher began really to feel very proud of his school.

As the appointed day drew near, Amsden, to make doubly

sure of a general attendance, was at the pains of calling on most of the parents and guardians of his pupils, to remind them of the time when the contemplated performances were to take place, and to urge them to be present. And so well did he prosper in obtaining individual promises of attendance, that he supposed there could be, this time, scarcely a possibility of a failure. His scholars, in the mean time, were full of ambition. He seemed to have succeeded, at last, in infusing into them a portion of his own spirit and enthusiasm for learning. Every thing went swimmingly on; and he felt himself justified in looking forward with certainty to the brightest results from the operation of his plan. But, alas! alas for the blindness and guilty neglect of the public, on a point so important to interests which we should hold, above all things, dear! We will not, however, anticipate.

The eventful day at length arrived; and our hero, having risen and breakfasted, left his lodgings for the scene of his daily labors, that morning, in high spirits. Every thing, thus far, seemed auspicious to his undertaking. On his way to his school-house, however, his attention was attracted by numerous hand-bills, posted on the doors, corners, and all other conspicuous places in the streets, announcing in staring capitals, for that evening, the wonderful exhibitions of the far-famed Potter, a professed juggler of those times, who proposed, in the present instance, as usual, to display the astonishing feats of swallowing swords and jack-knives, hatching chickens, frying eggs in his hat, together with an endless variety of other feats never before exhibited, but all equally miraculous. Performances to commence, in order to do full justice to the public, at the early hour of three o'clock, P. M.

As Amsden's examination was to begin only an hour before the time fixed on for opening these shows, and be resumed in the evening, for which the most interesting exercises, such as the reading of original compositions, declamations, and the speaking of a few select dialogues, were reserved,—it barely occurred to him that the coincidence might possibly be perhaps a little unlucky, as a very few unthinking persons, who otherwise might come to swell his audience, would, likely enough, be led away to witness the trumpery tricks of the juggler. But, supposing that no people of sense and character would do this, and especially that no parents would think of putting such pitiful shows in competition with the praiseworthy performances of their own children, when connected with a subject of such vital interest to them, he felt no uneasiness from the circumstance. And, very philosophically consoling himself with the thought that the presence of the few who would thus desert him would be no object, and that, after all, the poor mountebank, who would doubtless be the greatest loser in the rivalry for spectators, would have the most reason to complain, he dismissed the subject from his mind, and passed on unconcernedly to his schoolhouse. But, on opening his school, some doubts of a different character soon began to rise in his mind. Though he had no fears that the attendance of his audience would be materially endangered by the presence of these shows, yet he knew not but the excitement they would occasion among the boys of the village might distract the minds of his pupils, and cause them to acquit themselves less honorably than they would otherwise. For he was not long in discovering in them an unusual lack of interest respecting the performances in which they were in the afternoon to engage. A portion of them appeared too much excited to confine their minds to their tasks; others appeared absent, and yet others seemed wholly indifferent about preparing themselves for their allotted parts. Some other object of interest, in short, was obviously getting uppermost in their minds. And so great, indeed, was their listlessness, that their instructor at length began to entertain serious apprehensions that many of them, even those who had all along given the most evidence of improvement, would appear to great disadvantage in the approaching exercises. Nor did these unfavorable appearances at all improve as the morning wore away. At the recess of the boys, parts of exclamatory sentences, such as "*real live chickens!*" — "*great sharp swords, handle and all!*" frequently reached Amsden's ear from excited groups that were eagerly discussing the subject near the door; and on passing round among the seats just vacated, he saw the word *Potter* written on this slate, *Potter* on that copybook, and *Potter*, with his hat full of chickens, pictured out on the wall.

On returning to his school, after the usual intermission at noon, he found matters even worse than he had left them. The first boy he called up to read, after being shown his place, which he had forgotten, commenced, "B-a — yes, a — k-e-r," and stopped short.

"And what does that spell?" said his master, giving him an impatient jog, to recall his wandering ideas to the subject, "what does that spell, sir?"

"Potter!"

"What?"

"Potter — baker, I mean, but I was thinking" —

And so it was with most of them: their eyes might be upon their books, but their heads were full of Potter and his kickshaws.

All this looked rather ominous, to be sure; and Locke began to tremble for the credit of his pupils: but, believing they would be brought to their senses by the presence of the company, now shortly to assemble, he restrained his anxieties, and awaited, as patiently as he could, the hour set for commencing the exercises, and the arrival of the spectators.

Two o'clock at length came, but with it no company. At half-past two it was still the same; and the anxious teacher, now becoming really alarmed on a point on which before he had not suffered himself to entertain a single doubt, began to glance uneasily through the windows, and keep an eager ear listening for the approach of footsteps at the door. But he looked and listened in vain. Another hour came and passed, and yet not a single individual of all the expected audience made his appearance!

By this time, most of the scholars began to be restless, and show sundry other symptoms of impatience. The hour for opening the shows had come and gone. They were evidently thinking of this, and as evidently longing to be gone themselves. Locke, at the time previously set for the purpose, had commenced his examination, and thus far continued on with it, in the most unimportant parts of the exercises; but the business dragged every moment more and more heavily, and it now became obvious that the school could not much longer be kept together. First, one would ask to be dismissed; then, another; then, a third and fourth. And if refused, or put off, they would not sit five minutes without repeating their request; alleging, in many instances, that they had leave of their parents for so doing. Finding he might as well argue to the winds, as to a school in such a state — seeing, indeed, that it was wholly useless to attempt to proceed with the exercises, and having now no hope of any company, if he should, he reluctantly concluded to yield to the necessity of the case; and, calling up his scholars, he dismissed them till the next morning, without saying a word in comment. And no sooner was the welcome word pronounced, than the whole tribe, bursting out into an exulting *whorah!* hastily seized their caps, hats, &c., and rushed into the street, on their way for Potter's, where their more childish parents had gone before them — leaving their unregarded teacher to return home, more vexed, more chagrined, and more truly discouraged, than he had ever felt in the whole course of his life.

The next morning, on his way to his school, Locke encountered his friend and employer, Dr. Lincoln, and related to him the mortifying occurrences of the day previous.

"Your story, Mr. Amsden," said the doctor, "involves a satire upon us, which should well make us blush. Sensible of the importance of your most praiseworthy attempt, I was not only intending to go myself, but rally others; and an unexpected summons to a distant patient only prevented me from so doing. But, as provoking and truly discouraging as this affair must have been to you, do not allow yourself to despair."

"I shall not, of bettering my school in some measure; but what hope can I have of making it what it should be, while parents so plainly tell their children that they hold their improvement in science of less importance than the tricks of a juggler? Did they not so tell them yesterday? For, as somebody most truly says,

> "Words speak in a whisper, actions through a trumpet."

"True, true to the letter; and the sarcasm is richly deserved, though those to whom it applies are less conscious of their fault, I presume, than you imagine. Are you not expecting too much from poor human nature, especially here, where so many circumstances have long combined to blind people to the importance of popular education, and the best methods of promoting it? Men are generally more inclined to go where Folly leads than where Wisdom points. And here they have so long trod in the path of the former, that their blindness, on the point in question, has become chronic, and cannot be cured in a day. Your exertions will not have been lost on your school. Something has been gained in acquirement, something towards fixing good habits of study — all help. You must still persevere; and though it may not be expedient to renew your yesterday's attempt at present, you yet shall have my aid in trying to get parents and pupils mutually interested, as well by my occasional visits, as by my influence to procure the visits and enlist the interest of others. Yes, persevere; and, while you do so, remember that our village is not the only one guilty of the same faults. Our country schools are before those of our villages, in regard to the interest taken in them by both parents and children. In our country schools, a good degree of interest in learning is felt, and the pupils do learn; though, through the incompetency of their teachers, they too often learn error. But our village pupils do not even learn that. How important, then, that our schools, both in town and country, be, for different reasons, wholly revolutionized? And you, sir, are the man to begin the revolution."

"But what can I do towards such a work, supported as I am, and shall be, by the public, in the undertaking?"

"A good deal. While your persevering labors will eventually reform one school, you will be setting an example that will be surely, if slowly, operating upon others. And while doing this, you may enjoy the proud consciousness that you are doing more to perpetuate the liberties of your country, than the arrogating congress-man, who is spouting wind to the tune of eight dollars per day."

The judicious and spirited remarks of Lincoln were not without their effect on the kindred mind of young Amsden. He had long entertained similar views himself, and had laid out his course with reference to them. But he was by no means prepared for the obstacles and discouragements by which he found his path beset; and he was beginning to look on the prospect before him with a cold and doubtful eye. The wise and timely counsels of his employer, however, encouraged and reässured him, and he again returned with patient determination to his task. He now found, indeed, that patience and determination were alike needed by him, while trying to revive, in his pupils, the interest and ambition which he had succeeded in raising in them, previous to the failure of the little plan we have described. For, although the juggler and his shows, now they had seen them, had lost their charms, yet the course taken by their parents seemed to have removed all inducement to any future exertion. Instead of the pride which they had been told by their instructor those parents would feel, on seeing them acquit themselves well — instead of the praises they would get, they had seen their exertions pass unrewarded by either the praise or the presence of a single individual. And they were not slow in drawing the disheartening inference. For all this, the untiring efforts of our schoolmaster, directly applied, and the many pleasant little devices and amusing exercises that he contrived to get up, illustrative of the different branches he was teaching, and at the same time instructive in themselves, at length began to produce their effects in awakening some degree of the spirit desired. Dr. Lincoln and his lady several times visited the school, and their example was soon followed by some others, who seemed to think, that, under the sanction of so respectable a precedent, it would now possibly do to be seen in a common school. These visits much contributed also to encourage the instructor, and give efficiency to his exertions. And he finally had the happiness of seeing his school, if not all that he could have wished it, at least in a highly prosperous condition.

But although Amsden had at last found himself in a fair way of surmounting the obstacles that had here impeded his success as a teacher merely, yet there were, in the mean time, other trials attending his situation, which he was left to experience, and which he felt none the less keenly, for being compelled to endure them in silence. If the neglect and lack of interest which the inhabitants had exhibited towards his school had caused him so much chagrin and disappointment, it is natural to suppose that a still greater neglect of himself, in all those little courtesies and marks of respect which are usually extended to all respectable members of society, would not long escape his notice, or fail to make him feel unpleasantly.

There had been in the village, during the winter, a continued round of fashionable parties, some for the lively dance, but most of them for social converse, the occasional song, and such other light diversions as are usually introduced on these occasions. To these parties, all, of any thing like fair standing, had, in turn, been invited. Spruce mechanics and their journeymen frequently received their invitations; the pert merchant's clerk was sure to be remembered; even Locke's older pupils were not neglected, and sometimes, indeed, they were sought out and invited before his face. But nobody remembered the poor schoolmaster. Nobody seemed to be aware that he was born with social feelings, or that he had any sort of claim to mingle in society, like other people; and, throughout the whole, he was never complimented with a single invitation.

At first he did not pay any attention to this circumstance; or, if he did, he concluded it arose from some excusable inadvertence. But, being generally apprised of these assemblages, the next day after their occurrence, when he was often asked why he had not attended, the constant repetition of the neglect at length forced itself upon his observation, and caused him more pain than he would have been willing to confess. Let it not be supposed, however, that the unpleasant feelings he thus experienced arose from the disappointment of any particular wish he had to mingle in fashionable society. For, believing with his favorite poet, that

> —— "e'en while Fashion's brightest arts decoy,
> The heart, distrusting, asks if this be joy,"

he felt conscious that he should have little relish for its frivolities and amusements. No, it was not this that disquieted him; but it was the inference, the unavoidable inference, which he drew from the circumstance, that caused the pang; awakening reflections as wounding to his sensibilities, as they were discouraging to his prospects, in the path of life he had marked out for himself. And what was this inference? Did it grow out of the narrow jealousy that there was any thing relating to his manners, his person, or his poverty, that had shut him out of society? By no means; for his dress was good, his person what few could boast of, and his manners — he had no manners, he never tried to form any, but was wisely content with the unsophisticated demeanor of his childhood, which let his native benevolence, his kind and cheerful disposition, his strong sense and ready perception, shine out undisguised and clearly, and find their way, as they did, to every heart not foolishly shut by the conventional restrictions of modern society; while they imparted to his appearance an ease and dignity that fitted him for every company. No, it was nothing of that kind. It was the low estimation in which, he could not but perceive, the occupation of the common teacher was held by the public; an estimation, which, besides depriving that teacher of half the very influence he is expected to exercise over the minds of the young, virtually ostracises him from society, and leads even parents to place him whom they intrust to form the minds and characters of their own children for life — to place him, unconsciously, we hope — upon a level with the servants of their kitchens and the grooms of their stables!

Such were the difficulties, such the trials, which our schoolmaster was doomed to experience. But is the example, which his case exhibits, a solitary one? Let the public answer; and, if in the negative, let them reflect on the consequences of suffering this state of things to remain for ever.

How well and justly was all this appreciated by the good and charming Cowper:—

"Respect, as is but rational and just,
A man deemed worthy of so dear a trust.
Despised by thee, what more can he expect
From youthful folly than the same neglect?
A flat and fatal negative obtains
That instant upon all his future pains:
His lessons tire, his mild rebukes offend,
And all the instructions of thy son's best friend
Are a stream choked, or trickling to no end."

CHAPTER X.

"Ah! Envy, how I love thee, never!
  Let us wake the spiteful jest
And malignant sneer: how clever
  'T is to mar another's rest!
But this with rage I 've often noted:
  When they let our shafts alone,
Back they bound all double-bolted,
  And, except ourselves, hurt none."
Malice and Envy, Poetic Dialogue. — PERRIN.

THE author's task now draws to its conclusion; and, from what we fear will have been deemed by many as but the dry and unromantic scenes of a schoolmaster's usually monotonous life, we will turn to others, of a somewhat varied and more exciting character, at once preluding the little denouement of our story, and leading to an unexpected change in the apparent destiny of its hero, which called him from his present limited field of laudable exertion, to one where the same noble objects could be pursued with more extended usefulness.

One evening, while the situation of affairs remained as we last described them, Amsden walked out, after supper, for the purpose of visiting a sick pupil, the daughter of very poor but worthy parents, living in a wretched abode, near the outskirts of the village. On entering the house, he was no less gratified than surprised to find his fair favorite, Mary Maverick, standing by the pillow of the invalid, soothingly ministering to her necessities and comforts. A slight tinge of color overspread her sweetly eloquent countenance, as, inviting him to a seat near the sick-bed, she expressed her happiness at seeing him so mindful of the situation of their suffering friend. We said a slight tinge of color — it was so; but not the blush of shame at being found in a hovel, to which, unknown to the proud and fashionable family of which she was a member, she had come to bring some little delicacies of her own preparing for the sick girl. On rising to depart, she proffered still further assistance to the girl's mother, and requested to be sent for when she should be needed as a watcher or otherwise. After witnessing the broken but heartfelt outpourings of gratitude of the poor woman to her kind benefactress, Locke offered to attend the latter to her home; and, the offer being accepted, the couple left the humble abode, and were soon at the door of the princely mansion of the Carters. When Mary left home, Mrs. Carter and her two eldest daughters had gone out with the expectation of spending the evening; and for that reason, probably, she urged her attendant to go in, in a manner which, contrary to his previous determination, he was unable to resist; and he was accordingly ushered into the usual sitting room of the family, where, to the surprise of Miss Maverick, they not only found the supposed absentees, but their self-styled professor, who had found the latter abroad, and, as usual, gallanted them home. Although Mary felt painfully conscious that the circumstances were inauspicious for her friend's introduction to the family, she yet had the firmness to perform her part in the ceremony with composure and dignity. The professor, with a sneering air of mock politeness, bowed very low to our hero, on the announcement of his name. Mrs. Carter returned his salute with a freezing nod; and her daughters just moved their lips, exchanging with each other significant glances, as they were severally introduced. Perceiving at once the character of his reception, Amsden felt at a loss to decide for himself whether silence, speaking, or an abrupt departure, were the course demanded of him; but, in his hesitation, he adopted the former, and sat, as did the rest of the company, some moments, without uttering a word. At this embarrassing juncture, however, Miss Maverick fearlessly came to the rescue, and, with the tact and well-timed effort which a just and discerning woman will alone use on such an occasion, and a generous and discerning man alone appreciate, delicately opened the way for a conversation where all could join, and none offend, unless wilfully. But there was one present, conscious perhaps that he had others about him to support him in the course, who was not disposed to act the part which even ordinary good breeding would have then dictated. From the first, the professor had conceived the deepest aversion to Amsden. He had been secretly nettled that Miss Maverick, whose good-will, but for his interest to pay his court in other quarters, he would have gladly obtained, — that Miss Maverick should leave his school for another which he had so affected to despise. And his animosities, as is often the case with base and contemptible minds, settled on the person who had won, and, in spite of all the pains he had taken to frustrate it, continued to retain his pupil. In addition to this source of dislike, the growing estimation in which his rival's school was held had lately begun to alarm him for the safety of his hitherto undisputed dominion over the wealthy and fashionable part of the village. And he had therefore determined to lose no opportunity to disparage the man who was now before him.

"Well, Miss Maverick, what studies are you pursuing this winter?" asked Tilden, thinking thus to pave the way for his meditated attack on his hated rival.

"My spelling-book, grammar, and arithmetic, sir," replied Mary, playfully, yet with sufficient significance to apprise the interrogator that she understood the motive which prompted the question.

"Ay!" said the professor, "well, you seem to have been advancing backward quite rapidly, since you left us; you were upon rhetoric and select geometry, I believe."

"True, sir," rejoined the other; "but when I found myself unable to answer questions, not only in some of the first principles of arithmetic, but even in those of orthography and pronunciation, I thought it might perhaps not be *amiss* for me to advance backwards a little, as you term it."

"O, it is all correct, doubtless," sneeringly remarked the professor. "Your instructor, I presume, sees the propriety of taking a young lady from the elegant and refining studies of rhetoric and geometry, and placing her back upon the school-boy drudgery of the spelling-book and common arithmetic."

"The propriety of this," replied Amsden, thus insolently challenged to defend his course, "is sufficiently obvious from Miss Maverick's own acknowledgment, that she did not fully understand some of the first principles on which the sciences she had attempted are based. I cannot see how rhetoric, which teaches the art of using language correctly and effectively, can be studied understandingly till the construction of the language itself is first understood. And it is so with geometry and its correlative and basing study, common arithmetic, which must be first mastered. When pupils have done this, they may, with some hope of profit, enter upon geometry, in which they need not then be limited to a few pretty problems of this interesting branch of science; or they may enter upon rhetoric without being confined for illustrations to the stage-readings of Shakspeare, or the Melodies of Thomas Moore."

The professor, whose superficial teachings and manner of illustrating were known to Amsden, was touched by this reply even more nearly than the latter was himself aware. But, though evidently disconcerted, he contrived to conceal his feelings, under an affected disdain to offer at this time any rejoinder — leaving his fair worshippers now to take up the discourse.

"I wonder," said Miss Ann Lucretia, "what pleasure one can take in common arithmetic: for my part, I always hated it. And as for the spelling-book — why, I learned all there is in that before I was seven years old."

"Well, I am willing all should follow their taste," observed the next sister; "but as for myself, I have no notion of giving up the elegant pursuits of our select academy; at least, not for a common school, I am sure."

"Nor I," said Miss Matilda Mandeville, as usual bringing up the rear of this refined and accomplished sisterhood. "O! it would be so excessively *vulgaire!* Now, do n't you think so, Professor Tilden?"

"Why, I have only to say on the occasion, ladies," replied the professor, who by this time had prepared himself for what he supposed would be an annihilating discharge of his spleen, "I have only to say that there are those in the world whom you would labor in vain in trying to impress with any sense of the beauties of elegant literature."

"And there are again those, you might justly add, sir," promptly rejoined Locke, "whom you can never impress with any sense of the beauties of the sound sciences, for the reason that they do not understand them."

Upon this, the professor chose to consider himself insulted, and so much disgusted withal, that he could no longer endure the presence of Amsden. And, hastily gathering up his hat, gloves, &c., from the table by which his rival had been sitting, he moved towards the door with the show of departing, when the three sisters with one accord rushed after him, and begged of him, for their sakes, to remain. Mrs. Carter, also, muttering something about its being very strange that some folks could not understand their true position in society, earnestly joined in the request of her daughters. The soothed professor, being thus over-persuaded, returned to his seat. And Amsden, to relieve the company from his presence, rose to depart. Miss Maverick, whose pride and high sense of honor and justice had alike been deeply offended by this wanton attack on her friend, waited on him to the door with the most marked respect; and then, returning into the room with a face flushed with indignation, replaced the light she had taken, and instantly left the apartment without uttering a word.

Previous to the entrance of Amsden and Mary, the professor had been showing the ladies a guinea, upon the centre of which had been stamped, by some mechanic through whose hands it had passed, probably, some enigmatical letters and other signs. And this coin, when the former came in, had been left on the table at which the professor and his fair friends had been sitting, and by the side of which, when the position of the company became thus changed, Locke happened to be placed.

"What are you looking for, Professor Tilden?" blandly asked Mrs. Carter, as she observed the former turning over the books and other articles on the table, as if in search of something missing.

"O, merely the little coin we were amusing ourselves with, when our refined visiter, who has just left, entered the room; but it is no matter; it is somewheres about here, I presume," said the professor carelessly.

This announcement brought all the ladies round the table. A thorough search was made; but the coin was not to be found.

"Let me see," said the professor, musingly, pretending not to remember the fact; "who sat down by the table when we rose, on the entrance of this visiter?"

"Why, it was Mr. Amsden himself," replied Mrs. Carter.

"So it was — to be sure it was — it certainly was; and the gold piece was lying on the table after he came in and took that seat," severally responded the sisters, exchanging surprised and significant glances among themselves and with their mother.

"I perceive what you think, ladies," said the professor, after permitting them to look at each other long enough to reach the conclusion to which he had artfully led them; "I perceive what you think; but I beg of you," he continued, with an air of generous forbearance, "I beg of you not to mention the circumstance. The little coin is really of no sort of consequence to me."

"Why should we keep it secret? I think the fellow should be exposed," said Mrs. Carter, indignantly.

"I highly appreciate your indignation, madam," replied the professor, loftily; "I wonder not that you should feel such a bold insult on your house and family, to say nothing of the requirements of justice. But what proof could we make? Nothing that would answer the law. I must therefore insist that no public charge of the kind be made."

"It is just what I should expect of a vulgar pedagogue," exclaimed Miss Matilda Mandeville.

"And to think that Mary should have suffered him to come here!" said another sister.

"Yes, and the girl is still attending the fellow's school! — but that must be stopped," added the mother.

"Perhaps that were unwise," said the professor, here interposing. "By taking this step, you must give her the reason; and I really ask it as a great favor that not a syllable of the unfortunate affair be named to her, as it would be so very mortifying to her feelings. Whatever opinion you may consider it your duty to give your confidential friends respecting the man's true character, nothing must be named to her.

Indeed, for my part, I could wish that the transaction should be kept a secret from all; for I really cannot but pity the fellow."

The professor, having thus arranged the affair to his liking with his willingly duped worshippers, departed; secretly exulting in the thought that he had now struck a blow which must result in removing from his path the man whom he no less feared than hated. And, for a while, every thing seemed to promise fair to operate as he had designed it should. The story was studiously kept from Mary, and, in the shape of dark hints at least, confidentially whispered to others, who, in their turn, imparted it to a second round of friends, till it thus passed, in constantly widening circles, to the public.

Meanwhile the intended victim of this suddenly-devised and detestable plot to destroy his fair fame, continued diligently to discharge the daily duties of his fast improving school, having not the least suspicion of the withering whispers of detraction that were in progress around him. He was not permitted, however, to remain long without perceiving indications that something intimately affecting his interests was secretly operating to his disadvantage; but what that something could be, he was wholly unable to conjecture. He at first noticed a certain air of coldness and distrust towards himself among many of his village acquaintance, by whom he had been before met with respectful cordiality. His feelings were next tried by a withdrawal by their parents, on different pretexts, of some of the best pupils of his school. And, among the rest, his lovely friend, Mary Maverick, was unconsciously made to add poignancy to his regrets, and increase his growing uneasiness at the inauspicious appearances that seemed to be gathering over his path. She had been requested by her aunt to leave her school to assist in some business in the household line, which, as it was pretended, had unexpectedly arisen, but which, it was also urged, must immediately be executed. And, feeling herself under obligations to comply, she had left the school, without giving her instructer, or deeming it necessary to give him, any definite reasons for so doing, since she then had as little suspicion of the true motives of the hypocritical request that had induced her to forego the pleasures of her pursuits at school, as she had of the existence of the contemptible plan laid for undermining the influence and character of her respected instructer.

But, although Amsden was made, for a while, to suffer, in the minds of many, by this pitiful conspiracy, intended to put the finishing touch to the other means which had been used to disparage and destroy him, he was yet destined soon to be exonerated from every injurious impression, in a manner, which, had revenge been any part of his nature, would have afforded him all the triumph he could have desired over his despicable foe.

One evening, as Dr. Lincoln sat in his study, a boy entered, and, handing him a closely-sealed billet, disappeared. On opening it, he was surprised to find it a confidential note from Mary Maverick. He had before heard several vague hints relating to Amsden, which, owing to his unlimited confidence in the man, he had not understood. Some of the multiform aspersions, indeed, which had grown out of the professor's notable scheme of ruin, had lately reached his ears; but he had considered them so little worthy of notice, that they had passed from his mind. The note before him, however, brought the subject again to his thoughts, and he paused in its perusal to try to recall what he had heard. The writer commenced by mentioning the various attempts of the professor to asperse Mr. Amsden, related briefly what took place at Carter's while she was present, described the coin which she herself had noticed lying on the table, and concluded by divulging what she had that day accidentally overheard in the family — the whole circumstance attending the pretended loss of the piece, which she so much feared was being made use of to injure one whom she believed innocent, that she would not rest till she had taken the present step, though by the act she run the risk, she said, if her name should be brought in question, of making still more unpleasant her present not over-happy position in the family.

"Well, well, my dove among jackdaws, you shan't be hurt for the noble act you have here performed," said Lincoln to himself. "But that insufferable puppy — ay, villain, as he has now proved himself! Why, there 's not a doubt that he slyly caught up this guinea with his gloves, and pocketed it himself, as she evidently suspects. Well, he will be a lucky fellow if he do n't eventually find himself in the pit he has been digging for another. If I could get hold of that same coin! — stay, what is the reason I have not seen one with similar marks on it lately, somewhere? — yes, somewhere — let me think. Ah! I have it — and if I am right, no time should be lost," he added, springing from his chair, seizing his hat and cane, and hastily leaving his office for the destination to which his conclusions had directed him.

Prompted by his hatred, rendered more inveterate by the conscious defeat he had received in his insolent attack on Amsden at Carter's, the professor had taken a bold step, and one which, to be successful, required, on his part, no little management and caution. But, having seen the story, or rather the odium of the charge put afloat in the shape he had contrived to make it, intangible to his opponent, and having already exultingly witnessed many flattering results from his scheme, he soon became unmindful of one point which he should have particularly guarded. With the infatuated blindness with which Providence seems often to visit the secret perpetrators of crime, to make them become the instruments of their own detection and punishment, he had recently put away the coin, and thus thrown within the reach of his intended victim a weapon which the latter could not only wield triumphantly in his own defence, but hurl back upon the head of the aggressor with fatal effect.

The professor had put off the coin in question at the shop of a jeweller in the village, where he often made purchases in the line of trinkets. And it was to this shop that the aroused and indignant Lincoln was now directing his steps; having, the day previous, accidentally had a glimpse of the important piece, as he was receiving change for a bank-note offered in payment for some surgical instrument. The doctor was completely successful in his object. He not only obtained the desired coin, in exchange for an equal amount of his own money, but ascertained that it came from Tilden's hand but two days before. And having effected this, without making known to the jeweller his purpose in so doing, he immediately returned, with the prize in his pocket, to his office, compared it with the description in Mary's note, and found it must be the identical piece that Amsden had indirectly been charged with purloining. Amsden was instantly sent for, and in a few minutes made his appearance.

"My temper has been sadly ruffled, Mr. Amsden," said the doctor, pointing the other to a chair beside him.

"Indeed, sir?" inquiringly replied the former, in surprise; for he knew not for what purpose he had been summoned.

"Ay; but here, read this note from that paragon of a girl, Mary Maverick, and heed her request about bringing her name in question. The necessity of the case must be my excuse for showing it, even to you."

Locke read the billet, part of it, at least, with the utmost astonishment.

"And what do you think now, sir?" asked Lincoln, as the other finished the perusal of the paper.

"As I judge she does. I was aware of Tilden's disposition to injure me; and I have been conscious, for a week or two past, that some secret influence was operating against me and my school, in which I suspected the fellow was exercising an active part. But I little dreamed that he would resort to a measure so base and reckless. Why, sir, what would you make of a man who could do this?"

"An arrogant, but mean and revengeful puppy. He has not wit enough even to dignify him with the name of villain. Look here! did you ever see that coin before?" said the speaker, taking out the piece he had just obtained from the jeweller, and handing it to Amsden.

"I have," replied the latter, as he inspected the piece with a look of joyful surprise. "I saw it lying on the table at Carter's, on the evening in question, and noticed these marks on the face of it. It is the same, and lucky the chance that has brought it to the hands of a friend. I should not fear this story with those who know me; but with others, this would furnish the only testimony that would save me from disgrace. Where did you get hold of it?"

The doctor then related the circumstances we have already mentioned, and concluded by saying, —

"Well, Mr. Amsden, what do you propose to do about this despicable business?"

"I shall not suffer it to rest here, sir," replied the other, decidedly.

"Nor I; but what course are you thinking to pursue?" asked the former.

"To arrest the mischief at the fountain-head," answered Amsden, with increasing energy. "I had heard of the course of this pitiful traducer towards myself, previous to encountering him at Carter's; but I was not much troubled by it. And even when I there met him, and received from him what I felt was most ungentlemanly treatment, it did not disturb me so much as some other circumstances that have occurred since my residence among you. But this subsequent attempt is of a different character. And in justice to my school, and to you, sir, my employer, as well as to myself, I shall take prompt means to clear myself from the aspersion. He shall bring me before some legal tribunal, or, if possible, I will bring him."

"Well, said Lincoln, musingly, walking the room with his hands in his pockets; "well, I do n't see why you have not now the staff in your own hands. But have you thought of all the results that may flow from the measures you propose? If I predict right, your course will end in driving him from the town. Where then," continued the speaker, assuming a look and tone of sarcastic irony, "where then will be our Select Academy of Elegant Literature, '*so very distingué*'? where then will be obtained the accomplishments it affords, '*so very recherché*'? Think, sir, of the luckless situation in which the fashionable society of Cartersville would then be left — think of the half-drawn landscapes which must be thrown aside — the unstrung harps and pianos that will have been purchased at such cost but to be abandoned — think of the public calamity that must ensue from compelling the sons and daughters of the wealthy and genteel to depend only for their accomplishments on those old, worn-out, unfashionable, and vulgar studies which you still persist in teaching — and, above all, think of the deplorable condition of our young ladies, if they were thus driven from their French, and could only converse in nothing but common English."

"Ay, ay," said Locke, laughing; "but we will leave it to the professor to chant the elegy, if such sad consequences are to follow from his own acts. In the mean time, let me ask you to furnish me with pen, ink, and paper."

"What! are you going to send a note to the professor, to set before him the alternative you mentioned — that of pros ecuting or being prosecuted?" asked the other, handing the required materials.

"I am, sir," replied Amsden, beginning to write.

"Do so," rejoined Lincoln, approvingly. And I am glad to see you act with so much spirit and promptitude on the occasion. You shall not want for one friend to stand by you. But perhaps you had not better let him know that we have got possession of the guinea. And, further, I think I would give him some little time — say a fortnight, to undo all the mischief he has done; that is, to retract, confess, and follow his slanders through every channel where he has sent them, and honestly refute them, if he prefers that course: if not, then let him take one of the alternatives you have just named."

"I will follow your suggestions," answered Amsden. "The first may be a wise one; the last is certainly merciful, and if he will profit by it, I shall have no disposition further to molest him."

The note was completed, and immediately sent off to its destination by one of the servants of the house; when Locke and his friend separated, to await with patience, and silently, the result of their movement.

We will now turn to the soi-disant professor, with whom we shall have but little more to do; for his career, in this place, as Dr. Lincoln had shrewdly predicted, was now a brief one. He was alone in his room when the doctor's servant entered and delivered Amsden's letter, which, as he knew the servant, he received with rather a doubtful and uneasy expression. And no sooner was the messenger's back turned, than he tore open the note, and eagerly ran over its contents, at which his usual air of swaggering assurance instantly forsook him. Crumpling up the paper, and thrusting it into his pocket, he rose, and for some moments paced the floor in visible agitation.

"Perhaps it is not too late to defeat him now," he at length began to think aloud. "But that guinea must be secured, and the man must be bribed to hold his tongue. I wonder I was so thoughtless; but these shopmen are so clamorous for their debts. Yes, I must have that before I sleep, and luckily I now have what will bring it."

So saying, he threw his gaily-tasselled cloak over his shoulders, and took his way to the shop of the jeweller, whom he found preparing to retire for the night.

"You recollect that curiously stamped gold piece I paid you the other day?" said the professor to the man.

"Yes."

"Well, it being a present from a friend in town, whom I would not for the world have know that I had parted with it, I have brought the amount in other money to get it back again."

"Why, sir, I'm sorry, but you are a little too late."

"How so?"

"I parted with it this very evening."

"To whom, pray?"

"To Dr. Lincoln."

The professor actually turned pale at the announcement; but he made shift to stammer out, with an effort at indifference, "O, well, it's no sort of consequence, sir," and abruptly departed.

He was now in a dilemma, from which he could see no way to escape without disgrace to his character, or ruin to his prospects. Turn which way he would, the difficulties seemed equally insurmountable. Whether he prosecuted or was prosecuted himself, an investigation must ensue, which he well knew would place him in a light alike fatal to his pretensions and prospects. Should he take the other alternative, confess, and try to recall his slanders, he must not only virtually proclaim himself a liar and a contemptible calumniator, but at the same time elevate his rival at the expense of his own degradation. In short, he plainly foresaw that the days of his glory in Cartersville were numbered. And he soon concluded to shape his course accordingly.

It was among the very last of the unimproved days of grace that had been allowed the professor, when one morning, as the Carter family assembled for breakfast, Miss Ann Lucretia, the eldest daughter, failed to make her appearance. A search was made through the house; but she was still among the missing. All was now confusion and alarm. Messengers were despatched to all those places about the village, to which it was thought possible she might have gone out before the family had risen. No tidings, however, of the object of the search could be obtained; and one of the messengers, on his return, further reported that Professor Tilden was also missing. A painful suspicion crossed the minds of the weak and blinded parents. They now recollected that their daughter, for the past week, had been much of the time alone with her instructor; and that she had also, during the time, found some excuse for sleeping in a room by herself, from which an easy access could be had to the outer door. And they ran instantly to the apartment she had occupied. Her bed had not been used the past night, and all her best apparel had disappeared. The whole truth was now disclosed. She had eloped with the professor. Mrs. Carter was deeply chagrined, though she said little, except to express her surprise. But Mr. Carter, who now saw his folly in leaving every thing relating to his daughters to his wife, was loud in his denunciations of the conduct of both of the absconding couple, and at first declared his intention to pursue them. But, reflecting that before this time they were probably married, and thirty miles distant, on their way to one of the cities, he soon gave up the thought. There were others, however, in the village — in which the occurrence made much stir — who, for a different reason, actually made preparations for pursuit. These were the merchants, tailors, shoemakers, &c., who had been favored by the liberal patronage of the professor, during his year's residence in town. But they, too, soon discovered, on recurring to their claims, that their man had prudently placed himself out of their reach for the present. It appeared that, during the past fortnight, he had not only obtained all that was due him from his patrons, but had taken the precaution to settle with all his creditors, paying off some of the least, and giving his notes to the rest, payable in one or two months. And, it being thus found that pursuit would be alike useless to all parties concerned, the measure was at length abandoned, and the distinguished pair left to pursue their journey unmolested. During the forenoon, the following note, which had been overlooked in the first search, addressed to the oldest remaining sister, was found in the room last occupied by the fair fugitive: —

"Dear Angeline,

"Before you receive this, I shall be Mrs. Manlius C. .W Tilden. We have engaged a fleet pair of horses and a rapid driver to take us to ———, where a magistrate will be in waiting to tie the knot, and where, having been joined by a friend of Mr. T. as bridesman and *compagnon du voyage*, we shall take the stage at four o'clock, A.M., for New York — Mr. T.'s former residence, you know. He has been for some time getting disgusted with the petty annoyances of a country village, which, besides, he says, is no field for his talents. But he could not bear to leave me. He offered his hand; and, fearing papa would object, especially to so sudden a match as he was resolved to make, or none — he proposed the present romantic manner of making our adieus to Cartersville — it is so like him! Well, Angeline, what would you have done? But if you had felt the tender sentiment, I know what you would have done. And then think of the enviable station I shall fill among the very *élite* of city society, surrounded by all the elegancies and refinements of city life! All this he feels free to promise me; and I do suppose he is soon to come in possession of a splendid fortune, though he is so modest about it that I only obtained the secret from him by some inadvertent hints he has dropped. I anticipate how surprised you will all be, and I hardly expect papa will fully approve my course at first — perhaps mamma will not; but I know *you* will appreciate me, and so will Matilda Mandevelle. I will write you again when we reach the city, till which,

"With all the sensibilities of a refined nature,

"I remain affectionately, your

"ANN LUCRETIA."

The name and character of the friend and *compagnon du voyage*, mentioned in the foregoing epistle, was more fully disclosed the next day, by the following editorial notice in *The Blazing Star*, which came into town, all damp from the press of Mill-Town Emporium: —

"BASENESS EXPOSED!

"Our flourishing village was thrown into confusion this morning, by the discovery that our village schoolmaster, Blake by name, — if that be his true name, — had decamped, having artfully obtained the wages for the full term of his engagement, but a little more than half of which he had fulfilled. Some fears are also entertained respecting the value of a pretended jewelled watch which he lately sold to one of our citizens for fifty dollars; but enough has been said to caution the public, which, as faithful journalists, was our duty to do. There can be but little doubt that the fellow was an impostor. And our political patrons will not be surprised to learn, that his politics, though he at first professed to hold to our true doctrines, turned out to be in unison with those of that party from whom such things are to be expected. — *Ed. Blazing Star.*"

It was now evident that the dashing professor, and his less accomplished, though scarcely less superficial friend, Blake, who, as the reader will remember, was Amsden's successful rival in the competition for the Mill-Town school, were confederate impostors. But what had been the nature of their previous connection, or whether their career had been marked by outright villanies, or merely by petty impositions on the public, was not known for nearly a fortnight; when a young merchant from New York, arriving on a visit to his relatives in the village, reported that he had encountered, soon after leaving the city, the bride, her husband, and his friend; and soon recognized the two last-named worthies as a couple of fourth-rate actors, or some other unimportant adjuncts of one of the city theatres, from which they had both been driven in disgrace about two years before; after which they had occasionally been heard from, perambulating the country in the same direction; one — that is, Tilden — pretending to lecture on elocution, the art of reading, &c., and the other obtaining unauthorized subscriptions for periodicals. And these important and honest employments, it was thus made probable, they had pursued, till the former found an inviting opening for his versatile talents in a new character among the would-be fashionables of Cartersville, and afterwards another, for his congenial friend, in Mill-Town Emporium.

This was indeed a mortifying development for the proud Carters; and the females especially, who had never dreamed of any of their number marrying any thing short of counts, congress-men, or something equally high-sounding, could hardly hold up their heads, under the keen sense of the disgrace which they conceived had been brought on their family. Mr. Carter, however, who cared little for any other family distinction than what property, or at least the certainty of a good living, would confer — still had some hopes that his daughter, rash as she had been, might after all have married a man of enterprise, integrity, and capacity sufficient to maintain her respectably from his own resources. But the solace of even these faint hopes was soon taken from him. In a few days more, he himself received a letter from his deluded child, the main points of which were evidently dictated by her husband.

After excusing herself for the step she had taken in the best way she could, and speaking of her prospects in a much more moderate tone than that which pervaded her letter to her sister on her departure, she told her father that she felt very sure, whatever might happen, that he would never let her want money to support her in the style in which he had brought her up; and then she added, that Tilden — it was now plain Tilden — had met with a chance to invest her portion to very great advantage, and was very anxious, *for her sake*, to have it sent on, in drafts on some bank or commercial house in the city. The amount, she said, could not be less than twenty thousand dollars; but she would be content, at present, with ten thousand. This she begged of her father not to neglect sending in a few days, as it would make her husband so much happier. And in a postscript she repeated, "Do not fail to send on the drafts."

This was too much for the old gentleman, who, being by no means wanting in sagacity, now at once read the true character of Tilden, and the base motives which had governed him in drawing the weak and unsuspecting girl into this clandestine marriage.

"Ten thousand!" he exclaimed to himself, as, hurling the letter into the fire, he hastily strode round his counting-room in a paroxysm of exasperated feeling — "ten thousand! Quite modest, truly! O! the worthless, fortune-hunting scoundrel! Ten thousand! He will be apt to get it, I think. But what will become of the poor, deceived, ruined girl?" he continued, his indignation softening into pity. "If she ever gets rid of the villain, I hope there may be that sum left for her. But the rig these women have run! And I, like a fool, have yielded to it! I fear — I fear, that this disaster to my family will prove but the forerunner of worse ones. Heaven help me!"

The words of the distressed and foreboding father were but too prophetic; for this was the first of a series of misfortunes which were destined to fall, in rapid succession, upon this house of folly, and level its vain-glorious pretensions with the dust. But, as this will appear by pursuing the main thread of our narrative, we will now return to our hero.

As the reader may have perhaps already anticipated, the disgraceful flight of Tilden, and the disclosures that followed, respecting not only his character and false pretensions, but the base slanders he had originated, operated as a proud triumph to Amsden and his school. Many a man is indebted for his character almost wholly to contrast. And if such be the effect — as under favoring circumstances it often is — of a contrast between the demerits of one, and the mere negative qualities of another, in conferring character on the latter, it would be strange, indeed, if the operation of this principle, under circumstances so well calculated to call it into action, did not greatly tend to bring one of Amsden's high desert into notice, and place him on the elevation to which his merits entitled him. It did so. The very measures that Tilden had taken for the disparagement and ruin of his rival were now the means of turning the minds of the public to a comparison between the two, and of causing thereby to be done to the latter that justice which he otherwise might never have obtained. All the pupils that, on different pretences, had been withdrawn from his school, were at once permitted to return. The professor's Academy of Elegant Literature became, by the association with its doughty projector, a theme of ridicule; and the empty, and worse than empty, accomplishments it afforded, soon began to be accounted — as the miserable scientific tinselings imparted by hundreds of other similar establishments in our land under the name of accomplishments deserve to be accounted — less a term of honor than reproach. Even those ultra genteel families who had only patronized the select or private school system, now sent in their children, and began to open their eyes to the solid advantages to be obtained from common schools, under well-qualified instructers. The remainder of our hero's term of engagement, therefore, was marked with a success that amply repaid him for all his previous toils and vexations; and his labors now became as pleasant for himself as they were profitable to his pupils.

It was now past the middle of April. The period for which Amsden had concluded to continue his instructions had at length drawn to a close; and the time had arrived when he was called to that interesting yet mournful task for a teacher — the parting with his pupils, on the last day and hour of his school.

The tie that obtains between instructer and pupil, where the right feelings have been cherished and reciprocated, is one of peculiar interest. It consists, in the bosom of the one, of that tender regard, that disinterested affection, which is made up of several of the best and strongest propensities of our nature — the compassionate and kindly inclination which the conscious strong are prone to entertain towards the weak and dependent; the regard which is engendered towards those with whom habit has made us familiar, and the peculiar favor with which we are wont to view our own creations, as the minds, manners, and characters of those we have successfully taught, may be considered; — in the bosom of one, it consists of this. In that of the other, the tie is composed of that reverential esteem which is founded in the blended principles of gratitude for benefits received, and the inherent respect which is ever felt for superior powers, all combining to form the purest and the most exalted friendship that ennobles the human heart. The connection, indeed, has about it a beautiful patriarchal character, which renders it one of the most interesting relations in the world. And few can look back to the final parting with a respected and beloved instructer, without the most grateful emotions.

The parting hour, as we have said, had come — too soon come. The farewell address, fraught with many an allusion to all that could be remembered for praise in the past, many a kind word of advice for the future, and many an affectionate wish for the individual prosperity and happiness of each and all of the eloquently silent and often tearful little auditory, was spoken, and the word of final dismissal reluctantly pronounced. With a thoughtful and solemn quietness of manner, little resembling the noisy glee of other occasions, the books were gathered; and one by one the dispersing band came up, took the proffered hand of their loved instructer, uttered the subdued *good-bye*, and departed. But why was that hand, as if too busy with other occupations, so long withheld from one more tenderly regarded than all the rest? And why did she, without concert or request, still linger, till the last adieu had been spoken, and the last retreating form disappeared from the room — still linger to receive it? And why, in the hesitating, tremulous, and prolongued grasp that then followed, was no farewell, no word, no syllable, or sound, uttered? Why were these two, whose thoughts on science, literature, the sentiments, or other general topics, ever seemed to flow together, like two uniting streams from fountains of kindred purity and clearness, and whose tongues ever before grew eloquent in the converse which was sure to spring up between them, and which never wearied, — why were two like these dumb now? There are states of feeling, when the strong, deep-laid elements of the heart are stirred, which seem wholly to reject the utterance of language, — sometimes because words must fail of an adequate expression, and sometimes because those feelings are so consciously sacred, that they involuntarily shrink from the conceived profanation of such a medium. Both of these cases might have been combined at this parting between Locke Amsden and Mary Maverick. Be that as it may, the quivering lip and the agitated countenance of the one, and the quick-heaving bosom and the gushing eye of the other, as, from the long mute grasp they turned hurriedly away, constituted the only language that told the sensations of their hearts. It had never spoken before; but it had spoken distinctly now, revealing to them, for the first time, their own and each other's secret, and apprising them that the deep, unanalyzed, unacknowledged feeling, that had been sleeping and gathering strength in their attracted bosoms, had a name; and that its name was only to be found in the magic word, *Love.*

CHAPTER XI.

"A long-lost friend, or hapless child restored,
Smiles at his blazing hearth and social board;
Warm from his heart the tears of rapture flow,
And virtue triumphs o'er remembered woe."
CAMPBELL.

BIDDING adieu to the now deserted and lonely mansion which to him had been, for the four past fleeting months, the scene of so many mingling pleasures, toils, and trials, our hero, with slow and pensive steps, returned to his lodgings. He had contemplated making several calls that evening, both for the transaction of business, and the reciprocation of courtesies received, preparatory to leaving town the next morning. But the strong and varied emotions which had been excited in the scene he had just passed through, added to the state of his health, that, for several days, he had felt to be giving way, had so much disinclined and unfitted him to meet company, that he soon concluded to defer his visits till the following morning, and retire, as he early did, to the more congenial seclusion of his own room, where he could indulge the moody reveries of his mind, and the physical languor of his feelings, unrestrained and unmolested. Here his thoughts reverted to the past. He recalled the interesting incidents described at the opening of these pages, forming, as he was ever sensible, the first marked era of his life. He recurred to the unconsciously prophetic intimation then given him of his subsequent career by her whose image, while she thus indicated the way, imparted an ever-during impulse to pursue it. And with pleased and curious thought, he ran over the events that followed: the persevering exertions which had resulted in bringing him before the public as a teacher; the engagement in his first school, attended by the singular circumstances that led to an acquaintance with the only man who would have brought him to Cartersville, and the only man, who, when this was effected, would or could have placed him and the fair prophetess and seeming maker of his fortunes together in the relation they had lately sustained to each other. He saw, or thought he saw, in all this, a train of circumstances which formed the connecting links of a chain of destiny, which, from the parts disclosed, the ministering sisters, Hope and Fancy, now tempted him to trace onward into the dim confines of futurity, gilding the way for him, as usual, with many a bright illusion, and opening to his enchanted view many a fairy scene of love and happiness for him and the fair cynosure of his waking dream. But Reason and Conscience, here interposing, checked the lured heart in its rising anticipations, and coldly whispered of present destitution, — of the distant prospect of worldly means, on the one hand, and, on the other, of orphan innocence, inexperience, and perhaps love, that might listen to a connection involving circumstances which must defeat its own object, and bring poverty and its attendant miseries upon one who was worthy of, and who would otherwise meet with, a happier destiny.

Such were the conflicting emotions that now strangely agitated the usually tranquil mind of Amsden, as, for hours, he slowly paced his solitary apartment, sometimes cheering himself with the visions of Hope, and sometimes, as he looked upon the stern realities of his present situation, and those which his judgment told him would be likely to succeed, sinking into despondency. The latter feeling, however, as little good cause as he could assign for it, in any thing relating to the past, or the rational prospects of the future, seemed more and more to predominate. And, as the evening wore away, he became conscious of an unusual depression of spirits, a certain boding solicitude and restlessness of mind, for which he could not account, but which he could not but feel to be vaguely suggestive of some jeopardized interest, or some approaching crisis of his fortunes. After endeavoring awhile, in vain, to shake off these constantly intruding fancies, he betook himself to his pillow, and soon fell asleep. But sleep brought no repose to disturbed sensibilities. The sweet restorer had lost the power of tranquillizing. It is Dryden, we believe, who says, in a couplet alike remarkable for neatness of expression and condensed poetic thought, —

> "Dreams are but interludes that Fancy makes; —
> When Reason sleeps, her mimic monster wakes."

But whether this contains the true philosophy of dreams or not, it is certain that the idea here conveyed seemed to be strikingly exemplified in the visions of the sleeper, that now succeeded. While the same dark current of thoughts and undefined solicitudes which occupied his last waking moments continued to run in his mind, those thoughts, as reason ceased to control and regulate, soon began to shape themselves into a succession of wild and mysterious fantasies. In all of these, however, one characteristic prevailed. They all presented Mary Maverick as the principal figure, and always in circumstances of difficulty or danger. In the last mimic scene that was conjured up by the changing fancies of the troubled dreamer, he at first seemed reclining on the flowery bank of a sun-lit lake; a light boat came wafting before the ruffling breeze towards the spot where he lay; as it approached, he distinguished, seated within, the same angelic form and face which, in different situations, had been constantly rising on his vision. She raised her white hand in token of gratulation. He even thought he could trace the sweet dimpling smile with which she was wont to receive him, playing upon her countenance. "In one moment more," he thought, "she will be safe and happy, and all her fearful trials and perils will be over." But while he yet spoke, the sun became suddenly hid by doubling racks of dark and angry clouds, that seemed, with magic quickness, to have been gathered from every part of the horizon to a point directly over head. In another moment, the black convolving mass burst downward, and fell, in hurricane blasts, upon the lake; converting at once its mirror-like surface into a wild waste of tumbling, breaking, and raging billows, upon which the frail little bark of his fair friend — by this time almost within reach of his hand, now eagerly extended to grasp it as it came — began to pitch and whirl with a violence that threatened instant destruction. Now it was borne off on the eddying surges, and lost to his sight in the clouds of wind-driven mists and mingling atoms, that were sweeping over the face of the agitated waters. Now again it appeared on the refluent billows, and again it was lost. Once more it was revealed to the eager and strained vision of the distressed lover; but it appeared now only to complete his despair. It was foundering amidst the raging waves; and its lovely freight, with an imploring look, was stretching forth towards him her arms for aid. With a cry of agony, he plunged into the angry flood for the rescue, and awoke — awoke, and thanked Heaven that it was but a dream. But, although the illusion was dissipated, and the particular excitement it had caused soon allayed, the same feelings with which he fell asleep, the same boding, undefined solicitude which had attended, and probably given character to all his dreams, still continued to haunt and disturb him. The feeling grew even more painfully oppressive, and, after trying awhile in vain to sleep, he arose, lighted a lamp, and dressed himself. He consulted his watch, and found it past midnight. He listened for some sounds from without; but all, for a while, seemed hushed in repose. The silence, however, was at length broken by the noise of heavily-rolling wheels and the splashing of horses' feet, proceeding, as he soon concluded, from the southern stage, which, owing to the bad travelling, had but just arrived, and was now passing on its way to the post-office or stage-house, at the other end of the village. As these sounds receded, he turned from them with indifference; for they were not those which he seemed to have expected. But what did he expect? He knew not; and yet he felt a strange consciousness that something unusual was about to happen. And in obedience to an impulse which now seized him, he took his hat, descended to the door, and gained the street, without being able to tell why he did so, or where he was going. As he stood hesitating, a distant voice, in the earnest tones of one calling for aid, reached his ears; he sprang round a corner, in the direction of the sound, and the next instant heard repeated, by a nearer and more startling voice, the appalling cry of *fire!* "*Carter's house is on fire, and the family perishing in the flames!*" Heeding not the inquiries that now assailed his ears amidst the creaking of the opening doors, or hastily-raised window-sashes of almost every house around him, Amsden bounded forward by the lurid light that now began to glimmer along the street, with the speed of the wind, towards the spot indicated by this awful and, to him, agonizing announcement. The turn of another corner brought the eagerly-sought building into plain view. It was completely enveloped in one black, eddying cloud of swiftly-mounting smoke, through which the flickering flames began fiercely to gleam, as they burst successively from the windows along the lower story. The domestics, who slept in this part of the house, had just escaped. At that instant, a window was dashed out from the second story; and Mr. Carter, his wife, and daughters, were heard shouting and screaming for aid. Arousing the stupefied servants, Amsden, by their aid, and that of one or two others, who by this time had reached the spot, procured a ladder, and placed it to the window from which the cries had been heard; when, one by one, the family were seen emerging, half-suffocated, from the thick smoke that enveloped the upper part of the ladder, and hastily descending to the ground; the last one having barely time to avoid the broad gush of flames that now burst from the window below, and cut off all further chance of egress by the avenue through which they had so narrowly escaped. Standing at the foot of the ladder, and eagerly examining the disfigured persons of each of the females, as they came down, Amsden uttered an exclamation of despair, on finding, as the last one reached the ground, that she whom he most anxiously sought was not there!

"Where is Mary? O! where is Mary?" burst from his agonized lips, as he cast a wild and frenzied look on those around him.

"Yes, where?" responded Carter, throwing a startled and agitated look upon his wife and daughters, as he now for the first time discovered that the object of inquiry was not among them.

"She ran back to add another article to her scant dress, just as the ladder was raised for our escape," now recollected one of the females.

"Her retreat then was cut off by the flames," said the former; "mount at some other place and find her, or in another moment she is lost!"

Waiting only to catch the import of these replies to his question, the maddened youth flew to the ladder, planted it against another window, sprang up the rounds, and with a billet of wood before caught up for the purpose, cleared both sash and glass at a blow, and leaped in, to rescue his perilled friend, or perish with her. While this was transpiring, a well-dressed gentleman, whom no one appeared to recognize, came rushing, with distracted looks, through the crowd. He had evidently been apprised, on the way, of the peril and probable situation of the lady left in the burning building; for, calling aloud for assistance, he seized a spare ladder, and, with such help as was at hand, bore it round to an opposite side of the house, reared it, ascended, beat in a window, and quickly disappeared in the smoke that came pouring through the breach he had thus effected. For many minutes, nothing was seen or heard of the two individuals who had thus bravely hazarded their lives in the search. And as the fire, which had commenced on the lower floor, was plainly seen to be rapidly making its way upward, the spectators, now equally alarmed for the fate of all within, awaited, with breathless anxiety, for their reäppearance. Suddenly, the crash of a breaking window, in a different room from those which either of the two bold adventurers had entered, was heard; and they were seen, in the flying fragments and outpouring smoke, throwing themselves headlong through the opening, to the ground. They had rushed through the half-fired chambers in the fruitless search for the supposed perishing girl, till, their retreat being cut off, they met, nearly suffocated by the vapor, and took the only course left them to save their lives. The stranger, though not materially injured by the fall, was yet so much stunned, that he was taken up and borne off nearly senseless, out of the crowd. Amsden almost instantly gained his feet, and rushed, convulsed and gasping for breath, out of the stifling smoke and heat that encircled the spot, into the fresh air. The eyes of all followed him, and many gathered round to hear if he brought hope or information on the subject of the general solicitude. He did not, could not, utter words; but his woe-speaking countenance, as he looked upon the burning pile, and turned hopelessly away from the overpowering sight, told the sad tale that his tongue would have uttered. And the next moment brought confirmation, to the minds of all, of the dreadful supposition. A general burst of flames through every window below the roof of the building, disclosed the whole interior in a mass of flames, glowing with the bright heat of a furnace. "She is lost! she is lost!" now rose, in the low, deep murmurs of grief, from the shuddering throng, who stood appalled at the thought of a fate so awful, for one so good, so loved, and so lovely. With the subsidence of this burst of anguished sensibilities, a funereal silence for some moments pervaded the whole assembled multitude. The tumultuous shouts and varied commotion that had marked the scene, seemed hushed into awe; and nought was heard but the ceaseless crackling of consuming timbers, and the dull, far-sounding roar of the mounting flames. The gloomy silence, however, was soon broken by a cry of mingled joy and horror which now arose from a new and unexpected spectacle. She, whom all had given up as lost, was discovered, emerging from the scuttle, on to the nearly flat roof of the building, and advancing, with hasty, agitated steps, to the low terrace that ran round it at the eaves. Here, in the occasional openings of the eddying smoke that was swiftly whirling over and around her, she was seen, looking hopelessly down from the dizzy height, upon the anxious throng of friends below, who saw no way to rescue her from the fiery tomb, in which the already trembling fabric gave token she must soon be engulfed. In a moment she appeared to single out her distressed lover from the crowd; and she stretched forth her arms towards him, with the same imploring look with which he had seen her in his dream. Aroused by the mute appeal from the stupor with which his overmastering emotions had chained him to the spot where he stood, at the thrilling sight that had been so unexpectedly revealed, Amsden sprang forward to the very verge of the flames, and, calling aloud for assistance, looked distractedly round for some means by which she might yet be snatched from the fearful doom that hung over her. But how was any effectual assistance to be rendered? The body of the building, which was isolated from all others, was now but a bright mass of fire; while the whole compass of its exterior, on every side, from the base nearly to the eaves, was wrapped by the flashing gusts of the same fearful element. There was no ladder to be had long enough to reach the roof, or near it, if placed at an inclination in which it would be out of reach of the flames. Other expedients were, indeed, hastily suggested; but each in its turn, was quickly rejected, as wholly fruitless. And the seemingly fated girl was again about to be given up as beyond the reach of all human assistance, when an encouraging shout, as of approaching aid, was raised by those standing in the outer circles of the crowd. Eager to grasp at every appearance of hope, Amsden turned his eyes to the quarter from which the sounds proceeded, and beheld a small party rapidly approaching, with a long spliced ladder on their shoulders. As they drew near, the former unexpectedly recognized, in the burly frame and energetic manner of the foremost, his old friend Bunker, who, it appeared, having been aroused by the alarm from an inn nearly two miles distant, reached by him on a journey, a few hours before, had arrived just as the present emergency arose, and, with a quick glance at the means of relief, ran back to a neighboring barn, where he procured, and hastily lashed together, the implements with which he and others were now rushing forward to the rescue.

"Be ready there with pike-poles and pitch-forks to raise it," he exclaimed to the receding throng, as with long, rapid strides he came sweeping with his end of the load to the spot. "She may be saved! Now up with this ladder; and ho! there, you firemen! bring round your engine to bear on this side of the building to deaden the flames! What! can you neither think nor act? I tell you she must be saved!"

With that sort of half-mechanical obedience which superior energy and promptitude will always command, in a crisis of difficulty and danger, the before uncertain and paralyzed crowd, now aroused by the startling and authoritative tones of the speaker, began to move with alacrity to do his bidding. While the fire-engine, soon adjusted for the purpose, was pouring its torrents upon the space of flames immediately required to be held in check, the tall ladder was hurled into the air, and carefully lowered, till its upper end was brought on to the roof, almost at the feet of the perilled maiden.

"Now, young lady," shouted Bunker, in a voice that rose distinct above the noise of the multitude and the roaring of the flames, "if you have a head and hand steady enough, come down; for you have not a moment to lose!"

Evidently understanding the words that had been thus addressed her, the agitated girl instantly advanced, and stepping over the verge of the dizzy pinnacle, placed her foot upon one of the first rounds of the ladder — when, at the sensation which appeared to come over her, as she glanced down from the fearful height to the earth, partially disclosed to her recoiling senses in the disrupturing clouds of smoke and flame that were seething and raging beneath her, she suddenly stopped, put her hand to her head, and, with a shudder, sunk back unnerved and prostrate upon the roof.

"May the Lord have mercy on her!" cried Bunker, in tones of distress. "She has not the nerve to do it, poor thing! And this ladder may give way under the weight of two. But I cannot stand and see her die so. No, it must be tried," he added, turning to those around him, and preparing to mount himself. "So, under there with your longest poles to sustain and steady the ladder, as well as you can when we come down; for I will save her or go with her."

He was anticipated, however, in his intended ascent. Amsden, who had stood by, watching every movement with an intenseness of anxiety that had deprived him of the power of utterance, now rushed past his brave old friend, and, with a look of mute desperation, rapidly mounted the ladder, and soon disappeared in the smoke, on his perilous destination. The eyes of all were now turned upwards, with intense and eager gaze, to the vapor-screened roof, as they stood awaiting, in silent and trembling suspense, the result of the last effort which they felt could be made to snatch the luckless girl from her doom. But more than a minute elapsed before their senses were greeted by either sight or sound from the objects of their common anxiety; when "They come! they come!" burst from a distant part of the crowd. And the next instant the heroic young man was seen by all, sliding slowly and cautiously from round to round, down the ladder, with one arm firmly grasping his lovely burden, as she lay shudderingly clinging to his bosom, and the other employed in aiding his difficult and dangerous progress. The first fifteen feet of their descent was luckily accomplished without disaster or alarm. And this brought them so far out of the upward current of smoke and heat, that they now could breathe with comparative freedom. But the most perilous part of their passage still remained. And this became so frightfully manifest by the bending and cracking of the frail implement, as they approached the middle, that it was apparent the over-strained sides were about to give way, and precipitate them to the earth beneath or hurl them back among the blazing ruins of the tottering fabric from which they had so far escaped.

"Hold! hold there, above, or you are lost!" shouted Bunker, from beneath the ladder, as he and others were endeavoring to support it with their poles.

A moment of awful suspense followed. But while all others seemed to be deprived of the power of thought and action, by the awful spectacle of two human beings suspended, as if by a hair, over certain destruction, the coolness and presence of mind of the man who had already effected so much were again conspicuous. Casting an uneasy and hurried glance around for some means of averting the fearfully pressing evil, his eye fell upon an old carriage, standing in a distant part of the yard. This, by the loud and rapid orders which he then instantly gave, as he still stood, straining every nerve, at his post, was hastily rolled forward, and run so far within the line of the fire beneath the ladder, that it at once became nearly enveloped in the flames. Then calling on the firemen to turn their engine full upon himself, he mounted the top of the carriage with his pike-pole; and, while a drenching column of water was pouring directly upon his person, he soon gained a hold upon the ladder above, at so high a point as to secure it from any further danger of giving way, so long as he could remain in the hazardous and nearly insupportable position in which he had thus placed himself.

"Now be on the move there, above!" he exclaimed, in tones which plainly told what his effort was costing him. "The house is on the point of falling in; and, for your own sakes as well as mine, I warn you to be lively!"

Before these ominous words were out of the mouth of the speaker, Amsden, who had remained, in the mean time, stationary on his weak and failing support, without stirring a muscle, was rapidly gliding downward, with his still uninjured charge. In a moment the point of danger was passed. In another, Bunker was seen leaping from his stand to avoid the falling ladder, which, with the crashing roof above, now came down in a blazing mass together. But the irrepressible shout of joyful exultation that the next instant burst from the assembled multitude proclaimed to the ringing welkin around, that both the delivered and the deliverer were standing upon the earth in safety.

At that moment, a gentleman, hastily making his way through the crowd, rushed up to the rescued party, exclaiming, "My daughter! my daughter!" and, clasping the bewildered girl in his arms, and murmuring an ejaculation of thanks to Heaven for her deliverance, he led her away from the spot.

Amsden cast a surprised and inquiring look at the person who had thus unexpectedly appeared with the claims implied by the exclamations just uttered, when he recognized, in his general appearance, the stranger with whom he had so nearly perished in the burning house. But the condition in which he now found himself precluded all further thought or inquiry on the subject. A strange, giddy, and sickening sensation came over him; and, staggering, and grasping for something to support him, he was caught by Bunker, who immediately conveyed him, sick and helpless, to his lodgings. The unwonted exertions, and the fearful excitement of the night, had been too much for his already debilitated system; and his failing strength and overtasked nerves had given way together. He rapidly grew worse, and, before morning, was delirious with a raging fever.

O! who can follow the here confused and tangled thread of the sufferer's intellectual existence? Ay, who can give an adequate description of the aimless operations of a mind unsettled by disease — the dark and ceaseless turmoil of ever-changing, yet ever-recurring images — the vague, fleeting, mysterious, half-formed shapes, that are constantly rising on the troubled vision, passing through a thousand rapid and startling mutations, and sinking away to make room for others, seemingly different, yet felt to be the same — the haunting, hurrying, impelling consciousness of objects to be sought, but never obtained, and the deep and distressing sense of perplexity and helpless wretchedness that continues through the whole oppressively to brood over the distracted mind? Who, we repeat, can describe operations like these? No one. No pen, though guided by one who speaks from experience, can draw a picture bearing even the stamp of resemblance; and yet every one who thus speaks, feels that, while in that state, he was conscious of the passing of incidents enough to compose the varying scenes of a whole life.

For more than a fortnight, in despite of the daily, and often hourly attendance of the assiduous and skilful Lincoln, and the unwearied ministering of the kindest of friends, lay Locke Amsden; his prostrate body the helpless and almost hopeless prey of disease, and his sympathizing mind the sport of those troublous and distressing fantasies of the fevered brain, which we can name as such, but never describe. The taper of life, however, though often seeming but to flicker in its socket, continued to burn on; and, at length, nature began slowly to rally, and the invading enemy to retire from the long-disputed field of contest.

It was the beginning of the third week from the night which proved so eventful to the leading personages of our story, that Amsden, after several hours of calm and refreshing slumbers, awoke in full possession of his reason.

"What a long, long, troubled dream!" at length he faintly uttered.

A slight rustling in the room now attracted his attention; and, turning his head, he caught a glimpse of a female figure, quietly gliding out through the door. In a moment more the door was reöpened, when a matronly-looking woman entered, and, approaching the bedside of the evidently surprised invalid, gently asked, —

"Locke, do you know me? Ay, you do now, do n't you, my son?"

"My mother — but how came you here?"

"I came nearly ten days ago, to nurse you, Locke. You have been very sick, though for the last two days you have grown much better; and you would have known me before, probably, had we thought it best to arouse you so thoroughly from your sleep as we might have done."

"Then my mind has been wandering the whole time, I suppose — perhaps it is *all* a dream. When you came in, I was trying to recall, and to distinguish what might be reality from what was not."

"It may be you are mingling reality and your disordered fancies together. People will do so, on coming to their reason, it is said. But what do you allude to, in particular?"

"The burning of Carter's house, — our escape, — and then a great many other confused scenes, which I thought at first I could recall."

"The house you name *was* indeed burnt; and the same kind Providence that has preserved you through this distressing sickness, permitted you, and all that were endangered, to escape from the dreadful element. It must have been an awful scene. It made me shudder to hear Captain Bunker describe it."

"Captain Bunker? Did he remain with me till you arrived."

"Why, he came after me, my son, brought me here, and continued with us several days afterwards, watching over you with all the seeming anxiety of a parent. And, on taking his leave, and looking on you, as he believed, for the last time, it was a moving sight to see that strong man weep."

The patient now, at the suggestion of his careful nurse, refrained from further conversation, took some nourishment, and soon fell again into gentle slumber, from which, at the end of an hour or two, he awoke, much refreshed, and evidently less feeble than before.

"Mother," he said, after lying awhile in thoughtful silence, "mother, who was that lady that left the room just before you entered, the first time I awoke to know you?"

"Why, it was Miss Maverick," replied the other, hesitatingly, as she cast a surprised and rather searching look at the countenance of her son. "She has been here almost every day since I came; and so, indeed, has her father, who expresses —"

"Her father?" interrupted Locke; "O — why, I now recollect. Then that was in truth her father, whom all supposed dead? He arrived the evening before the fire, I presume?"

"No: he arrived in the belated stage, I understood, about the time the alarm was given, and, hurrying to the spot, rushed into the building, where he heard, as he drew near, his daughter was left to perish. The rest you remember, I suppose."

"I do now; but where has the Colonel been, these many years, that nothing should have been heard from him?"

"In Brazil, South America, I think Mary told me, where the country was in such commotion that his letters miscarried. He was at first made a prisoner, and carried into the country, when, effecting his escape, he was drawn into the wars, became an officer, and acquired wealth from his pay, and the services he rendered some rich Spanish families, in saving their lives and estates. He came away, he says, as soon as he could turn his property, and get out of the country with his money, which he has brought home with him, to a large amount, it is generally thought. And it certainly seems like it; for he immediately bought back, of the agent of his old creditors, the beautiful house and farm he formerly owned, and has already moved into it. He has also very generously bought another comfortable house for the Carter family."

"Indeed! but why should he do that, mother? Mr. Carter, notwithstanding the loss of his house and furniture, must have been abundantly able to purchase another, himself."

"Why, did n't you know — but of course you could not — that Carter had failed?"

"You surprise me, mother."

"Yes, he has totally failed. And it is now said he has been a bankrupt for some time, though most people supposed there was scarcely an end to his wealth. His losses by the fire in some way brought his true situation to light. His creditors — and it was found that, besides his immense city debts, he owed almost every body here — his creditors struck on him a few days after, stripping him of every thing that the fire had left; and he is now a poor man, owing thousands, it is said, which he can never pay, and still having the same unprofitable and helpless family on his hands, whose extravagant habits have been the chief means of his ruin. Every body pities *him*, but nobody his wife and daughters."

"What a striking concurrence of events has been here!" observed Locke, thoughtfully; "and what a strange reversal of fortunes has a few days brought about between the dependent, and I fear misused, Mary Maverick, and the vain and haughty Carters! Well, Mary, I suppose, is considered a wealthy heiress now," he added, with a sigh.

"She may be, and justly, too, I presume," rejoined the mother, seeming instinctively to comprehend what was passing in her son's mind; "she may be thought so, and really be so; but let me tell you, that, although the Carters are humbled, she is not exalted. O Locke!" she continued, with earnestness and rising emotion, "I cannot express how much I think of that good, good girl! But I am wrong to lead you to such agitating subjects," she added, suddenly checking herself, as she glanced at the other, and saw him grasping for a handkerchief to conceal his starting tears. "We will converse no more now; and in a few days you will be out, I hope, to see and judge about all these things for yourself."

Amsden possessed a sound and vigorous constitution; and so rapid was his recovery, that, in one week from the time at which the delirium left him, he was able to leave the house. During the whole period of his convalescence, he had seen nothing of Colonel Maverick or his daughter; the former having recently become too much indisposed to appear abroad, and the latter making that circumstance an excuse for the sudden discontinuance of those calls which were so frequently repeated so long as her friend was considered in danger. These facts Amsden learned from Dr. Lincoln, who, gracefully sinking the physician into the companionable friend, still continued his daily visits. And the former was the more concerned at the information thus obtained, as the doctor began to express some apprehensions, that the colonel's indisposition, though appearing like an ordinary cold merely, was the effect of a permanent injury to his lungs, which he might have received from the smoke and heat encountered at the fire, and which, though but slightly developing itself at first, might yet assume a serious aspect. But although Colonel Maverick for the reasons just named, and his daughter for those she had assigned, or others which we will not be very particular in scrutinizing, had not called on the recovering invalid, yet they took means to apprise him that he was not forgotten. A freshly-installed domestic of the new family establishment now regularly made his appearance every morning to inquire after Mr. Amsden's health. And, before the latter was permitted to leave his room, he received a note from the colonel himself, insisting on a visit as soon as his health would possibly allow. There was a roguish postscript to the note, in another hand, which made it none the less welcome to the receiver.

The season of the violet and the opening leaf had come; and the spring-tide of returning health, as if responsive to the action of reviving nature, now everywhere bursting into young life around, began to mount, and course with quickened impulse in the veins of him who was so lately the pale and helpless victim of disease, bringing with it that peculiar buoyancy of spirits, that sort of spontaneous joyousness of animal sensation, which is experienced only by those recovering from long and wasting sickness.

And throwing aside the loathed habiliments of the sick chamber, and spurning the further restrictions of prescribed diet, and confinement within, he now came forth from his prison-house, rejoicing in the conscious glow of physical regeneration, and seemingly sucking in happiness at every grateful inhalation of the open air. Finding himself daily revived and strengthened, instead of harmed, by the exercise of his new-found privilege of wandering abroad, he set out, on the first pleasant afternoon that occurred after his release, for the charmed residence of the two beings who not only for years before had occupied the conspicuous place in his mind, but who now seemed the centering points to which his every thought and inclination irresistibly tended.

On arriving at the gate, he could not but pause a moment, to admire the neat and effective arrangement of the surrounding grounds, the ornamental trees, and every thing connected with this beautiful establishment, all of which seemed to have remained in the form originally laid out by the tasteful owner. He then glanced within the enclosure, in the thickly budding shrubbery of which the not large, but elegantly constructed mansion was nearly embowered; when he caught a glimpse of a female figure, which a second glance told him was Mary, unobservantly bending, with busy and fostering hand, over her geraniums and violets,

"Herself the sweetest, fairest flower of all."

With a beating heart and tremulous hand, he opened the gate and entered. The next instant she came bounding to his side with the graceful lightness of the young fawn; and, with an extended hand, and a countenance all eloquent with blending smiles and blushes, exclaimed,

"O Mr. Amsden, Mr. Amsden! how happy am I to see you looking so well — and how gratified to see you here — *here*, where I can welcome you to a house of my own, — or rather, and what is better, to the house of a father, — who will be no less pleased to see you than myself. Come, come, let me lead you to his room."

The joyous girl immediately ushered her friend and late deliverer into the house and apartment where her father was setting. As they entered, Colonel Maverick, who was reclining on a sofa with a newspaper in his hand, instantly rose, and greeted Amsden with a warmth and cordiality which abundantly made good the assurance that his daughter had just uttered. The colonel, though thin and sallow, from the effects of his long residence in a tropical climate, and though troubled with a bad cough, to remove which, he was now confining himself within, under a course of medical treatment, appeared so much better than his visiter expected, that the latter soon forgot the apprehensions which Dr. Lincoln had excited, relative to the situation of the former, and gave himself up to the delights of a conversation which now ensued among the happy group, and to which the pleasant remembrances of the past, the grateful and gratified feelings of the present, and the congenial tastes of the parties, all combined to impart a reciprocal interest. To Amsden, indeed, that afternoon was one of those halcyon spots of moral sunshine to the heart, which, in this world of care and cloud, occur but once or twice in the course of our lives, when the soul, unconscious of a single ungratified wish, neither turns to the past nor reaches forward to the future, but is fully content with the happiness of the present. And when, with a feeling of surprise, he perceived the unwelcome shadows of evening stealing over the landscape, and warning him that the time at which he had proposed to return had arrived, he wondered how the winged hours could have flown so quickly.

Now, reluctantly rising with the intention of bidding his kind entertainers adieu, he proceeded to announce to them, with an effort at calmness which he was far from feeling, his previously formed determination of leaving town the next morning, on his long-delayed return to his college studies, upon the last term of which his class had, many weeks before, entered. Colonel Maverick, though silent at first, seemed evidently disappointed; and the countenance of his daughter instantly fell at the unexpected announcement.

"Is such indeed your purpose, Mr. Amsden?" asked the colonel, seriously.

"It is, sir," answered the other.

"But why this haste in leaving us?" resumed the former. "Your health, which needs more firmness, will be gaining in the delay; and a few days can certainly make no essential difference with either your studies or your interests at college."

"If those few," replied Amsden, "were not to be added to the many already lost, it might vary the case. As it is, however pleasant to me would be a further stay in town, I think I can tarry no longer."

"I confess I can hardly reconcile myself to this," observed the colonel thoughtfully. "I had counted on a week's inter course with you, at least. I have much to say to you on subjects connected with recent events, which, though it may appear strange, I feel hardly prepared to say now. But you will hear from me again. And, if you must go," he continued, advancing and offering his hand in a kind, feeling manner, "I will bid you, with many good wishes for your welfare, a good-bye for the present, but for the present only. I must insist on your visiting us again, as soon as your term of study is closed, and before you make any arrangement for the future."

Reciprocating the kind wishes of his almost revered friend, and bidding him, as he supposed, an adieu, at least for months, Amsden left the room for another parting, in which he felt far less prepared to act his part; for Mary, who had not uttered a word during the foregoing dialogue, now attended him, in silent agitation, to the door.

"Miss Maverick!" he said, with an effort, as he paused at the threshold, and took her trembling, but frankly-offered hand.

She raised her eyes inquiringly to his, but read there that which caused her to drop them again instantly to the floor.

"Miss Maverick!" he repeated, after a hesitating pause, "your circumstances in life, since our last parting, have become much changed."

"They have, Mr. Amsden," she replied, "and I feel very grateful for the unexpected blessing—but," she continued, with a half-blushful, half-challenging smile, "it do n't follow that I should be changed also."

Another pause of delicate embarrassment succeeded.

"Mary!" once more began Amsden; but as he glanced in thought at his own situation in life, and her altered condition, he could not go on.

"I know what you would say," said she, looking up in sweet confusion; "but come, say it before my father, my confidant, my adviser. You have as little to fear from him as from me — come, come!" And she drew him, hesitating and irresolute, back towards the room they had just left; and the next moment they stood before Colonel Maverick, who, though evidently surprised, yet welcomed their return with an affectionate smile.

"I have returned, sir," said Amsden, diffidently, but with manly firmness, "I have returned, at the suggestion of your daughter, to say before you what I was about to say to her."

"I am much gratified at your course, my daughter," interposed the colonel; "but proceed," he continued, turning encouragingly to the embarrassed lover; "proceed, Mr. Amsden."

"To say, sir," resumed the former, "that, however strong have been the feelings and hopes I have secretly cherished towards her, I will not presume, in the new and high position which she" —

"Stop, stop! Mr. Amsden," interrupted the father; "you do injustice both to us and yourself. We both feel, independent of the high estimation in which we hold you, we both deeply feel how much we have recently become indebted to you for those exertions which cost you so dear. And if this," he continued, advancing, and with much emotion placing the readily-yielded hand of his daughter into that of her almost overpowered lover, "if this is to you the most desirable boon, then be it your reward. The gift, for me, is indeed a great one; but who, by noble exertions, can ever better earn it, and who, by intrinsic worth, more richly deserves it? And now, Heaven bless you, my children!"

A few more words, and the task of the narrator is ended. With a heart made light and joyous by the prospects which had so unexpectedly and so brightly broken on the path before him, Amsden returned to college. The few weeks now remaining to bring him to the close of his collegiate career rolled rapidly away; when, with the highest honors of the institution, and the distinguished esteem of his fellows, he left this spot of hallowed associations, and flew back, as if on the fleet wings of love, to the scene where his affections had learned to cluster; and where the wedded felicity, that now speedily succeeded to the happy and deserving pair, who became its mutually blest recipients, was only clouded by the event which had hastened their union, — that of the still gradually failing health of the accomplished and high-minded Colonel Maverick, whom his sorrowing children were, in a few months, called on to bear to the silent tomb; a bereavement for which they felt themselves but poorly compensated by the ample fortune he left them, not only to ensure the means of their own comfort and happiness, as far as such means have effect, but to enable them to become, as they soon did, the dispensers of comfort and happiness to others individually, and of general usefulness to the society at large, of which, ere long, they were the acknowledged ornaments.

Pass with us, now, gentle reader, over a short period of time, and we will bring to your view a brief picture of results, which involve at once both the conclusion and moral of our tale, or, at least, so much of the latter as you may not have gathered by the way-side, as, not unpleasantly, we humbly hope, we have journeyed on together. A dozen years have not elapsed since the events whose attempted delineation have occupied us through the latter portion of our unworthy performance; and yet Cartersville, the scene of their occurrence, is almost entirely a different place, in all that should give character to a village community. The old school-house, before described as constructed after the miserable fashion of the times, and situated on a busy street, amidst a clump of noisy shops, has been pulled down; and, to supply its place, a neat little edifice, of interior construction, as regards space, seats, means of heating, and ventilation, calculated alike for the convenience, comfort, and health of the pupil and teacher, is seen standing on a retired slope, surrounded by shade-trees, fancifully grouped over a spacious enclosure. This commodious and attractive establishment was built and given to the district by the wealthy and liberal Mr. Locke Amsden, now a member of Congress for that part of the country. That gentleman and his amiable lady having, in conjunction with their friend Dr. Lincoln, early been the means of introducing adequate teachers at an adequate compensation, have made it their rule to visit the school as often, at least, as once every month, through the whole of its continuance. Captain Bunker — who, as we must pause to inform the reader, has been induced to give up his farm in the "*Horn-of-the-Moon*" to his two eldest boys, and, with his surplus capital, purchase, and settle down on a small farm, adjoining that of his friend Amsden; through whose influence, with the aiding effect of a scurrilous attack upon him, that, on his being announced as a candidate, appeared in "*The Blazing Star*," which, with this effort to extend its political supervision over the affairs of Cartersville, soon expired, he has been advanced to a seat in the State Legislature, where he has become the champion of the farming interests — Captain Bunker, we say, has also lent efficient aid to the common school, having become a convert to the principle of high wages for teachers, since, as he says, he is now satisfied that nobody who is a sufficiently "*good thinker*" to be a good teacher, can be got at the old rate of wages. Incited to emulation by the example of the now most wealthy and influential family in town, the people of most of the neighboring districts in the village and country around it have built new school-houses, and supplied them with good teachers;

while school visiting has become as fashionable as it was formerly the reverse; and whenever a select party is got up, the master is now not the last to be invited. An entire revolution, indeed, seems to have taken place in the public mind on these subjects. Ornamental education is now here never thought of, till the solid and useful sciences are first secured. The demand for piano fortes, water-color paint-boxes, drawing-paper, &c., is at a low ebb, while that of the standard works of science and literature is daily increasing. Professors of Elegant Literature now find poor picking in Cartersville; and the race of fashionable fine ladies, who were once their patrons, are lamentably in the back-ground. Fops, formerly the leaders of society, are as scarce as owls in the sunlight, the two last that remained of the tribe having gone off some years before with the two younger Misses Carter; who, finding themselves no longer *appreciated*, concluded to emigrate, with the best offers they could obtain, to some more congenial residence. Nor are the more general results flowing from these circumstances less observable. The village, instead of a trifling, has become a reading and a thinking community; doing every thing for the encouragement of popular education at home, and now yearly sending off, to the academies and colleges abroad, some half-dozen scholars, where one, and oftener none, were sent before. The proportion of vice and crime has already very sensibly decreased; while that of industry, general competence, and rational happiness, has still more sensibly increased. In short, the whole tone of society has changed; and that change, kind reader, great and beneficial as it is, has been effected by the nobly begun, and, subsequently, the no less nobly sustained efforts of THE COMMON SCHOOLMASTER.

A LIST OF BOOKS

PUBLISHED BY

BENJAMIN B. MUSSEY AND COMPANY,

NO. 29, CORNHILL, AND 36, BRATTLE STREET, BOSTON.

MUSIC BOOKS.

THE MODERN HARP,

Or, BOSTON SACRED MELODIST.—A Collection of Church Music, comprising, in addition to many of the most Popular Tunes in common use, a great variety of new and original Tunes, Sentences, Chants, Motets, and Anthems, adapted to Social and Religious Worship, Societies, Singing Schools, &c. By Edward L. White and John E. Gould.

This Book, in the short space of twelve months, has passed through no less than sixteen editions, and is now used in all the best Choirs and Societies in New England, and is universally considered as one of the best books of Church Music now in use.

"So far as we have been able to examine this work, we should judge it to be superior to any modern work that we have seen."—*Skowhegan Democrat.*

"In bringing this work before the public, no time or pains have been spared to render it not only a popular, but a useful Collection. More than the usual number of new Tunes occupy a space in it, and most of this new Music is of a high character, and possesses the true attributes of Church Music. There is also to be found an unusual number of Sentences, Select Pieces, Chants, &c., suitable for the opening and closing of divine worship, among which the entire service of the Protestant Episcopal Church is given in the order of performance.

"The whole Collection is judiciously arranged, and will undoubtedly take a rank second to none of the numerous publications of Church Music now in use."—*Atlas.*

"This Book is composed mostly of Music new to the American public, and embraces every variety of metre now in use, with numerous Sentences, Chants, Motets, and Anthems, suited to particular occasions." - *Salem Observer*

[*Extract of a Letter from Rev. M. K. Cross, of Palmer, Mass.*]

"I am free to acknowledge that I have been very highly gratified with the musical taste and talent exhibited by the authors. It seems to me that a larger proportion than is usual in books of this kind, will be found suitable and edifying for common choirs and congregations. The selection of *words*, set to the Music, is very chaste, and well adapted to devotional purposes; which gives an additional interest to the work. I am happy to learn that it is soon to be introduced in our own congregation."

M. K. CROSS

THE OPERA CHORUS BOOK,

Consisting of Trios, Quartets, Quintets, Solos, and Choruses, selected and arranged from the most popular Operas of Von Weber, Rossini, Meyerbeer, Bellini, Benedict, Donizetti, Mercadante, Auber, Balfe, Verdi, and Bishop. By EDWARD L. WHITE and JOHN E. GOULD.

[*We select the following from numerous Notices of this Work.*]

"SALEM, NOVEMBER 1ST, 1847.

"MR. B. B. MUSSEY — DEAR SIR — I have examined the new publication which has lately come from your press, called the 'OPERA CHORUS BOOK,' and do not hesitate to commend its design and execution. The Selections are well made and well arranged, and are, almost all of them, gems of high musical value. The field from which they were gathered, has not, until now, been explored. It is rich in fruits, and it is to be hoped, that such success may attend this first gathering, as to induce the reapers again to try the sickle."

Your friend and servant, H. K. OLIVER.

"On every page there is evidence of much patience, care, and industry, on the part of the Editors, and we question if among all the volumes of Secular Music that have been published in this country, there will be found one that has more real claims to the admiration of the musical public than this. The Work abounds in those delicious gems of the Opera, any one of which is beautiful enough to tempt our readers to the purchase of the whole collection." — *Boston Daily Whig.*

[*From Thomas Power, Esq.*]

"BOSTON, DEC. 29TH, 1847.

"GENTLEMEN, — Having examined, with some care, the 'OPERA CHORUS BOOK,' of which you are the publishers, I cheerfully give you my opinion of its particular merits. As the study and practice of

Secular Part Music has been pursued with increased zeal and success, within a few years, it has been a leading object to find accessible advanced works of a good character. The practice of the old standard Glees, however excellent, has lost its novelty, and some of its interest. A higher grade of compositions has been required; and the graceful and charming choruses of the modern Opera have given an increasing desire for that class of compositions.

"In selecting from the standard works of the day, a knowledge of the requirements of performers, and a good judgment as to what shall meet these requirements, were imperative. The collection of the Opera Chorus Book has been made with good discretion, combining what is in advance of the current standard, and, at the same time, affording to social parties, for which it seems to be particularly prepared, the easy means of studying gems of some of the best masters.

"Whatever motive of ambition or interest suggested the idea of this Collection, the Book is exactly what is wanted at this time; and it will be taken as a favor to the musical public, inasmuch as it cannot fail to be a great acquisition for practice, and a means of creating a better taste. A book got at with such good properties, cannot fail to be well received."

Respectfully yours,

THOMAS POWER.

THE TYROLIEN LYRE,

A Glee Book, consisting of easy pieces, arranged mostly for Soprano Alto, Tenor, and Bass Voices, with and without Piano Forte Accompaniments, comprising a complete collection of Solos, Duets, Trios, Quartets, Quintets, Choruses, &c., for the use of Societies, Schools, Clubs, Choirs, and the Social Circle. By Edward L. White and John E. Gould.

The sale which this Work has already met, is evidence that its merits are well known to the public; but we extract the following from "*The World of Music:*"— 'It contains many subjects from different popular Operas, very beautifully elaborated, among which we recognize many gems of melody from Rossini, Auber, Bellini, Balfe, &c. Also some sterling Glee compositions from Bishop, Spofforth, Danby, &c., and a large number of those Tyrolien melodies which Malibran and the 'Rainer Family' used to electrify their hearers. The Work will not only be a pleasant social companion, but will be found extremely useful for Choirs, Schools, &c."

"It is a large and well executed volume of two hundred and thirty pages, containing easy pieces, arranged mostly for Soprano, Alto, Tenor, and Bass Voices, with and without Piano-Forte Accompaniments, comprising a complete Collection of Solos, Duets, Trios, Quartets, Quintets, Choruses, &c. The names of Edward L. White and John E. Gould, by whom the Music is composed, selected, and arranged, is a sufficient recommendation of its excellence."— *Olive Branch.*

THE BOSTON MELODEON, VOL. I.

A Collection of Secular Melodies, consisting of Songs, Glees, Rounds, Catches, &c., including many of the most popular Pieces of the day; arranged and harmonized for Four Voices. By Edward L. White.

THE BOSTON MELODEON, VOL. II.

A Collection of Secular Melodies, consisting of Songs, Glees, Rounds, Catches, &c., including many of the most popular pieces of the day, arranged and harmonized for four voices, vol. 2, by E L. White.

The above Books have been before the public some two years, during which time, more than 23,000 of them have been sold, and their reputation is too well known to require any commendation.

THE WREATH OF SCHOOL SONGS,

Consisting of Songs, Hymns, and Chants, with appropriate Music, designed for the use of Common Schools, Seminaries, &c. To which are added the Elements of Vocal Music, arranged according to the Pestalozzian System of Instruction; with numerous Exercises, intended to supersede (in part) the necessity of the Black-board. By Edward L. White and John E. Gould.

"This Work is just the thing for Schools, Juvenile Concerts, &c.; consisting of Songs, Hymns, and Chants, with appropriate Music, designed for the use of Common Schools, Seminaries, &c., to which is prefixed the elements of Vocal Music. In many of the Public Schools out of the city, as well as in, Music has recently constituted a part of the studies of the pupils. This we are glad to see, as many advantages may be derived from such a course. And the experiments, as yet, have proved quite satisfactory. For such purposes, we have seen no better work than the 'Wreath of School Songs.'" — *Olive Branch.*

"Wreath of School Songs." — "The above is the title of a New Music Book, just from the press, and is peculiarly calculated to interest the young singer and make him acquainted with the Elements of Music." — *Eastern Mail.*

"It is a charming little volume, and we recommend it to all who have families." — *Signal.*

BAKER'S ELEMENTARY MUSIC BOOK,

Comprising a variety of Songs, Hymns, Chants, &c. Designed for the use of Public and Private Schools. By BENJAMIN F. BAKER.

"This little Work is designed for Children, as its title indicates. MR. BAKER is an accomplished and successful Teacher of Music in our Public Schools; and his experience in teaching Children to sing, has enabled him to prepare a work adapted to their wants. The introductory part is simple and comprehensive; and, in the hands of a good teacher, cannot fail to lead the learner to a thorough knowledge of the science of Music. The Songs are for the most part lively and interesting, containing just and moral sentiments; and the Music is admirably adapted to them. We commend it to the attention of all those interested in school education." — *Atlas.*

"The Book is prepared with knowledge and judgment, and is admirably adapted to the purposes for which it is designed; and our Committee, wisely regarding the interest of our Children, have authorized its use in those Schools of which MR. BAKER has the care." — *Mercantile Journal.*

"We have examined this Work, and do not hesitate to recommend it to all who are desirous of obtaining a useful book. The Elements of Music are arranged in the most natural and convenient order for the use of Singing Schools and Private Classes. After a few Introductory Remarks, the Scale is introduced to the learner, and explained in the author's peculiarly plain and happy style. Next in order is the Staff, Clefs, Notes, Rests, &c. The whole Work is regularly laid out in the most comprehensive form, illustrated with appropriate Remarks and Examples. The Examples on the transposition of the scale, are the most plain and the easiest for the pupil to understand of any we have ever seen. The Book also contains about one hundred and twenty pages of Music, 'designed for the use of Public and Private Schools.' Teachers of Music will find this a very useful text-book, as it will enable them to go through with the Elementary department of instruction in one half of the time which it usually requires." — *World of Music.*

THE SABBATH SCHOOL LUTE;

A Selection of Hymns and appropriate Melodies, adapted to the wants of Sabbath Schools and Social Meetings. By E. L. WHITE and J. E. GOULD, authors of the "Modern Harp," "Tyrolien Lyre," "Wreath of School Songs," "Opera Chorus Book," &c., &c

SCHOOL BOOKS.

Hitchcock's Bookkeeping. — A New Method of teaching the Art of Bookkeeping, by J. Irvin Hitchcock.

Hitchcock's Key. — A Key to Hitchcock's Method of Book keeping.

French Spoken. — A New System of Teaching French, by Edward Church.

Cutter's Physiology. — Anatomy and Physiology, designed for Academies and Families, by Calvin Cutter, M.D., with over 200 Engravings.

Cutter's First Book. — First Book on Anatomy and Physiology, by Calvin Cutter, M.D., with 84 Engravings.

Colburn's Sequel. — Arithmetic, upon the *inductive* method of Instruction, being a Sequel to Intellectual Arithmetic, by Warren Colburn, A.M.

Boyer's French Dictionary. — Boyer's French Dictionary, comprising all the Improvements of the latest Paris and London editions, with a large number of useful Words and Phrases, selected from the modern dictionaries of Baiste, Mailly, Catineau, and others, with the pronunciation of each word, according to the dictionary of the Abbe Tardy: to which are prefixed Rules for the Pronunciation of French Vowels, Diphthongs, and final Consonants, with a table of French Verbs, &c.

Sherwin's Algebra. — An Elementary Treatise on Algebra, for the use of Students in High Schools and Colleges, by Thomas Sherwin, A.M.

Sherwin's Key. — A Key to the Elementary Treatise on Algebra, by Thomas Sherwin, A.M.

Worcester's Dictionary, in 1 vol. 8vo.

Webster's Dictionary, complete, unabridged, crown quarto

F. A. Adams's Arithmetic and Key.

PRONOUNCING BIBLE.

Just Published, a new edition of Alger's Pronouncing Bible, in 1 vol. octavo.

"This is an invaluable edition of the Bible, and should be in every family where there are children."

CLASSICAL BOOKS.

Crosby's Greek Grammar. — A Grammar of the Greek Language, by ALPHEUS CROSBY, Professor of the Greek Language and Literature, in Dartmouth College.

Crosby's Greek Tables.

Crosby's Xenophon's Anabasis.

Pickering's Greek Lexicon. — This is the *best* Greek Lexicon in use.

Leverett's Latin Lexicon, 1 vol. 8vo.

Gould's Ovid. — Excerpta exscriptis Publii Ovidii Nasonis, accedunt Notulæ Anglicæ et Quæstiones, in usum Scholæ Bostoniensis. Cura B. A. GOULD, A.M.

Gould's Horace. — Quintii Horatii Flacci Opera, accedant Clavis, Metrica, et Notæ Anglicæ Juventuti Accommodatæ. Cura B. A GOULD, A.M.

Gould's Virgil. — Publius Virgilius Maro's Bucolica, Georgica et Æneis, accedunt Clavis, Metrica, Notulæ Anglicæ, et Quæstiones. Cura B. A. GOULD.

Xenophon's Anabasis. — Xenophon's expedition of Cyrus, with English notes, prepared for the use of Schools and Colleges, with a Life of the Author, by CHARLES DEXTER CLEVELAND.

Greek Delectus. — Delectus Sententiarum Græcarum ad usum tironum accommodatus ; cum Notulis et Lexico.

MISCELLANEOUS BOOKS.

Encyclopedia Americana. — A popular Dictionary of Arts, Sciences, Literature, History, Politics, and Biography, a new edition. including a copious collection of original Articles in American Biography; edited by FRANCIS LIEBER, assisted by E. WIGGLESWORTH. 14 vols., library style.

A General Biographical Dictionary, comprising a summary account of the most Distinguished Persons of all Ages, Nations, and Professions, including more than One Thousand articles of American Biography, by the Rev. J. L. BLAKE, D.D., author of the Family Encyclopedia of Useful Knowledge, and various other works on Education and General Literature. Eighth edition, revised.

Tappan's Poems. — Sacred and Miscellaneous Poems, by W. B. TAPPAN.

The Green Mountain Boys. — By the author of Locke Amsden, or the School Master; May Martin, &c. Revised edition.

"This is one of the most stirring Tales of the day."

www.ingramcontent.com/pod-product-compliance
Lightning Source LLC
LaVergne TN
LVHW050515100826
845148LV00002B/348